Won Race

Choose Your Ways

I0535307

D.F. Laborde

D.F.Laborde

Copyright © 2010 D.F. Laborde

Version 8.00
4/10/2019

ISBN: 978-0-9834485-1-8

Choose Your Ways

Commander Atera was a war hero when she was young. Now, she trains fighter pilots who have never known a day of war. She thinks they are young and reckless. They think she is old and overbearing. But then suddenly, the Puratist Wars overspill onto an uncharted and unsuspecting world, Earth.

Earth had been safely out of the reach of the Puratist Worlds and their wars of ethnic cleansing, but not anymore. Atera's pilots are defeated and overrun at every turn and just when things seem like they can't get any worse, a new enemy emerges.

An evil from a bygone era. The Beast, if ever there was one. He is older than they are, wiser than they are, and he seeds their hatreds to keep them divided. The legend of an ancient weapon is their only hope, but they have no idea that the weapon they seek is the weapon he wants.

All that one generation experiences, so too will the next.
Love is love.
Fear is fear.
Hate is hate.
And
War is war.

CONTENTS

CHAPTER 1: THE SECRET

The airship engines roared as they swooped down over the island and hovered there while Captain Helforn awaited confirmation from his Navigator. "Sir, this island, it's not on any of the maps. It's uncharted!" Helforn looked quickly at his wristwatch and then again at the sun that was setting low on the horizon and realized that time was running out. "Down, down… put us down on that grassy patch."

Without a moment wasted, all eight of the VTEC airships dove down and landed. Just as soon as the landing skids hit the ground, the doors popped open and troopers rushed down the ramps. As they gathered in the grassy clearing, Captain Helforn shouted his orders. "Time is running out people! We've got to find that energy signal. It's either underground or it's in those old ruins on the hilltop. We'll split up so we can search faster."

He pulled Sgt. Anil close to him. "You know what to do. Get the Neferan equipment unloaded and run the search grids. I'll take another team to the hilltop." With his rifle in one hand, he began running backwards as he gave his final order. "Keep the Neferan and the Lycerene apart…don't let them anywhere near each other!"

Helforn's troopers scrambled to catch up with him as he ran across the two hundred meters towards the ruins on the hilltop. They stopped about twenty paces away from the entrance which was sealed by a heavy wooden door with old iron braces. By then, Helforn, had already realized that the buildings were not ruins at all. They were old and in disrepair, but occupied nonetheless. He approached the entrance along with two troopers at his sides. He knocked on the old wooden door and waited. Minutes passed and they knocked again. No answer, not so much as a footstep could be heard.

The knocking grew louder and just as Helforn threatened to break down the door, he heard a muffled clicking. Slowly, the heavy door cracked open revealing a dark passageway from which a solitary Monk appeared. As the door opened wider, the Monk raised a hand to shield his aged eyes from the bright sunlight. Carefully, the old Monk stepped forward into the light. Bent over and limping with age, he spoke slowly and with a thick accent. "Good day, Sir. I am Brother Sarrow. How may I serve you?"

"I am Captain Helforn. We are under direct orders of The President to search the premises. Please have your staff assemble out front."

The old Monk turned around to face the handful of other Monks who had gathered inside the passageway. His turn was slowed by the weight of his heavy grey robe and his vision was obscured by the thick hood that hid most of his face. He waived his crooked hands at the other Monks motioning them to come outside and in that same moment, Helforn motioned his troopers to enter the building and begin the search.

As the last of Helforn's troopers entered the building and disappeared into the dark passageway, the old Monk spoke. "Captain, this is a private monastery, a place of solitude. Whatever are you searching for?"

Helforn had to think carefully about his response. "Brother Sarrow, are you aware that Earth has been attacked by people from an outer world and that two of our cities burn?"

The old Monk seemed to shudder with concern. "No sir. We are an isolated monastery...visitors are rare." He slowed as if to catch his breath and then paused a moment to clear his throat. "We will add additional prayers to the day's sermons."

While the troopers searched the monastery, Brother Sarrow turned about slowly, taking careful steps toward a small mound where he could look out and see the rest of Helforn's troopers who were busily working near the VTEC airships. His aged eyes caught sight of a small group of troopers who were slowly making their way towards the monastery. Even though they wore full body armor, he couldn't help but notice that one of them was different. "Who is she?"

Helforn immediately knew who the monk was speaking of. "I assume you are speaking of the one with the limp and walking cane...that is Commander Atera." Helforn paused for a moment to remove his helmet. "Brother Sarrow, the attacks...they caught us by surprise. There was no stopping them until Atera's squadron arrived. Nobody trains Pilots like Atera....she is a real one-of-a-kind."

Slowly, the monk raised his hand to shield his eyes from the bright sunlight. Further in the distance he could see teams working hastily among the VTECs. He noticed that some of them wore armor unlike Helforn's armor which was painted in camouflage. Curiously, the monk formed his question. "Who...are they?"

Helforn cleared his throat. "The soldiers wearing the black armor with gold markings are Neferan soldiers. The other ones, with armor painted like...like...the shades of a Wolf, they are Lycerene warriors. They are enemies to each other and it was their war that found its way to Earth. All we know is that there is an energy signal that led them to Earth. We believe the energy signal is here...somewhere on this island."

Helforn continued impatiently. "Listen carefully Brother Sarrow, there are technicians out there running search grids on this site. If something is there, they will find it sooner or later. If you know anything at all, then you need to tell us now....right now. Lives may depend on it."

Taking a couple steps forward, as if the weight of the world were suddenly pressed down on his shoulders, the old Monk replied. "Captain Helforn, all I know is that I am a simple servant and this is a place of solitude." His eyes never turning from the sight of the black armor as he mumbled. "I would not understand the nature of such things."

Sarrow stood there watching the Neferan technicians with such focus that he hadn't noticed Commander Atera approaching. Even with her limp and walking cane, her pace had quickened as something seemed to concern her. "Monk, if this is a house of worship, then what need have you of guards?"

Brother Sarrow suddenly stood straighter and turned about. His old and weakened voice now a bit clearer. "What do you mean...guards? Where?"

Brother Sarrow motioned for two of his lesser Monks to investigate. They rounded the corner of the old monastery and stood directly behind Atera. Immediately, one of Atera's pilots, named Scout, handed a view scope to the monks that they might see the silhouettes off in the distance, under the trees, but the monks ignored her. Moments later, they turned back to Brother Sarrow. No words, but clearly something was happening.

Clapping his hands twice to get their attention, Sarrow's voice resonated with some concern. "My friends, the time has come for you to depart. Come, come, I will see you to your airships." Motioning with his hands to encourage them to move along.

Scout ran to the East and gave a loud shout. "More of these guys to the East. I'd say maybe ten or twelve...and they are armed!"

Stepping directly in front of Brother Sarrow, Captain Helforn stood sternly and demanded an answer. "What is going on here? Who are they?"

Brother Sarrow seemed to struggle to raise his words. He stood there looking to the East and then to the West. Twice and three times he scanned the horizons and each time the concern drew heavier on his face until he turned sharply to Helforn and stared him directly in the eyes. His old and bent body suddenly stood straighter and his words came through loud and clear, "My friends, I urge you to leave." Suddenly, the air rang aloud with the sounds of mortars launching into the sky followed by a bone chilling sound as the mortars screeched through the air.

All eyes turned upwards as if they might see the incoming mortars, but the sun blinded their eyes. As the sounds drew imminently closer, they dropped to the ground, all of them except for Brother Sarrow.

Sarrow stood alone, staring intently at the silhouettes that scurried among the tree line as the first volley of mortars erupted. Mortars like no other with their searing white flashes followed immediately by deafening blasts that mimicked the crack of thunder. Even though the troopers wore advanced armor, their vision was temporarily black spotted by the flashes and their ears were deafened by the blasts.

The ground rumbled as the mortars struck the soft soil to either side of the roadway, but still, Brother Sarrow stood there. With no regard for the blinding flashes or the thunderous concussions, he stood there motionless, as if his body were made of solid lead. Standing straight, barely flinching as the wind whipped at his robe and the dirt sprayed his face. Just a quick twist of his head to shake the dirt free from his face before he again shouted at Helforn. "Get up! Get to the monastery!"

Helforn barked right back. "Not until I get my troops out of those VTECs." He turned and raced towards the VTECs crossing maybe twenty yards when he was suddenly spun around by Brother Sarrow. In disbelief that the old man could have caught him from behind, Helforn pulled his arm free. "What the...?"

Cutoff by Brother Sarrow who insisted, "You cannot save them! It is...too late!" And the skies were again filled with the sounds of mortars screeching through the air as Brother Sarrow grabbed Helforn by the neck collar and shouted directly in Helforn's face. "They mark their distance...they adjust!"

The mortars crashed down around them, this time closer. Again, the air was singed by the white-hot flashes that blinded them and the concussions that made their ears ring. Helforn could barely hear Sarrow who was shouting directly in his ear. "They mark their distance. They won't miss again!"

Even as Helforn waived for the VTEC's to lift off and rise to safety, the third volley of mortars rained down. One by one, the VTECs were engulfed in rolling flames. From across the distance, Helforn could only watch as troopers tried to escape from the burning wreckage. Caught out in the open, they had but one chance, to cross the open field and seek refuge in the Monastery.

Again, more mortars rained down as Helforn and his troops opened fire aimlessly at an enemy who was hidden behind the tree line, all but invisible. Trying desperately to provide cover fire as their comrades ran towards them, dragging the wounded as best they could. But, the old Monk saw the trap that was being set. "I told you, they mark their distance. Stay here...and you die!"

With that, the old Monk shoved Helforn back towards the monastery. "Get to the monastery! We will protect you there!" With mortars crashing all about them, troops ran to the monastery to find the old wooden door already opened and the Monks ready to receive them. They raced in and took cover behind the thick stone walls. Lastly, the survivors who had crossed the open field poured in and collapsed upon the stone floors.

With his hands, Helforn motioned for his men to take up positions at the windows and upon the rooftops. Immediately, the troops began firing across the long fields. Firing at an enemy whose speed was inhuman and whose pace was relentless.

"Sir...Commander Helforn...look here," yelled Scout. She gave him her view scope and pointed in the direction of the dark silhouettes running across the field. Helforn peered through it and his throat closed tight, then he backed away in disbelief, unable to find the words. Scout's voice rang like an alarm as she called to Brother Sarrow. "Monk! Monk! What the hell are those things?

They looked like men, but their bodies were unusually long and horribly thinned as if suffering from starvation. Flesh that was colored dark green and deeply wrinkled as if raised from the grave and their fingers were stretched long and pointed. Mouths that were blackened and teeth that were yellowed and stained foul. Some ran upright like a man, but most ran on all fours, like wild dogs.

Brother Sarrow yelled back "You cannot fight them! You cannot win!" For a moment, the roar of gun blast and the mortar concussions deafened their ears. Whatever Sarrow was screaming at them was muted by the thunderous pounding, but for sure, he wanted them to follow him. Down the long stone passageways turning and turning until they had arrived in a library located at the south corner of the courtyard.

Once inside, Helforn shoved his way through the troops until he stood face to face with Sarrow. "What the hell are those things? Don't give me this crap that you don't know!"

Just then, above the sounds of battle, a new sound rose in the distance. Not the sound of mortars and not the screams of wounded men, but a sound that made the skin crawl.

Immediately, the Monks froze still and began to mumble something, like a prayer, as if protecting themselves from the unclean sound. As the sound intensified, so too had their prayer unto the point where they were nearly unresponsive. Shuffling and stumbling about in odd fits.

The sound moved like rolling thunder and when it had passed them, the Monks slowly returned to their senses. Simultaneously, they all rushed to Brother Sarrow's side.

Without opening his eyes, Sarrow looked upward, and then slowly, the words escaped his lips.

"He has found us."

Again, the sound rose up from the distance. One of the lesser Monks called to Sarrow.

"He calls...to us."

He...and his legions!"

This time the sound was louder, much louder. It rolled forward with more intensity and then seemed to pause directly over them. As the sound hung there, the Monks returned to their prayers, slipping deeper and deeper into meditation. It was then that Helforn and his troops felt it for the first time. Even with their advanced armor, the sound crept in, slipping in through the ears and crawling down the spine, as if it were a living creature. In a fit of twitching and scratching, Helforn grabbed Sarrow "What is it?"

But, Sarrow could not respond. He was lost in prayer, mumbling things, speaking words that Helforn did not recognize; words from ancient languages. But, there were two words that Helforn did recognize. And just two words said it all.

The Secret...

CHAPTER 2: ATERA

Before anyone could speak, one of Atera's young pilots staggered from blood loss and she immediately turned to his aid. Quickly, she identified a small hole in the armor that protected his lower leg. It started with a slow drip, but as the boot filled with blood, the drip turned to a flow. "Get it off! Pull the boot off now! It's an artery….Ready the coagulating agent!"

Her other pilots held the man down as she injected his leg with the coagulating agent over and over; almost stabbing all around the wound until it swelled shut.

As the man's screaming subsided, Atera's thoughts raced backwards. How unprepared her young pilots were for the battle to come. She had handpicked them, every last one of them. She trained them, mentored them, and disciplined them, but they were young.

Just one day earlier, before Earth had been attacked, she had caught them in the middle of the night, doing mischevious things that young soldiers do. They should have known that she would be watching, as she always had.

On that night, Atera hid in the shadows outside the flight simulator room where she was sure her young pilots had gathered for their fun. Watching and listening, but mostly waiting for the moment that she knew would come. It didn't take long for the argument to begin, followed immediately by the sounds of a fight. First, she could hear the body armor clashing followed by a loud thud. With that, she knew that her young pilots had fallen off the platform and onto the concrete floor. Armor or no armor, that fall knocked the wind out of them.

It was the moment that she had been waiting for. The perfect opportunity to surprise them and put an immediate fear into the lot of them. At that very moment, while her pilots were still groaning on the floor, Atera stepped forward and pivoted sharply into the doorway. With a sharp stomp of her right foot, she barked. "Form ranks!"

She waited there until the last of her Pilots had formed ranks, then she began to walk down the long ramp. She walked slowly, to let the fear set in. Each step was amplified by the antiquated clickers that she wore on her boots while her perfect cadence was timed by the metallic-sounding tip on her walking-cane. Each click, each pivot, each spike of her cane was a language unto itself.
"Where shall I begin?
　　The fight,
　　　The game…you hacked into the simulator-pods,
　　　　The arrogance…to think that you could get away with it. That I might not notice?"

At that moment, her pilots wished Atera would yell and scold them like any other Commander would do, but nothing about Atera was like the other Commanders. Especially the way that she punished them; the 'crank' as she called it.

Again, she let the silence speak for her. She tipped her chin high and stood like a statue, a machine, void of all human emotion. Then, she spoke one single word. The one word her pilots dreaded more than any. "Begin!"

With that word, every soldier in the room simultaneously dropped to the floor and began doing push-ups. After a few moments, she walked over towards the two men who had been fighting and she spoke in her military, demeaning tone of voice. "Stalker and Prowler. Both of you look especially tired today. Please, find a chair, and take some rest while the others...carry on."

She stood there apart from her pilots, looking in their direction, but not at them. Looking only to read the stress upon their bodies, the way a lion studies a heard. To see the sweat, to see the trembling, to see the muscles twitching. Studying their breath, reading their eyes, and noticing as their backs bent under. To take note of the weak.

She began to pace back and forth never taking her eyes from them. Tapping her cane to the ground, gripping it and twisting it over and over again. Then, she turned her eyes downward, staring down at the metal tip at the end of her walking cane as if it had some special meaning. Suddenly, she looked up just as the last of her pilots collapsed from exhaustion.

"On your feet", she snapped at Stalker and Prowler.

Using her cane rather than words, she directed them into the middle of their exhausted teammates, leaving them facing each other. And then, she said one more word and it clearly meant that she was drawing the final line. "Swords!"

A tremor passed through everyone for real swords were never drawn in training. They were the most technically advanced ever produced by humans. The blade being a mastery of both strength and flexibility. When unsheathed, the blade was no longer than a man's forearm, good for close quarter stabbing. But when snapped outward, the blade would hinge over and double in length, good for open swordplay.

No words, but a sharp whip of her cane upon their breastplates. Again and again, she whipped and smacked them with her cane. "What are you afraid of? Two of you, against one old woman!"

She pivoted sharply, face to face with Stalker and then she eyed him with discontent. "Stalker...tell me the weakness of your trusted armor? Tell me where even I can strike you down?"

Rather than injecting any opinion of his own, Stalker cleverly cited a metric from the military training manual, for he had it memorized. Every last word of it. "This armor can withstand up to five-hundred degrees, it can protect against..."

Before he finished, she took her cane and smacked Stalker's helmet sharply below the left ear where the electronics were tightly packed. The metal tip on her cane caused a brief disruption to his vision and hearing. Just enough time for her to strip the sword from his hand and smash him with his own sword, like a child.

Not to leave Prowler unscathed, she whipped her cane around and smacked Prowler on the forehead with blistering speed. Before he regained his focus, she used her walking cane and the sword together, as if she had two swords. She spun them around faster and faster and then she swung them like hammers against Prowler's sword. Beating it down and down until she knocked it out of his hands.

"I know what you people think; that there are no wars."
But, I warn you, history is full of fallen empires.
Because of fools...fools like you!"

CHAPTER 3: THE FALL OF LYCERA

The carrier was named Longspear and its battle accolades were legendary...when it was young. Even now, old and outclassed, it still performed duties, but not on the front lines. Not with the other battlements of the Deep-Space Pack. Serving always at the same remote quadrant in roles ranging from Rear Guard and sometimes Search and Rescue. Longspear was nothing short of a dreadnaught, a behemoth. Still, the name Longspear was a haunt to the enemy and they would sacrifice much for the chance to destroy her.

Longspear and her crew were born into a war that was generations old. A war with no end, not until the genocide was fulfilled one way or the other. Two worlds, two ways; Lycera and Nefera.

Lycera, a race of humans, noble as any. A people whom despite their advanced technology, still valued the ways of the animals. Defining themselves around one particular animal, a beast of legend; long extinct on their world. The legends of the beast and its ways were so revered that they became the basis for the social structure and the basis for their military strategy. Living in groups, hunting in groups, and warring in groups. Likened to that of the wolf...The Pack.

And of their enemy, a planet called Nefera and its people called The Neferan. A race easily compared to that of a Wasp; with its High Queen, Subordinate Queens, and countless drone soldiers. A social structure likened to that of a Hive and a military strategy likened to that of a Swarm.

For generations, no battle grand enough could be enjoined to settle the account for the two worlds existed at opposite ends of an impassable void. A great emptiness where no vessels dared to travel for as long as history recorded. A silent place where instrument signals never reflected and probes never returned. A hollow place where ships had simply disappeared.

Ancient religions declared The Void an unholy place; to be avoided at all times. Hence, from the beginning, vessels traveling between the two worlds navigated around the great sphere. A journey that consumed massive resources. But of recent, the Neferan had set themselves to conquer all the worlds. One by one until they were on the doorstep of Lycera.

The alarms rang out as they had done so many times before and Longspear's crew scrambled to their stations assuming it was just another drill. Running nearly half the length of Longspear, Reza and his fighter squadron raced to the flight deck, but as Reza passed the Combat Intelligence Center, he caught a glimpse through an open door. He paused for a moment and then kept running. His second in command, a female named Chel, called forward to him as they ran. "Why did you stop? What did you see?"

With crew members running all about, weaving in between them, Reza shouted back. "I'm not sure, but something is different."

Rounding the final corner to the flight-deck and rushing up the stairs, Chel couldn't hold back her curiosity. "What's different?"

As they reached the flight-deck, Reza turned backwards to Chel. "That broadcast was coming from COMCEN...and it wasn't encrypted. Something big is happening!"

Just as the rest of Reza's squadron reached the flight-deck, he motioned for them to gather around. "Whatever it is, it's big. I saw the Generals at COMCEN giving orders for all Class-One and Class-Two ships to make immediate jump preparations. All Class-Three ships are on stand-by."

Even before he finished talking, the Tech Crews had arrived, rolling in pallets of body armor and immediately began assisting the pilots with the task of suiting up. Just before Reza's face disappeared behind his helmet, he shouted. "As soon as you are jacked-into your fighter-jet, patch into the Priority-Two station and await orders!"

Longspear was no longer considered a Class-One or Class-Two ship. She was now a Class-Three with orders to hold. Even had she been called to duty, she was currently under repair and it would be at least one, maybe two days before she could be ready for a jump.

Moments later, Priority-Two station was patched through to the display monitors for Reza and his pilots. The message was being broadcast from inside COMCEN. Battle status from the Deep-Space Pack was being delivered to the War Chiefs at COMCEN.

The Chief-of-Fleet, a man of many battles, had been born of the Tuctomah Chiefdom and his name was Cree. His voice rumbled. "Outnumbered at least ten to one. I say again, we are currently outnumbered at least ten to one.

Good Sirs, even if every Class1 and Class2 platform arrives, that would still leave us outnumbered eight to one."

Not a sound from the War Chiefs at COMCEN. Not a whisper from anyone on Longspear. Seconds of silence and then one of the War Chiefs at COMCEN tried to make sense of things. "Chief Cree, this cannot be. Our Intelligence indicates that all enemy ships are still at their normal patrol zones. Are you sure your sensors are not experiencing technical malfunction?"

To which the old Chief, Cree, sank in his chair stunned at their disbelief and amazed at their denial. "Good Sir, I am certain of it."

Still confused and unwilling to believe that after all these years, that the best of their Lycerene Intelligence had been thwarted. That the Neferan Swarm now held the element of surprise as well as having them outnumbered. "Chief Cree, just what makes you so certain?"

Cree paused for a second and then gave the simple reply "Good Sir...because I can see them." He patched through a visual of the massing Swarm as seen from his bridge viewport. Before their eyes, for everyone at COMCEN to see, the largest Neferan Swarm they had ever seen. Ships of every size from the largest of Carriers to the smallest of Fighters.

Gasps could be heard coming from the War Chiefs at COMCEN. "Chief Cree, the Deep-Space Pack must hold. It cannot break. If you cannot stop them, then you will slow them down with every ship you have. You are the front line Sir. Do you understand me?"

Expecting no less, Chief Cree looked dead ahead, his once polished and pressed uniform now soaked with sweat, he thought of only one thing. "I will tend to my front line. As for you Good Sirs, assemble the Reserves, the Rear Guard...Everything, and I do mean everything!"

To that, Chief Cree switched off his communication radio. From that moment forward, everyone on every ship and every post understood the old chief implicitly. The Deep-Space Pack would not survive the day.

The old Chief closed his eyes as his thoughts turned inward. Images flickered in his mind...he surmised that the Deep-Space Pack could at best only stall a Swarm of that size...a second line would only meet the same fate...Lycera's planetary defenses would fall in the coming weeks...Ground Packs could not sustain combat ops without reinforcements and supplies. In all, maybe four to six weeks until open genocide.

Urgent as the impending battle was, his first thoughts shifted. He opened a secured communication channel that stretched far across deep space to Longspear. To another member of a higher military order known as The Keepers. An order of a select few who were believed to hold the secrets of the Ancients. Being the eldest and most respected among them, Chief Cree was ordained as Keeper Prime. To him and only to him, were entrusted the greatest of those secrets.

As Chief-of-Fleet, Cree knew his priority to be a battle plan, but as Keeper Prime, he knew his priority to be the preservation of those secrets. Now, in his last hour, he needed to transition those secrets to another member of the Order. But, in short time every Keeper would be on scene and he knew that they would all perish in battle; all but one. The youngest and least prepared among them. And he was far from the front lines. With his communication channel opened to Longspear, and his young Keeper at the ready, he began.

"Keeper Reza, I trust you have seen the Priority broadcasts, so listen carefully as I have only moments to spare. I am sending you two sets of coded files. The first files are the translations of the holy scrolls. The secrets of the ancients. Understand that by days end, you will be the sole Keeper. The burden is upon you now."

Even now, Chief Cree's crew called to him, "Neferan Swarm at eighty-five percent. They are repositioning...they are preparing to attack".

But, he stole a few more precious moments. "Second, and more importantly, are the files of my personal research. Set yourself immediately to studying my files. To you alone they will make sense. I chose you unto this purpose. You must convince them, you must!" The young Keeper interrupted with questions, but Chief Cree was out of time. "Keeper Reza, in the darkest of hours, keep the faith...the faith in our ways. Good day young Sir." And the communication channel closed abruptly. Leaving the young Keeper stunned and confused.

Amid a pure panic, Chief Cree turned and addressed his crew. Across the bridge from port side to starboard side, he looked at the faces and felt their despair. He gave a sharp and sounding command "People, surely we will not win the day... but I swear to you...We will find the Queen. We will find that Bitch and when we do, we will give her hell."

That name, 'The Bitch' is a name that he had reserved for one very special Queen. A Subordinate Queen, known as the 'Warrior Queen', Anak Re Sun.

The lines were forming fast as ships from both sides were jumping to the scene. A Neferan Swarm nearly ten times greater than the Lycerene Deep-Space Pack. Some twelve Super Carriers, twenty-five Heavy Cruisers, eighty Fast Destroyers, and hundreds of Neferan Wasp Fighters. All against the Lycerene Deep-Space Pack which was able to assemble nearly two thirds of all Class-One and Class-Two ships and their Packs of Fighters. Even so, the Deep-Space Pack could scarcely hold against such numbers.

The mass that had appeared as a Swarm of ships jumping in at a rapid pace began to see the pace slow. Like a clock winding down until it finally stopped. Finally, the gigantic Neferan Swarm lurched forward.

But, the Lycerene Pack were steadied and set to their own plan; Cree's plan. "All ships retreat! We've got to buy time for the War Chiefs at COMCEN to form up a second line… and most importantly, to find the Queen".

Cree's orders flowed. "Communications Officer, take the entire auxiliary Sysplex and load your search algorithm. Run those scans on multi-thread…submit them on max-priority."

The look of confusion stared back at him from his Communications Officer. "Chief Cree, the scan algorithms are old; almost useless against the Neferan encryption. They are unreliable at best."

They could see by the look in Cree's eyes that it mattered little now and he reconfirmed his order. "I know she is here. No chance she would sit this one out. Even with encryption and shielding, we should see something. Triangulate on her signals by sync'ing your scans with the Carriers North Wind and Dark Cloud. Find me that Queen!"

For a time, Cree's retreat worked. Then the Swarm changed shape yet again, forming a giant crescent. The smallest among them being the Wasp Fighters now raced ahead of the larger vessels along the outer perimeters. First in singles, then in groups until the mass stretched out like arms that would ensnare the Pack and attack it from all sides. Upon that, Chief Cree could buy no more time. "Communications Officer, what is your status?" The voice replied right back "Chief Cree, scans are running. Nothing yet."

It was time for Chief Cree to ready himself for the battle. He strapped himself into the Captain's chair located center of the bridge. Surrounded by his monitors and the battle grid from which he could control his entire Fleet as a single Pack. Control them with nothing more than the swipe of his hands over the battle grid.

His thoughts flickered again…an outflanking maneuver against such a massive Swarm would prove futile…a traditional line attack was suicidal…but the worst possible option was to stand still and be attacked…and so he did the unthinkable.

As the crescent shaped Swarm encircled the Pack, he swiped his hand across the battle grid drawing a thick red line directly across the Swarm's center.
"All ships:
Shields to low,
Maximum speed,
Disable targeting….fire at will! ….fire at will!"

The Lycerene Pack hurled itself directly into the center of the crescent Swarm with all its cannon blazing. With shields low and the targeting disabled, the Pack's cannon roared at twice their normal rate. With nonstop sparks and fire spitting from the gun turrets until the point where they glowed red hot. The Packs ships gave no pause as their speed and momentum carried them deep into the Swam. Spinning and twirling as many of them slammed into the Neferan Destroyers and Cruisers.

From where Queen Anak Re Sun sat, hidden far back among her Swarm, she could see as the battle quickly became a massive debris cloud. "What is happening? I cannot see what is happening. Switch to infra-red!" Even with the best of Neferan scanners, the fire storms and smoke clouds obscured her vision, but she could see enough that the fear of it struck her. With her eyes so fixed on the battle, she knew not that her polished and sharpened fingernails had dug deep into the armrests of her throne.

As the Pack began to emerge on the other side of her crescent swarm, her stomach knotted and her breathing ceased. Counting and weighing the damage to the Lycerene Pack against the decimation of her Neferan Swarm until the moment when she could see how few of Cree's Pack emerged. All of them bearing heavy wounds, some listing, some sputtering, all of them ablaze in one place or another.

The Queen's relief burst out from her chest:
Beaten!
Beaten!
Beaten! Finally you are beaten…old man!
Turn your tail and run you old dog…but I will catch you!

Hardly had she regained her composure when voices called to her. "My Queen, surely they are defeated. We will finish them with ease. Might I suggest you depart now to avoid any undue risk?"

Queen Anak Re Sun turned to greet him with the look of dissatisfaction "First Officer, Sun Keptra, I trust you know me better than that. Never will I depart! Not until I see the last of them defeated. Never!"

"Yes my Queen. They are but a tattered few and our Wasp fighters are running low on fuel and ammo. Shall we have them press the attack?"

Queen Anak Re Sun responded slowly, gloatingly, and full of self-confidence "No. No, time is on my side today. Recall my Wasp fighters; refuel and rearm them."

Her First Officer responded sharply "Yes my Queen. I will make preparations for another assault."

The Queen replied gracefully. "No...no, not an assault. When the time is right, I will unleash my Swarm. My Swarm will dive down upon them like rain from a storm cloud. A single pass over those howling bones and we will break their backs once and for all!"

Immediately, her orders were observable from across the battlefield. Voices relayed it. "Chief Cree, she recalls her fighters....no doubt to refuel and rearm."

Already focused on his prime objective, the old Chief barked directly at his Communications Officer. "What about my scans? Where...is...that...Bitch?"

The Communications Officer responded half confident as his hands pointed to the battle grid "Chief Cree, the best I can figure, the Queen is somewhere in this cluster of ships." To Cree's dismay, the cluster contained a handful of Destroyers which hid the Queen well. In thought so deep, he clinched his teeth and a low growl emitted from his throat. "We'll find her. We'll use the old ways!"

Again, his hand swiped across the battle grid redirecting the Pack fleet to roll out and downward as if turning away from the fight; yet aligning his fleet towards the Swarm cluster that hid the Queen so well.

He was quick to decide just how to use the time. "Keep our backs to her so she thinks we are in retreat." As the tattered remnants of Cree's fleet made their long slow turn, damage control crews patched and rigged as best they could. Gun crews reloaded what scarce munitions remained and engineering crews rerouted all remaining power to the core thrusters and turrets. Anything to steady the ships for their final purpose.

The voices called forward again "Chief Cree, we are nearly out of time! She is massing her Swarm. They gather directly behind the cluster!"

Old and exhausted as he was, Cree's mind began to turn inward with images flickering…drawing a map of the Swarm that was gathering behind the Queen…but which ship was hers? How to find Anak Re Sun? Just as the image began to solidify in his mind, he was interrupted.

"Sir, the Swarm is nearly massed…at seventy-five percent capacity. We are almost out of time!"

For the first time in his long career, he sat back so exhausted that his mind was emptied and his body slumped. In that tiny space where his mind was empty, the flickering resumed. That image reappeared in his mind…the Swarm massing behind the cluster….and suddenly, the picture was complete.

He was ready for it. "All ships come about. Hard to Starboard ninety degrees. One quarter thrust. Form it up in two columns."

The Queen's First Officer, Sun Keptra advised her of the incoming Pack. "My Queen! They have turned into us. They are headed straight at us. Again, I advise that we evacuate you. The Swarm can finish them without you."

The Queen peered sternly at him. "Steady yourself First Officer Sun Keptra. I will do no such thing. My Swarm will make an easy pass of them."

Moments passed before Sun Keptra could hold his concern no longer. "My Queen, enemy is accelerating to attack speed. They are now at three-quarters thrust."

The distance now half closed and the intensity drew on her face. She could wait no more. "What is my Swarm capacity?"

Sun Keptra responded quickly. "My Queen, Swarm capacity is at ninety percent."

Her confidence now waned and it showed in the stiffness of her posture. Her eyes darted across the array of monitors; back and forth until she could wait no more. "Release my Swarm!"

At that distance, the Lycerene Pack didn't need scanners to tell them what was happening. "Chief Cree, here they come! Nearly a full Swarm bearing straight at us. Estimated time of impact is ninety seconds."

Again, Cree raised his hand this time to steady his Pack, sure that this was his final moment. Seconds passed before Cree voiced his plan.

"They are coming straight at us!
They are in dive formation!
Helmsman, no matter what happens, keep us pointed at that cluster. Dead on!"

Heads and eyes about the bridge turned sharply in disbelief. Voices erupted. "Chief, they are closing fast! Sir, we'll never make it through that Swarm. At least divert us around the Swarm!"

Cree could see their confidence wane on their faces, yet no time to steady them.
"Damn it Good Sirs!
Do as I tell you!
All ships....give me mines, stealth-mines, everything!
Rack'em and stack'em in the hangar-bays.
Configure to wide distribution, max distance!"

And now the old Chief turned like a caged beast ready to strike. His orders resonated crystal clear.
"Wait till they are upon us!
Wait! Wait for my command!"

With his fleet still in column formation, he waited until the diving Wasp Fighters were close. Waited until the Neferan Wasps had already fired their first volley. Then, his hands moved quickly swiping across the battle grid. His fleet suddenly sprung outward into a wide formation, speed accelerated, and the mines were fired forward using the very same electromagnetic catapults that launched the Lycerene fighter jets. Thousands of mines of all types were catapulted forward.

The simplicity of it was beauty enough. The Neferan Swarm that dived down in a single never ending column found themselves barreling into a wall of mines. A wall that stretched from side to side and from top to bottom like a massive net.

The first line of fighters had barely enough time to pull away, but for the fighters behind them, it was too late. Headlong into the mines they went. Burst after burst and their visibility quickly became clouded with smoke and debris. Wasp fighters now careened into mines, crashed into scattered debris, or collided with other fighters. And then the Pack accelerated forward with those blazing cannon that lit fire to the oncoming Wasp fighters. Obliterating wave after wave of them.

The Queen burned with confusion "What...What is happening to my Swarm? How can this be?"

Sun Keptra fumbled with his keyboard until his head popped straight up. "My Queen, I've analyzed their strategy. I think they are using mines, stealth-mines, to clear the way. Hurling them directly into the path of the Swarm. It is possible my Queen...that they may breach the Swarm! I suggest once more that we evacuate you...now!"

What little use his words carried now. "Have me retreat...hide? Do you think me a coward? Between me and that old dog is the mightiest Swarm ever assembled! Even if he makes it through, he still has to face the firepower of my ship and her Destroyers."

First Officer Sun Keptra leaned close to the Queen, to speak quietly, so as not to deface her before the crew. "My Queen...you have said it clearly yourself....between he and us, lies a Swarm, but also lies those mines; hundreds...maybe thousands of mines...and they are headed directly toward us."

Her head snapped around peering directly at him as if he were the enemy. And before she could speak, the first few mines struck her Destroyers. Fire bursts flashed and ruptured the hulls as the Destroyers buckled from the blasts. Slowly, the Destroyers rolled over and out of control exposing her ship to the incoming Pack.

"Mines…mines…those damn Lycerene mines! Get us out of here!"

It was the moment that the old Chief was waiting for. The moment when the Queen was forced to move her ship and reveal her position. Old and exhausted as Cree was, his eyes did not miss it.
"There she is!
The Bitch has flinched!
All ships…ramming speed!"

Sun Keptra, was fixed to his computer screens and saw it coming. "My Queen, they are in the clouds and coming straight at us!" The clouds continued to swirl around as explosions and fires raged everywhere. All eyes fixed on the cloud and then Cree's flagship burst through. Damaged so that it was hurling out of control, twisting and spinning onto its back.

Queen Anak Re Sun, The Warrior Queen, rose to her feet, backing away from the viewport. Half bent over as if the failure of it pained her so. The old Chief's ship simply spun at her as if it were falling out of the sky. Filling the viewport and blotting out the stars as it drew closer and closer.

Somewhere between his fear of death and the thrill of victory, Cree's young Communication Officer shouted. "Chief Cree, Neferan Queen, dead ahead. We have her Sir!" The old Chief now dropped back into his chair exhausted, and his head dropped hard to his chest. Then it hit. A flash so brilliant, it would rival the nearest star.

Amid the smoke, the fires, and the blaring alarms, Sun Keptra's familiar voice screamed…"My Queen, My Queen, are you alright?

Still dazed with her eyes half closed and fluttering, she appeared dead. Shaking her again and again until she blinked. She mumbled. "What…What…What has happened?"

"My Queen, the Destroyer Annacon rammed him. Just seconds to spare, but she hit him straight on. Chief Cree is dead…that dreaded old dog is dead for sure!"

Still dazed, she mumbled almost incoherently. "The Destroyer Annacon…sacrificed?"

"Yes. My Queen, most honorably. Even so, we have won the day. The Lycerene Pack is destroyed…it is finally destroyed!"

Then he stood straight, almost at the position of attention and delivered a most important message. "My Queen, it is time for you to return to Nefera. The High Queen, Ahmun Shepsut Anak, has summoned you to her side."

CHAPTER 4: EYE FOR REVENGE

Never before had Longspear been so quiet and so still. On that walk to the briefing room the young Keeper, Reza, saw not so much as one eye look upon another. The look of defeat infected every one of his Pack brethren. A look that he never expected to see.

Young Keeper Reza entered the briefing room and although he had never before seen the inside of that room, he knew where his seat would be. Like every other officer, he walked to it and stood behind it, waiting. Twelve seats in all, the highest of them being the Chief-of-Ship held by Chief Sazzi.

As the new Keeper Prime, Reza's seat was directly across from Chief Sazzi. When Chief Sazzi and the Executive Officer entered the room, the call to 'attention' brought every silent soul to focus. Only after Chief Sazzi had seated did Reza and the other officers take their seats. Then they awaited Chief Sazzi's first words.

"Our options are but two. First option is that we could make a run for it, flee to open space and take our chances. Second option is we could return home and fight. It's a long journey, and there is no telling what we'll see. There may be nothing left to save."

To that, the young Keeper sat there watching them, silently. Watching them agree with each other and watching them call for revenge. Young as he was, even he knew that Longspear alone would pose no real threat to the Neferan Swarm. But, he did have an idea. An idea that the Neferan would not expect and so at least it had the element of surprise.

Sitting there quietly and patiently while waiting for the right moment, he knew that there would be no second chance to persuade them. Waiting until the twelve had noticed that he had not yet spoken. They looked upon him. "What say you? What does the proud Keeper have to say?" Other voices burst out in anger. "He is no Keeper...Are we to take advice from one so young?"

Still, Reza sat there in thought staring at his pencil and not at them. He poked the pencil to the paper and slowly rolled it in his fingers for a few seconds. "I agree we attack, but I disagree on just what we attack." To that they scoffed. "Ah... he is young. We may have but one chance. Would you have us expend it on a convoy or troop transport?"

To that, they attempted to resume their talks, but he had to convince them. Pausing just a moment to collect his thoughts, remembering as had been taught. A change to his voice, a more commanding tone and he spoke sternly and loudly above them. "With a fleet so large to attack us, the Nefera home world must now be lightly defended."

To this their eyes drew to a blank stare as their thoughts now drifted inward. "So you have an eye for revenge....tell us young Keeper, how do you intend to reach their world? Where do you propose we find the fuel?"

Before he could address the issue, he needed to carry them a bit further into his train of thought. "Revenge is not the only reason. Think of it like this...Until now, the Neferan have been strictly on the offensive. If we can strike the Neferan home world, they will have to recall forces to defend their world.

Reza looked around the table, gazing into their eyes one by one. Looking to measure their response. Few if any gave their support, so he continued. "Can you win a fistfight if all you do is defend yourself? No, you must strike back, bloody their noses. I say we strike them! Strike them now and I say we strike them in their own homes. Let them know that terror works both ways!"

The room fell silent for a moment as they all knew that the young Keeper had spoken well. Far across the table, one voice spoke; Chief Sazzi. "Just what Chiefdom bears us such a young Keeper?"

Reza responded firm. "Sir, I am Reza of the Cherrkota Chiefdom."

Now Reza had to prepare himself for the hard part of his proposal, how to convince them that he knew a short-cut. He knew they would never accept his answer. It had been an accepted fact that it was not possible, that it could not be done. "As you know, my predecessor, Chief Cree was a man of many studies including history; ancient history. He spent his last years immersed in it. In fact, it was one relic in particular that commanded his focus."

At this point, Reza reached into his bag and produced his personal computer device, keyed in his password, and the image appeared. Hovering above the table, in a vision of charged air particles, appeared the image of an ancient box as long, wide, and deep as a man's forearm and made of metal. The ancient metal shined brightly and was untarnished having engravings cut deep into it. He pointed to one particular image. "The box is of unknown origin and is among the oldest relics ever found. We have yet to understand its symbols entirely. We don't even know the composition of the metal."

He pointed to the carvings on the box. "In these carvings right here you can see what Chief Cree believed to be the symbol of a passage, a Corridor as he called it." And before he could finish, Chief Sazzi interrupted "You are young, maybe too young. This is a military vessel, we don't dabble in ancient religions."

Sensing that his audience was losing patience, Reza took a slow breath and steadied himself for the worst was yet to come. "Chief Cree believed that The Corridor is a configuration of stars that are essentially a roadmap, a shortcut." Chief Sazzi responded "How can this be? Why haven't our instruments identified such a configuration?"

No sooner had those words left his own lips, when Sazzi had deduced it for himself. He stared blankly across the table, directly into the eyes of young Keeper Reza "This Corridor...it must be inside The Void." The room fell silent. Then the question returned, "I say again young Keeper, how do you propose we get there? The Void is impassable."

Reza pushed one more button and the image floating before them changed to a star map. Reza continued. "Chief Cree had recognized that the points in the carvings were stars, but they were largely uncharted. Cree was building a computer simulation to map the stars, but he never finished it. That's why he chose me to continue his work. I have an interest for such things, ancient symbols. And one of the symbols here I took to mean 'empty star'. I may be no expert with stars, but I can tell you that there are many types of stars, even those that we cannot see, black-holes."

They thought for a few moments and then the questions began. "Still, young Keeper, even if we could find this Corridor, we may lose weeks or months to get there."

To answer that question, Reza opened the last file and displayed it. "Good Sirs, does this star map look familiar?" They sat confused staring at an image of millions of stars, yet something within them recognizing the scene. It was the same scene visible from the Port side of Longspear. They had been staring at The Corridor with each passing day. "My guess is that you've all wondered why Chief Cree kept Longspear stationed out here, in the middle of nowhere, and now you know why."

They sat quietly for a moment, searching for any evidence to argue the contrary. "Gentlemen, here is the key point, The Void is impassable, this is true. But, if Chief Cree is correct, The Corridor is like a key to The Void; the one place where The Void can be entered. If this is true, then we would pass directly through the center of The Void rather than traveling around it. We would expend a fraction of the fuel and most importantly time, time Good Sirs. We could be in a position to attack the Nefera home world long before they could recall their Swarm…from our world.

An immediate objection was voiced by the Executive Officer citing that the risks were unacceptable. Others joined in and the argument grew stiff. But, young Keeper Reza had one undeniable fact and was prepared to use it. "Good Sirs, the time is short. Once the Neferan Swarm locates our position, they will come for us. We need to strike now, now while we have the element of surprise."

Reza had captured their attention and he proceeded with his final words. "Chief Cree, gave me this plan as his last order. I am to lead my Pack of twenty-five fighters into The Void and if we are successful, we'll send one fighter to return and lead Longspear through." With that, he made an assumptive close to his proposal. "My Pack will be ready to depart at zero-six-hundred hours tomorrow." To that, he closed his personal computer device, saluted Chief Sazzi, and departed.

Again, Keeper Reza stepped out into the hallway and passed through the defeated eyes, the fearful eyes, and the lost eyes. But his footsteps were different this time. Full of confidence and full of purpose, and they sensed it. This time, they raised their eyes and watched him walk along. His eyes no longer showed defeat, his shoulders no longer slumped, and they knew that something was going to happen.

Passing through the mess hall, passing through the officer's lounge, all the way to his squad bay, where his Pack awaited. He opened the heavy hatch, stepped through, and pulled it tightly closed behind him. Dogging-down on the hinges by pulling the heavy arm. Before he had turned to address them, they were on their feet standing at attention. Some half-dressed, some half asleep. All of them aware that Reza had been called to Chief Sazzi's quarters, but did not know why.

But, they were eager to hear the outcome. He faced them and looked in their eyes one at a time. All twenty-five of them. A long bond between them, for they were a Pack and Reza was their Chief-of-Pack. A Pack was a military unit comprised of lifelong brothers; a family. Among this Pack, the leaders were Reza and a female pilot by the name of Chel, of the Chenne Chiefdom.

Upon the slightest change to Reza's facial expression they knew something big was about to happen. "At zero-six-hundred hours tomorrow, we will attempt to pass into The Void. We will pass through based on the coordinates left to my care by the former Keeper Prime, Chief Cree. We will find the Nefera home world. When we do, we will send one fighter back to escort Longspear through. Then we attack the Neferan home world. Now take your rest."

The Pack immediately returned to whatever they were doing. Anything to pass the time. Reza walked through them straight to his bunk at the far end of the compartment. He sat down and leaned back to look up at the pictures he had fastened to the bunk above him. Just a few pictures of his wife and two daughters. Those pictures had always reminded him of home, someplace happy. Now, they brought a rush of fear, hate, and rage. As he was thinking deeply, one of his closest comrades, Nava of the Segosett Chiefdom, leaned over from the bunk above and dropped down.

"Move your arss over, I'm bored."

Reza replied "Nava, my arss is in no mood for company."

With his friendly smile, Nava continued. "Your arss doesn't know what's good for it. Never did. Now, let me get this straight, we're going into The Void yes? And we're going in using some really old coordinates provided by the Keeper Prime, yes?"

Reza looked at Nava and appreciated the humor, "It's not like that my friend. I've seen Chief Cree's files and the ancient scrolls. He was planning this for some time."

Again, Nava joked at the mission. "Hmm. Impassable void, ancient coordinates, mystical relics, you can't make-up this stuff." With a smile Nava added "We depart at zero-six hundred. I figure by zero-six-fifteen, we will all be dead. Still my friend, it is better than waiting for that Swarm to find us."

Not another man among his Pack could have pulled that off without annoying Reza. "C'mon Reza, or must I now call you Keeper Prime. Let's get something to eat. I'm hungry."

Reza smirked back. "Nava, you are always hungry. One day, you will not fit so neatly into that pilot armor that you keep so shined."

That night they slept on Longspear, what little they could amid the sorrow and fear. Then, they awoke and took to their pre-combat rituals, preparing their bodies with prayer and cleansing. They removed their personal effects. As for most of them, they still clung to the ancient religion. The symbol of that religion was hung from a chain worn about the neck. The beast of legend to which the ancient prophets proclaimed would one day return; to guide them. It would return at a time when man would be turned away from his technology and returned to the wild. It seemed an easy thing to shed those chains now.

Before suiting up in their armor, they applied their war paint. Sash marks of blues, reds, and yellows; all in accordance with their family burial traditions. These to be covered by their armor such that only the bearer or his grave digger would ever see them. The final step was to add the ornate headdress of colored feathers that was reserved only for pilots; symbolizing flight. Feathers that hung across the back of the helmet, facing downward, spread out like the wings of an Eagle. And when they were finished, they formed ranks inside their squad bay and waited for Reza to open the heavy hatch.

They marched in unison and the sounds of their footprints stepping on the metal decking was thunderous. All eyes looked to them as they passed and all eyes knew the time to retaliate was near. Reza and his Pack proceeded on through Longspear until they reached the flight deck. There they stood awaiting final orders to board their fighter-jets.

The flight deck was so large that it was the entire length of the Longspear. In the very center was electromagnetic catapult that used to launch fighter jets from the stem and retrieve them at the stern. To either side were conveyor systems that moved the fighter jets from their resting place to the catapult; for rapid deploy and retrieval.

As Reza made preparations with the Flight Deck Officer, he noticed Chief Sazzi and the twelve officers assembling upon the flight deck. He anticipated more objections and concerns, possibly even the worst, that the mission had been cancelled. Before they had a chance to object, Reza grasped the moment and reminded them of the urgency. "Only a matter of time before that Swarm will detect Longspear… and they will give chase!"

But, Chief Sazzi interrupted him. "Keeper Reza, this is my ship…I give the orders around here." Sazzi looked down at the report in his hands and immediately Reza suspected something urgent. Reza looked across at the twelve officers and by the look in their eyes, he was sure of it. Then, Sazzi continued. "Minutes ago, our sensors began to pick up signals….they have already found our position. That Neferan Swarm will be upon us within the hour, but Longspear's repairs won't be completed for at least twelve hours. There is no place to run."

Now, all eyes drew to the young Keeper who shuddered at the thought as Sazzi continued. "There is no place left to hide and Longspear can barely fight in this condition, let alone jump. But, she can make way under normal power, so we are left with one option. We stick to the original plan, but with one change…Longspear will follow your Pack into The Void."

All of this was not what Reza was expecting. It was almost too much for him to think through and his eyes went blank. Any failure, any miscalculation, any error would mean annihilation of everyone on Longspear. Chief Sazzi didn't like the look on Reza's face so he pressed the issue. "Unless you've got any better ideas in that mystical box of yours, this is it. You will enter The Void ahead of Longspear and you will relay anything relevant...anything at all. Longspear will make adjustments based on your findings. Minutes matter now so brief your crew and resume your mission!"

With a sharp about-face, Reza picked up his gear and scrambled down the centerline to his fighter-jet. Once seated, Reza opened his bag, took out his personal computer device, and jacked into the interface port. He quickly briefed his Pack of the mission change. Then, settled back reminding himself that he would soon pass through The Void. He wondered how old the box was, what he would see in The Void, but most importantly, he wondered how he would strike the Neferan home world.

He looked down at the small circle that was loosely attached over his shoulder armor and detached it. Holding it up to his eyes, he activated it and instantly, an image of his family appeared in the circle. Just a moment to think of them, but they too were among the millions facing genocide. Suddenly, the conveyor shuddered and he knew what that meant. Regretfully, he deactivated the image and he reattached the circle to his shoulder.

Immediately, the launch sequence began. One by one, the barrier doors revolved around and released a fighter-jet into the centerline where the electromagnetic catapult threw the fighters out into space. Briefly the fighters lofted there before the thrusters fired up and kicked in. In all of thirty seconds, twenty-five Pack fighters were now lofted and thrusting into formation an eyeshot away from Longspear. Once lofted, Reza watched the great hulking Longspear as he passed on by. He noticed every one of Longspear's battle scars. Scorched and twisted patches. With each passing scar, fear gripped him more. The fear that he would never see Longspear again.

CHAPTER 5: THE CORRIDOR

Now in standard flight formation, Reza assumed his role as Chief-of-Pack and took control of all twenty-five fighters, to fly them as one Pack. Within his fighter-jet and onboard Longspear, display panels refreshed depicting The Void with the twenty-five fighters headed into it along with Longspear trailing far behind.

Each refresh of the display panels brought the Lycerene Pack and Longspear closer to the line that represented The Void and in a matter of minutes, Reza's Pack would enter the outer rim of The Void.

Per Chief Cree's calculations, the entry to The Void was to be as slow as possible, so Reza announced the order, "All ahead, one quarter thrust." As they breached the outer rim of The Void, their communications began to encounter sporadic disruption. It gradually worsened so they switched to text messages. Further into the outer rim, their instruments began to behave strangely. Starting with subtle little flickers and blurs, but like the communications, it gradually worsened. Yet, the Pack pressed on. Messaging to and from Longspear like a safety cord. Always with the sense that they were still tethered to Longspear. But that also began to fade and become sporadic at best.

Chel worked diligently at her analysis trying to determine what type of energy was causing the disruptions. She sent a text stream to the Pack, "Disturbance caused by unknown energy type. Current rate of degradation will result in electronic damage in one, maybe two minutes."

Reza read it and quickly responded to his Pack and to Longspear "Prepare to switch to Analog." A switch from digital instrumentation to Analog was rarely ever necessary. It was considered a dangerous thing to do because Analog instrumentation was slower and less sensitive than digital. Most of all, they would lose the ability to fly under the singular control of the Chief-of-Pack. They would need to pilot on manual; each pilot to his own.

It was time to switch or risk losing key electronic systems. From every display panel, every eye watched as Reza made preparations for Analog. His first thoughts were that they could be separated, but there was no time to estimate the risks. Then, he keyed the final command. Instantly, the fighters felt different, felt looser, they swayed and pilots tried to adjust to steady their fighters, but they responded sluggish as if they were logs floating on the sea. Amid the sporadic communications and alarms they came close to each other, too close. All at once, the fighters passed the threshold into The Void; into the point where the disturbance was most concentrated. The fighter-jets now bounced around having little if any ability to navigate. Even Analog was now failing, leaving Reza with but one solution remaining. He powered down all non-vital systems, surely Longspear's sensors would see that.

They were now essentially being thrown into The Void cascading along as if they were free falling. That final tether to Longspear was now gone. In that very moment when the entire Pack was disappearing from the display panels of Longspear, the two fighter-jets at the rear of the Pack collided. The sensors onboard Longspear had captured the event and relayed it through the display monitors for everyone to see. There, in real-time, the disappearance of twenty-five fighters and confirmation that two of them had been destroyed.

But Chief Cree had proven himself yet again. For his assumptions had predicted rightly that The Void could only be penetrated in one place, at one trajectory, and at one speed. Had they impacted the outer rim at even a medium speed, they would have simply destroyed their electronics, and if they had survived that, they would have drifted endlessly. Surely, this explained why no sensors, probes, or vessels had ever returned from The Void.

Now, they were inside The Void and slowly, their fighters began to regain control. As quickly as possible, Reza switched back to digital and restored the automated flight controls. He made every effort to reestablish contact with Longspear, but as expected, no signals returned. Once inside, it was easy to see that The Void was not an empty space. It was a barrier that blocked anything from passing in either direction. Soon, they found that all systems had returned to normal function. Tedious text messages were no longer needed and the speakers burst aloud as everyone chimed in at one time. Frantically, they searched for the two fighters that had collided. But, only a few charred remnants of the machines drifted past.

Onboard Longspear, they had no sooner received the findings from Reza's transmissions when the alarms rang out once again. Something was creating an energy disturbance that could only mean one thing, the Neferan fleet was jumping to their position. Now, there was no time left. No time to confirm if the Pack had survived and no time to run calculations and predictive models.

On the bridge of Longspear, with alarms buzzing and people scrambling, Chief Sazzi withheld the order to enter The Void.

"Hold this position! I need those calculation. I will not throw two thousand lives at that Void unless I absolutely have to!"

Then, The First Officer turned to Chief Sazzi "Sir, it's not the attack that I'm concerned about. If we stay, we run the risk that they will find The Corridor!"

Chief Sazzi snapped back. "I have nothing! I don't have a navigational solution. I will not plow into that thing. You saw what it did to Reza's fighters!"

The First Officer responded with urgency. "Sir, yes, I did see. But, those fighters didn't just disappear. They powered down before they disappeared. That's our solution! We don't have time for an Analog cutover....Set this ship to the same speed and course as Reza's Pack and power down before we hit the outer rim. A full power down on this ship will take at least seven minutes, but that Swarm will be on us in twelve minutes. You've got to do it now!"

Chief Sazzi stood there thinking while moments ticked past. Before the First Officer could press the urgency, he raised his hand to calm the crew. He spoke slowly, as if he had fully detached from himself, knowing that there was no choice. "First Officer, you have my order.... Execute per your suggestion."

To that, the First Officer immediately set to his plan. Calling out orders and keying in command after command. While the First Officer orchestrated the solution, Chief Sazzi stood watching out the rear view port, watching and waiting as the Swarm fleet jumped into position.

Longspear was aligned to The Corridor and set to speed. Crews all over the ship were busy in preparation, especially those involved in the delicate power down. Even to the best of their abilities, they couldn't bring the ships systems entirely down in time. There was smoke, electrical bursts all over the ship, and fire. Fire in the berthing areas and mess decks. The massive ship passed into The Void while the Swarm continued to assemble behind her. When Longspear emerged on the other side, she was in trouble. Listing heavily to Port side with the bow down, powerless. A full day's time had passed before Longspear was repaired and ready for jumps. Reza and his Pack pressed ahead to scout the Neferan planet while waiting for Longspear.

The journey would take incremental steps traversing each star in The Corridor. Stopping at each star only long enough to reconfirm their position and prepare for the next jump. From star to dark-star and on and on. The repeated jumps went beyond their physical limits, beyond the number of jumps allowed per fleet regulations. They grew weary and sick with the effects of the jumps. If not for the automated controls, more of them would surely have been lost. Then slowly, the distance between the stars and black-holes grew longer until there was only one jump remaining. And upon that final jump, they were there.

CHAPTER 6: THE INNOCENT WORLD

The old Keeper Cree had predicted it so, he had plotted and assumed it correctly. A solar system that they had never seen, nothing but a glowing orange sun and the countless stars all around them. Exhausted to the point of confusion, they gathered their senses slowly, as if they had been asleep. Reza was the first to speak. "Where is it? Where is Nefera? It should be here!"

Chel slowly came to her senses and began looking all around. Looking up high and twisting her neck as far back as she could to see behind her. But, no sign of Nefera. Finally, she leaned far over to the right and looked downward. The words burst from her mouth. "Below us! Below us! It's right below us! We are right on top of it!"

No sooner did Reza look down than Nava had joined in. "To close! To close! They will know we are here! What do we do now? Longspear won't be here for at least a day."

Chel checked her computer for any planetary communication signals. "Multiple signal sources from the planet below...and satellites. The planet is rimmed with satellites that are already sensing our position. Reza, even if we retreat, they know were here."

Reza looked down at the planet and saw his opportunity slipping away. Not just because they were losing the element of surprise, but because they had emerged on the dark side of the planet; another advantage that he could not afford to lose. His eyes fixed on the black orb below, not the planet itself, but the glowing lights of the cities. Two of them were enormous; perfect targets for a night attack. "We attack! We attack right now!"

Reza continued. "We target those two cities.
Chel, man the gun turrets.
Nava, ready the bombs."

Before Reza finished giving his orders, he had already begun navigating the Lycerene Pack into attack position by rolling them over and diving straight down. Chel immediately took control of every gun turret in the Pack and prepared to defend against the Swarm. At the same time, Nava made his preparations, he stated the obvious. "Reza, those two cities are huge. We have hardly enough bombs for targets that big."

Reza had already thought of that and he had an idea. "We will drop Harmonics and Magnesium Thermocells on the cities; right in the middle of the city. The harmonic tremors and magnesium fires will spread outwards. Hopefully, it will keep them busy till Longspear arrives."

The Pack broke thru the planet's atmosphere at supersonic speed leaving a trail of fire and smoke across the night sky, and still, no Neferan Swarm. But, Reza kept his eye on his radar screen scanning and searching. Sure enough. "Chel, here they come. Neferan Swarm massing directly below us. Ready the turrets!"

Chel's hands glided across her control panel as she redirected every gun turret to rotate forward. Frantically, she pre-programmed the initial targets and as she did so, the Swarm grew larger and larger. Coagulating just below them in a giant mass that swelled by the minute. The distance closed and in the moment before they would be in range, Chel spoke. "So many. Reza, there are so many!"

That should have been the first hint that something was wrong, but Reza proceeded. "Chel, we will use diving speed to break through them. We will dive to the first city, then level off for the bomb-run, then dive to the second city. Nava, configure the detonators. First city, high-altitude. Second city, low-altitude."

Nava responded with the obvious. "What then? What do we do after the second city?" There was no reply.

As the Pack dove straight down and slammed into the swirling Swarm, the gun turrets erupted with pinpoint accuracy. The night sky was illuminated by the flashes of Wasp Fighters exploding into fireballs. As the Lycerene Pack careened deeper into the Neferan Swarm Chel worked at a panic pace to keep the gun turrets on target.

As the first city came into range, Reza leveled-off from the dive and prepared for the bomb-run. "Five, four, three, two, one! Nava, release the bombs!" The bomb doors opened and Nava released dozens of bombs that poured out from every fighter-jet of the Pack. Nava shouted back to Reza. "Bombs away...dive! Dive! Dive!" Immediately, Reza put the Pack into a dive and headed straight towards the second city. Behind them, the bomb blasts erupted and the city was swallowed in a boiling cauldron of fire and black smoke.

Minutes to the next city and the Neferan Swarm was right behind them. Chel's gun turrets fired nonstop trying to fend them off, but the damage to the Pack was mounting.

She could see several of her brethren were smoking and falling behind, but what caught her eye was one of the Wasp Fighters. "Nava, look at that Wasp Fighter off our starboard side. Do you see him?" She didn't wait for Nava to reply. "He is different. Not the usual mindless...drone attack! He is doing something!" Nava found the Wasp Fighter and noticed that it was holding one position. It hung there as if it were studying the Pack. Searching for some way to attack. Chel pointed the turrets at the Wasp and fired, but it waited till the last second and quickly rolled-out, then rolled-back exactly where it had been before. Chel fired again and again, but it the Wasp just rolled-out and rolled-in again. Always returning to the same position.

That should have been the second hint that something was wrong. Before Chel could say anything, Reza burst over the radio and disrupted her thinking. "Nava, second city in range! Leveling off for the bomb-run. Five, four, three, two, one. Release the bombs." With the Bomb-bay doors opened, Reza worked fitfully to hold the pack steady while the bombs poured out.

But, 'steady' is exactly what that single Wasp Fighter was waiting for. The Wasp Fighter had caught the Pack at its most vulnerable moment, 'steady' while the bombs were pouring out. That single Wasp Fighter rolled right in behind the Pack and opened fire. His tracers and bullets peppered the Pack as sparks and fires erupted everywhere. Chel redirected her turrets, but that one Wasp Fighter was too fast, too maneuverable, to instinctive. Before she realized it, she was totally out of munitions. "Reza, that's it! We are out of munitions. All turrets are inactive!"

The bomb blasts lit up the night sky behind them. At that same moment, Reza could see the first glows of the sun rising off the horizon in front of them. Those first glows revealed a forested patch on the ground below. Reza knew that if his Pack had any last chance, it was on the ground. "All hands, we will eject over that forested patch and make for the hills."

Even as he spoke, the few Pack fighters that had fallen behind were being overtaken by the Swarm. One by one, Reza's Pack was disintegrating so with seconds remaining, he pointed the Pack to the forest, dived down, and at the last moment, they all ejected.

Small thrusters guided the ejection crafts to the ground within earshot of each other. Touching down in a field just outside of a large forested patch, nineteen in all. In minutes, those who had survived exited the ejection craft, grabbed their gear and their weapons. Then, they located each other and disappeared into the woods.

The darkness of night had covered their escape thus far, but soon, daylight would break. They retreated deep into the woods as search craft blanketed the area. Searchlights filled the night sky scanning from side to side all while ground troops massed all around the forest. Soon, scanners and sensors would be on the scene and there would be no place left to hide. At best the Pack could evade detection for hours, maybe less, and they knew it.

Deep in the woods, Reza and his Pack stopped for a moment. Exhausted and breathless, most of them simply let their bodies collapse to the ground allowing their armor to shield them from rocks and branches. Lying there long enough to catch their breath, just enough air to speak. Nava burst forward still gasping "Get up, we've got to keep moving...they are right behind us." A few of them rose to their feet and then tried to help the others. Still on one knee, Reza muscled up enough air for a few words "Go where?"

A few more gasps and Reza resumed his sentence "They will find us soon enough! Look around, this is good fighting ground. We stand here! We fight here!"

More gasping and he stood up. The position was an open field surrounded by the dark forest on three sides with a fourth side being sheer cliff. Boulders scattered about the base of the cliff; boulders that were plentiful and large enough to provide cover for a man. It was a perfect trap for the Neferan troops, especially if the Neferan intended to capture them. "Put your backs to the cliffs....spread out along the rocks. They will come through the clearing. Then, we will catch them in a crossfire."

As if following his own orders, Reza turned and headed off to the cliffs taking up a position behind a boulder dead center of the clearing. The others followed and spread out crouching down, catching their breath, and making preparations.

The darkness of night now was transitioning to daylight as the sky glowed orange from the sun, but beneath the cover of the forest, it was still dark. The still night air carried the sounds of troops and machines as they closed in. Among those sounds was something new, not man, not machine, but something else, animal. Something that sounded ferocious like steel jaws snapping, over and over. Something else was in those woods.

Soon, very soon, whatever was coming would suddenly find itself bursting through the underbrush and into the clearing. By the sounds alone, they could tell that whatever approached in the darkness was heavy and armored, like themselves. They could hear the sound of armored feet upon the rocks, hear the sound of sticks and branch breaking with each step. At the same moment that the sun cast its first glows into the forest, something entered the clearing running at full speed; black silhouettes. In moments, they were halfway up the clearing when the Pack opened fire. What had been a peaceful and quiet forest was instantly filled with a deafening roar of gun blast.

A startling sound that echoed against the cliffs and rolled like thunder across the clearing. Each of the black silhouettes were struck by several bullets throwing some backward while others were spun about. A few of them collapsing to the ground, but alive. Their armor had fared well against the side-arms of the Pack. Yet, they laid there, twisting and crawling in pain.

A small force equal to Reza's Pack had rushed right into the clearing. Before they could use up all their ammunition, they were upon each other, hand-to-hand. They crashed together at such speeds that the first clash of blades found no marks. Instead, their bodies simply collided shoulder to shoulder and helmet to helmet. Bodies were cast in all directions and they thundered and cracked as they landed upon the rocks. Equally matched almost man for man, but the Pack was now nearly exhausted having spent most of their energy in the endless sequence of jumps. The casualties mounted quickly on both sides, not from sword alone, but from fist and rock and anything else. Soon both sides reached exhaustion levels to where they were on hand and knee gasping for air, all but two of them.

They were filled with revenge, these two; Reza and his enemy Wasp; still beating and bashing each other. Blades whisping around in the air emitting sparks as they matched each other blow for blow and thrust for thrust. For all Reza's training and skill, he could not defeat this Wasp who fought from intensity and instinct.

Just as they locked wrists, Reza's ears were suddenly filled with the sounds of those snapping jaws. Three of them had pounced on Reza from behind, knocking him to the ground. Before he could roll over, those teeth were snapping at his face. Unable to cover his face with his hands as two of them bit into his armored forearms, tugging and snarling. Leaving a third beast to stand over his face to scrape with its paws, to bark, and to growl. A ferocious beast indeed, and it had returned as prophesied. Not to lead the Lycerene Pack, but to hunt them.

The beasts held Reza to the ground while one of the planetary Officers shouted orders. "That's enough! We need them alive. Let's go people, pack them up. Medics, tend to the wounded!"

The voice came from the forest where it was still dark, but soon that man approached. As soon as he stepped into the light, everything changed. As if time stood still, as if the world had stopped spinning. The gaze of every Lycerene was upon him. Where all of the Wasp soldiers wore full body armor, black as night, this man did not. Something was wrong. Something was very wrong.

There standing before the Lycerene Pack was something that could not be, simply could not be. For the Neferan were of black skin. Black as the night sky and nothing but black; for that was their way. Not so of the Officer standing in front of them, for his skin was white.

Reza's mind spun with a singular question, "How...how...how." He recalled the images of the star maps and The Corridor. He recalled Chief Cree and his predictions, calculations, and assumptions. And there it was...the assumptions. Nowhere on the ancient box did anything state that The Corridor led to Nefera. Nothing on the box stated exactly what world The Corridor led to. Reza looked at Chel who was down on her knees and his voice trembled, "Not Nefera…it's not Nefera! What have we done?"

They were hurried into two land bound vehicles large enough to contain a dozen or more men. The trip lasted hours and finally they were moved to a secured facility. The facility was aloud with medics and soldiers at every station, all of them wearing protective suits. All at once, the medics exited out the rear door and another crew of medics rushed in. At the sight of their faces, Chel gasped. An impossibility beyond anything they had yet seen. She burst aloud "Reza!"

The room went dead still as Reza followed Chel's stare across the room at the incoming medics. Reza stood in total disbelief, a yellow face with slanted eyes and then a brown face with long black hair, and finally, a face that was black, black as the Neferan.

For generations, the twelve worlds that surround The Void had fought a war, a war of purity. Hence, they were known as the Puratist Worlds. Twelve worlds, each to its own kind; never anything more and never anything less. And yet here, a world where the races lived together, an uncharted world, Earth. By everything Reza knew, this world should never have existed. By everything he knew, this world was an abomination.

Even now, Earth's medics and soldiers could see that race had something to do with the attack, but they were unprepared for what they would see next. Within the walls of the sealed facility, they could now remove the armor of Reza and his Pack. For the first time, the people of Earth would set eyes upon the Lycerene. Recognizing that Reza was the leader, they approached him first and they used hand motions to indicate that he was expected to remove his armor. He did not resist. Rather, he motioned to one of his men to assist, Nava.

First, the neck collar that held the helmet to the neck. Then, each piece of armor was removed and placed on the rack. Still, under that armor, was a pure white under layer covering the entire body. The headdress was a form fitted material with openings for the eyes, nose, mouth, and ears. Blood had soaked the facemask and had run down the neck and chest area, but Reza stood straight and tall. Then, Reza put his hands to his shoulders and peeled back the layers of the headdress. He removed the headdress in one pull. With that first glimpse, Earth's medics and soldiers found themselves equally shocked for they set eyes upon a race of man for which they had never seen. Now, they understood, even if only a little more.

The body of Lycerene men was covered fully with hair of differing lengths, coarseness, and color. The head was covered by hair same as any, shoulder length and braided. The face was covered by two types of hair. The familiar hair about a man's mouth and chin which grew long. But the remainder of the body and neck was covered by a shorter hair. The very same hair that all races exhibit above the brow. Short, soft, and smooth. Lycerene Females were slightly different. Covered by a light tan hair that held more shine than the males. Females also had the distinct characteristic of a 'v' shaped hairline upon the forehead. It framed the face and bestowed an eloquence upon them, every one of them.

In their exhaustion, Reza and his Pack hadn't considered until now that they hadn't been killed or tortured. They had been treated for their injuries, photographed, measured, and examined. Then, all at once, the medics and soldiers departed the room and left Reza and his Pack to themselves. They settled back for their minds were weary and their bodies ached. All of them closed their eyes as if they would be allowed to rest. For the first time, they had a chance to speak among themselves.

Chel spoke first. "What have we done? We attacked an innocent planet."

Reza replied in frustration. "Everything went wrong. Everything!"

Nava joined in. "Be prepared, they will be back soon. This time to interrogate us."

Chel responded lost in her own words "We dropped harmonics on them…and Magnesium Thermocells, those cities will burn for weeks. These people will not know how to extinguish them. We murdered millions of innocent people! What are we going to tell them? How can we tell them about our war, our world, and…"

Then, Nava sat straight up and blurted out. "Longspear! We need to tell them…that Longspear will be coming through. Longspear will attack! We've got to stop it."

The room fell dead silent. Reza then thought one step further, "They need to know that there may be something else besides Longspear coming through…The Neferan Swarm."

Then Nava's face took on an expression of hopelessness "They will never believe us…never…What have we done?"

Chel then stepped forward as if taking the lead. "We've got to try. What purpose do we serve now if not for this? We'll make them believe." She walked directly up to the glass wall that was solid white. She knew that behind the wall was a team of interrogation technicians. She stood tall and spoke in a commanding, dignified, yet apologetic tone. Words they would not understand, but conveying an emotion that was clear. It was time to talk.

CHAPTER 7: EYE TO EYE

Nobody behind the glass wall understood her words, but they understood that she was going to tell them something important. They adjusted the shading properties of the glass. It now changed to a clear glass with a smoky tint of white. Two teams now stood face to face on opposite sides of a glass. Chel motioned for a writing utensil, something to draw a picture. In that picture she began with an illustration of this newfound world, Earth. Around it she illustrated The Void. Around The Void, she illustrated the twelve known worlds with Lycera and Nefera at opposite ends, with Earth in the middle. That much was easy.

Next, she illustrated the war between Lycera and Nefera. In that scene, she conveyed the loss of Lycera and they understood. Then, through the center of The Void, she drew The Corridor and illustrated that the Pack of twenty-five fighters had traversed through The Corridor to Earth. Behind the twenty-five fighters, she illustrated Longspear, and behind Longspear, she drew the Neferan carriers.

Again and again, she tried to explain that they had attacked Earth assuming it was Nefera, but the coincidence of it all was simply unbelievable. The interrogation crew clearly assumed it was a trick. Suddenly, the wall went solid white again, something was happening.

Seconds later, the door burst open and soldiers poured through. The soldiers carried with them airtight suits one for each member of the Pack, for they were being moved. All of them were loaded into some type of railcar that quickly headed toward a nearby mountain. They could see vehicles of all types rushing past them and people running in all directions. In the distance, they could see the plumes of smoke from the two cities. Raging fires with thick black smoke rising high into the sky. The valleys were thick with smoke and ash, but they drove on straight towards that mountain. Straight up to the heavy blast doors at the entrance of the mountain. As they entered the mountain, they could hear the alarms. They surmised that Longspear had arrived.

The railcar transported them deep under the ground into a bunker complex. The complex was not large, twenty meters by thirty meters. Guards hurried them to a room behind the combat intelligence center, again, separated by glass. From there, they could see the screens above them and they could hear everything. Most of the guards then departed and left two armed sentries behind to secure them.

There were two such rooms that were side by side, separated by a glass wall. The second room was empty and the Lycerene Pack found another opportunity to talk amongst themselves. Chel spoke with heavy guilt on her mind. "Reza, did you see the cities?"

Reza hesitated to reply. "Yes. They burn more than we anticipated. Far more."

He had a confused look upon his face so Nava tried to make sense of it. "They had no idea we were coming. And, they don't know anything about Harmonics and Magnesium

Thermocells or how to extinguish them. The Neferan know how, but not these people."

Just then, the second room on the other side of the glass wall began to fill with armed troops, Earth's own. Reza initially took no interest in them, but Chel did. "Look at their armor. They are pilots like us. I think they must be the ones we fought over the cities."

Nava gave little attention to it. "Probably here for a briefing...in preparation for a second attack from Longspear."

One of Earth's pilots was clearly agitated, pacing back and forth, staring at Chel. Without his helmet on, Chel could see his eyes. Every time he turned, his eyes darted right back to Chel who grew uneasy. She turned to Nava.

"He is the one! I just know it! He was the Wasp Pilot that shot us down! I can tell by the way he stares...he has the instincts of an animal."

Reza finally took interest and he saw something familiar. "His intensity is unmistakable...A pilot ought not to let his rage get the best of him." Reza paused for a moment as he dared to say what was really on his mind. "He is the one that I fought in the forest. I would know him anywhere."

By now, the pilot saw Reza staring at him and the pilot erupted with agitation. It took a handful of Earth's other pilots to drag him back and settle him down. Even though they did not recognize the language spoken by the Earth pilots, Chel heard one word over and over and she understood its importance. "Pro...Prow....Prow-ler. I think his name is Prowler. Look at him, he burns with rage. We have killed someone that he loved...very much."

They could see that Prowler had brown hair, brown eyes, and tanned skin with a stocky, muscular build. They could also see a remarkable difference between him and Stalker. Stalker had yellow hair, blue eyes, pale white skin, and was taller, leaner. And, they could see Scout, the female, who was Atera's most trusted. Black hair, golden-yellow skin, and dark eyes that were narrowed. Such differences among them.

More alarms rang out across the bunker complex and all eyes suddenly turned to the combat intelligence center. In the combat intelligence center were rows and rows of desks with computer terminals. Above the desks was an array of computer display panels. Even though they didn't share the same language, the illustrations were clear, Longspear had indeed arrived.

Onboard Longspear, they encountered a sequence of events almost identical to that which Reza's Pack had encountered. The final jump had put them right on top of the planet, in darkness, with the same multitude of communication signals.

Chief Sazzi immediately called for status.
"Operations Officer, have you located Reza's Pack?"
The response was disheartening "Sir, yes, all twenty-three fighters are down. Most of them are fully offline"

"Operations Officer, can you confirm if any of them are still alive?" The response was confusing "Sir, no, I cannot. Their armor sensors indicate no readings. Either they are all dead, or they are no longer wearing armor."

"Communications Officer, at least tell me Reza's Pack had attacked. Is there any damage?" The response made Chief Sazzi stand tall. "Sir, yes, two large fires have been identified on the surface of the planet. Harmonics frequencies are still resonating and temperature sensors indicate Magnesium

Thermocells still burning." That was enough information to confirm for Chief Sazzi that Reza had led the first attack. Now, it was Longspear's turn to join the attack.

"Officer of the Deck, call for Battle Stations." The OOD then snapped to attention "Sir, yes Sir."

Chief Sazzi then looked to his Communications Officer, "Have you parsed a signal yet?" The response was quick. "Sir, yes. A number of the outer satellites are beaming signals directly at Longspear. I'm still trying to match the language or dialect."

The Captain grinned "Stay on it! Let me know as soon as you have it."

From deep within the mountain, Reza and his Pack watched hopelessly while Longspear lofted its fighter-jets; Seventy-five in total. Below them was a mass of Earth's fighter-jets. Too many to count, but at least twice as many fighters as Longspear. Within minutes they would be close enough to engage.

In those last seconds, all eyes were on those display panels, but Chel turned away. She stared across the combat intelligence center watching and admiring the people who held steady amid their fear. Her eyes passed back and forth across the room thinking about the suffering to come and then she finally gave up, she simply tuned out.

Her eyes slowly turned back to Prowler. She couldn't help but feel the strain upon his face, the glossiness to his eyes and then his eyes quickly darted to hers; as always. She turned away stunned that he could feel her gaze. Her eyes went blank and settled upon the young man sitting two rows up. He sat there speaking into the microphone and each time he spoke, he pressed the same button. Each time, he rotated the dial with his left hand one tick to the right. She noticed that all three men who sat next to each other were doing the same, at a panic pace. Then it occurred to her. She moved quickly to get behind Reza, and Nava who were standing shoulder to shoulder. She stepped in between them with a nudge and whispered. "There, those three men, notice what they are doing. They are trying to intercept Longspear's communications!"

They studied the three men for a few moments and then simultaneously turned to Chel. Reza spoke quietly so as not to draw attention. "I believe you are right. If they knew what to listen for, they might find it."

Not risking any more words, Chel simply looked at them. First Reza, then Nava. It took them a moment, but finally they understood what she was thinking. If they could get a lock on Longspear's frequency, it could be used to send a message to Longspear. If just one Lycerene could get to that desk and radio to Longspear, maybe they could stop the attack.

Reza turned for another member of his Pack. A pilot named Sena. A brave pilot true, but at hand to hand combat, Sena was the master. Tall and thin, with the bulking legs of a sprinter, fast and agile. If any man among them could reach that desk, it would be Sena. Looking down at the metal bindings upon his wrists he then looked up at Reza…even with bindings, Sena would do it.

They waited and waited, watching each turn of the dial, each press of the button, each refresh of the display monitor. Then it happened, a familiar language burst over one of the speakers, they locked onto Longspear's radio frequency.

Reza gave the nod and immediately, the Pack slammed themselves against the door and it bust open. They grabbed at the Sentries weapons, pulling them down while Sena burst through the door and stampeded towards the desk. Sentries from all over the room converged to that point between Sena and those desks. Before the nearest Sentry could raise his weapon, Sena accelerated directly at the Sentry. Running low to the ground, he bashed his shoulder into the man's chest and threw him upon his back. Not a step lost, as the second Sentry blocked the isle with his rifle almost at the ready. Another crash as Sena stumbled over the body and when he looked up, he saw the third Sentry with rifle at the ready.

Sena knew it would happen, he braced himself for it and tensed himself for it. Growling as he charged headlong on those final steps. The weapon fired and it struck Sena in the shoulder and spun him half around, but his momentum carried him forward. Sena's momentum was enough to bring his full body to slam against the Sentry who simply buckled and slid back across the floor.

Just two feet remained and Sena collapsed upon the desk. He reached for the button and shouted "Longspear, hold your fire! This is not Nefera! I say…" And then a third shot rang out from across the room and Sena collapsed on the desk. And then he was no more.

Instantly, the Sentries and Atera's pilots were upon Reza and his Pack. Pinning them hard to the floor, the wall, and the desks, whatever they could. All the while, Reza made no movement; only staring at his friend lying dead upon the floor. Something both of them knew would happen.

The officers and crew of Longspear were still awaiting the Communications officer to interpret the language or dialect coming from the planet below when they suddenly heard Sena's message. Loud and clear. "Chief Sazzi, we've intercepted a partial message. It's one of our boys!"

Chief Sazzi suddenly snapped his head around to see the Communications officer. In disbelief he motioned to replay the message on loudspeaker. Everyone on Longspear's bridge could hear the transmission. "Communications Officer, can you match that voice? Who is that?"

"Sir, we have matched the voice. It's Sena, he is a Lieutenant under COP Reza. Voice pattern contains deviations that indicate extreme stress and or injury."

From the Communications officer, "Sir, it could be a voiceover. If the Nefera had intercepted transmissions during Reza's attack, they could copy and manipulate using Sena's voice pattern."

"Communications, have you matched the language or dialect of any other messages? It shouldn't take this long to confirm."

From the Communications officer, "Sir, no. I cannot. There are too many languages…and none match the known Neferan archives."

Back at the combat intelligence center, deep within the mountain, Reza struggled against the Sentries who held him against the wall, making his best efforts to garner the attention of Captain Helforn. With steady eye contact and careful hand gestures, Reza made it clear what he needed to do and Helforn gave an approving nod.
"Longspear, this is COP Reza.
This world…is not Nefera.
It's an uncharted world."

The First Officer on Longspear immediately warned the Chief Sazzi, "Sir, Reza himself led the attack. See there, two cities burn, Harmonics and Magnesium Thermocells are still active! I don't believe it. Either he is being coerced or this is yet another Neferan deception!"

Chief Sazzi's distrust resonated in his voice. "COP Reza, your seconds are running out! My Navigation Officer has confirmed that we have followed The Corridor precisely. We can see the traces of your attack and yet, you expect me to believe that this is not Nefera?"

Reza spoke slowly and clearly. "Sir, we did not cross The Void. I repeat, we did not cross The Void. We are somewhere within The Void. Check your signals, check your voiceprints. They are not Neferan."

Minutes ticked away with no response from Longspear. Hope faded fast as Reza considered just how valuable this surprise attack was to his proud warrior brethren on Longspear.

Reza turned away and looked over at Chel with a look of desperation. Yet again, another innocent city would be set to crumble and burn. And then a memory triggered inside of Reza, recalling that very moment when he first set eyes on people of the white skinned race. His eyes skirted immediately to Helforn. With one hand moving slowly, he reached up to Helforn's face and pinched Helforn's skin. Helforn knew what to do.

Then, Reza spoke clearly with an air of confidence, "Chief Sazzi, one image…one image is all you need. The image is being transmitted now. With your own eyes…you must see it."

An eerie quiet settled across the radio, with not one voice to be heard anywhere. As the silence lingered, all eyes were on the display screens except for Reza and Helforn who stared directly at each other. Suddenly, the display panels refreshed and one single craft could be seen lofting from Longspear. But this time, a shuttle-craft and not a fighter-jet.

Filled with science officers and representatives from Longspear, it descended slowly. Studying the planet as it descended, transmitting a multitude of images to Longspear where crews of technicians analyzed every image. In short time, they were busy establishing a common language. A basic language with as much as a couple hundred words and numbers. Now, they had attained a common language, but far from a common trust. A trust deferred by yet a more pressing issue as Longspear's Science officer made his first attempt at communicating the likelihood that the Neferan Swarm would follow Longspear into The Void.

CHAPTER 8: THE HUNT FOR LONGSPEAR

A fleet of five Neferan carriers had been dispatched to find Longspear. Five state-of-the-art ships, and their combined firepower was enough to make a fair challenge to the old dreadnaught. A firepower normally reserved for fleet-to-fleet encounters, but this was different, much more than a seek-and-destroy mission. The High Queen, Ahmun Shepsut Anak, wanted Longspear as a war trophy and a symbol of her absolute power, to display as a warning to the handful of Puratist worlds who still defied her rule. A legend to be captured and caged, like the ferocious beast that Longspear was.

Of the High Queen, Ahmun Shepsut Anak, a visionary was she. First enticing the other Queens of Nefera, uniting them with a vision of expansion. Expanding beyond their world, expanding beyond the stalemate and taking what she deemed rightfully hers. An authority that she deemed to be righteous for her blood was of the highest purity, thousands of years in the making. Not a genetic trace of any weakness, pure to her race.

Of the Subordinate Queen, 'The Bitch', Anak Re Sun, a conqueror was she, delivering world after world to the High Queen. Second only to the High Queen herself, born of the same royal bloodline. It was her misfortune to have been born one clan removed from the throne and she was all the more bitter for it. Never taking her eyes away from the throne, protecting it, expanding it, and strengthening it as if it were hers in the waiting. And an army that had remained loyal to her as if she were the one true Queen.

Generations of imperial breeding had yielded Anak Re Sun, The Bitch, and a Queen of physical perfection. Tall in stature with broad shoulders, a perfectly tapered waist, and legs of solid shining muscle. A face of structural perfection, balanced and proportioned in every facet with straight black hair that hung down to the middle of her back. Every emotion and every thought transferred through her eyes; eyes of opal shape. Colored with blue-azure paint that was stretched wider so her eyes appeared to be larger. Altogether, her eyes made her look more majestic, more intelligent, and more seductive. Eyes to be used, the same as any weapon.

But, now the High Queen wanted Longspear and she wanted Anak Re Sun to capture it. To that resolve, she had recalled Anak Re Sun on the very moment of her conquest over the Lycerene Deep-Space Pack. Not that Anak Re Sun was the only Subordinate Queen who could capture Longspear, rather there was another reason. Anak Re Sun's reputation had grown with each conquest and some among the High Queen's Court had noticed. A reputation that the High Queen was well aware of and one that she would be forced to deal with.

The hunt for Longspear was the perfect mission, and there could be no better timing. She had recalled Anak Re Sun to attend the victory celebration where her entire Court had assembled. There, before all the Court to see, the High Queen so cleverly challenged Anak Re Sun with the mission, one that could not be declined before the watchful eyes. A scheme to see Anak Re Sun discredited or to see her die trying.

But, Anak Re Sun was no lesser Queen and would have it no other way, to bring home Longspear, as her own war prize, her own personal trophy, or never again return home.

The five carriers, each a third the size of Longspear, were packed with the best of Neferan technology. The best of her ships and the best of her subjects. Including her First Officer, Sun Keptra. She referred to them all as one and named them 'Cher-a-bahl', meaning 'chosen ones'. The Hamunaph, The Ranakan, The Seraphes, The Arumose, and her flag ship which carried no less name than her own, The Anak Re Sun. Each carrier holding a compliment of three Swarms each comprised of ten Wasp Fighters. A total of one hundred and fifty Wasp Fighters at her disposal.

Having assembled her small fleet of five carriers, Queen Anak Re Sun set out to find Longspear. A ship such as Longspear, so feared, was well tracked by the Neferan intelligence teams. Longspear's last known position was far from the front lines, in a remote quadrant, at the edge of The Void. The Queen ordered the jump.

On the bridge of the Anak Re Sun, the jump completed just minutes before Longspear had slipped into The Void. Quickly the alarms on every Neferan carrier called crews to battle stations. Anak Re Sun entered the bridge to hear the familiar announcement. "Queen Anak Re Sun, on deck!" To which the crew within the bridge responded, "Sir, yes Sir", bowed briefly to the Queen, and promptly returned to their tasks. She marched straight to her station, more like that of a throne in the middle of the bridge with all other stations around her. Like the honeycomb of a hive.

On the six walls were a multitude of display panels, unique in the way that the data displayed in continuous streams rising bottom to top. With display panels all about her on six sides and each of them streaming data, the ship itself appeared to be alive, buzzing with intelligence. An entity unto itself. Such was the setting of every bridge on every Neferan warship. All identical, every one of them the same.

And her throne sat center of it all, higher than all the rest. About her throne were six more stations, each representing a key discipline: Engineering, Deck, Weapons, Communications, Operations, and Fighter-Control. Standing at opposite sides were her most trusted officers; the First Officer, Sun Keptra and her Commander of Ground-Swarm, Sun Anniz.

Sun Anniz was none other than her younger brother. On any other world, he would be the seat of power and not her. Of the same royal conditioning, of the same royal schooling, and of the same royal embodiment. Standing over six feet tall with muscles enhanced through years of genetic engineering. His sword, nearly twice the weight of the average, could cleave a man in two, armor and all. A killer and an unmatched commander of Neferan Ground-Swarm troops.

She stepped up to her station and spun about whipping her cape out of the way before she sat down. Draping the cape across her thighs to keep them warm and pliable. Her eyes immediately scanned the panels as her station spun around giving her all the info she needed within a couple of seconds.

"First Officer Sun Keptra, Where is Longspear? We should be in range by now."

"My Queen, Longspear is there...at the outer reaches of our sensors, just in front of The Void."

Difficult to see was Longspear, so close to The Void and so tiny next to it. She looked and leaned downward to the man sitting at her right hand side. "Fighter Control, ready your fighters!"

"Yes, My Queen."

Then, from the Communications Officer sitting to her left. "My Queen, Longspear appears to be maneuvering!"

The Queen took interest. "So, like her great Deep-Space Pack, she turns to engage us?"

"My Queen, No. It appears she is headed into The Void!"

The Queen was shocked and confused. "What? That's impossible. Your sensors must be malfunctioning. Run your diagnostics."

Again, more fearful than before, he dared not look up at her. "My Queen, diagnostic checks indicate that all sensor functions are within normal tolerances. My Queen, Longspear still approaches The Void."

With impatience, the Queen shouted. "Fighter Control Officer, we attack now… ready your launch!"

"Yes, My Queen."

Again, the officer to her left spoke. This time, with fear in his voice, for he knew that she would not take the news well. "My Queen, at her current speed, Longspear will impact The Void before our Wasp Fighters can engage."

Then, a long pause as she sat motionless studying the display panels. Staring at them like a Queen, as if she could command the screen to obey her will. Then she peered down to her Communications Officer and said, "You had better not be mistaken." To which he was too fearful to respond. She accepted the obvious. "Fighter Control Officer, stand down."

"Yes, My Queen."

Thinking aloud, the Queen muttered. "What is Longspear doing? How dare she not engage me?"

Then, another long pause as she thought deeply. Thought about anything and everything she could do to stop Longspear from destroying itself. To preserve her war prize and protect her credibility. But, each solution that ran through her mind was met with gaps and flaws. There was no way to reach Longspear and no way to stop her. And then…

"My Queen, sensors indicate Longspear is now impacting The Void."

She barked her orders. "Officer Of The Deck, bring us closer!"

In moments, the fleet was close enough for them to bring more sensors to bear. Sensors that could detect transmissions, and sensors that could observe energy emissions. "Track Longspear! Record every detail as she disintegrates! If so much as one fragment of that ship can be salvaged, I want it!"

Moments passed and the sensors detected massive energy discharges all around Longspear. An unrecognizable energy, but detectable nonetheless. Like a wall, the discharge shot outward from Longspear in all directions. More sensors detected transmissions within Longspear and still others detected explosions and fires. In a matter of minutes, Longspear slid into The Void and disappeared.

"My Queen, sensors indicate that Longspear impacted The Void at one quarter thrust."

Confused and agitated now, the Queen's thoughts had slipped past her lips. "No fight? Nowhere to run? Nowhere to hide? The Lycerene must have known we were approaching. Suicide? Suicide? They committed suicide?"

As if Longspear had gotten the better of her. As if Longspear had won something in its final moment of defiance. She sat still staring at the display monitors. Monitors that were now streaming volumes of data as they scanned for some fragment worth salvaging.

Her agitation now turned to raw anger. "I want one piece, no matter how small. One piece! Do you hear me?"

From every crewmember on that bridge, a resounding response "Yes, My Queen!"

And then she stood up and marched off the bridge, returning to her quarters. A room with six walls and in the center of it all, a berthing chamber of six sides. Golden steps surrounded the chamber on all six sides with thick columns that held a canopy above. She waited there within the berthing chamber, among her personal servants. Waiting for news of some fragment. And then came the expected sound announcing its arrival, a knock upon the door outside her quarters. Someone was requesting permission to enter. "My Queen, Commander of Swarm, Sun Anniz requesting permission to enter."

"Enter."

He entered through the doorway in the expected military fashion. "My Queen, scans for fragments are complete. Officer of the Deck and Communications Officer are standing at the ready, to deliver their findings."

She spoke sharply. "Officer of the Deck and Communications Officer, enter and deliver."

To this, they squared the door, marching in one after the other and stood according to rank. She rose from the midst of her servants and walked slowly toward them. Eyeing them as she walked them end to end.
"I trust you have found a suitable fragment, a bridge perhaps? Hmm…Or, maybe a one of those damned Lycerene gun turrets?"

The three of them stood motionless waiting for the First Officer, Sun Keptra to respond, for it was his duty. He stood there fearful, for he knew well what her response would be. "My Queen, we executed the scans twice over. Each time we found no fragments. Not one single piece."

Suddenly, she snapped towards him. As if he had spoken out of turn. "You disappoint me once again. Is this to become something of a habit for you?"

She motioned for her servants to seize him and beat him about the midsection. She took special pleasure from watching her victims gasp for air. Watching him as he twisted and curled on the floor until finally, she kicked him onto his back, to which she mounted him as if in pleasure. Taking her dagger and now pressing it to his abdomen. Pressing slowly and deeply, but not deep enough to penetrate the skin. She savored in the fear that way.
In the moment before the skin would give way and push itself up the still blade, he chanced and spoke. "Not one fragment…that cannot be!"

He captured her attention for just a moment. She leaned in to where her eyes were just inches away from his. Peering in as if looking into a window. Not a word from her, but he knew he had earned one more word with her. "My Queen, I...I propose that Longspear did not destroy itself upon The Void. I propose that Longspear survived."

Her mind so fixed that The Void was impenetrable. That The Void was as solid as a wall made of stone and brick. The thought of it did not register with her at first. But, she needed to believe that there was still some chance and so she retracted the blade a bit. "And just what gives you to such fantasy?"

"My Queen, aside from the lack of fragments, consider this. Longspear impacted The Void at one quarter thrust."

She snapped. "What of it?"

"My Queen, no ship travels through space at one quarter thrust. Such slow speed is useful only for docking and boarding. Anything that travels in open space either jumps or travels at max thrust. That Longspear entered The Void using slow speed...is curious."

"Curious indeed." she declared. Setting back now on her heels as if she had finished her pleasure. Returning her dagger to its sheath.

"My Queen, consider this as well. Our intelligence indicates that Longspear has been stationed at this same coordinate for her last five tours. An unusual coordinate with no strategic value. Might there be something special about this place?"

"Curious again my First Officer, Sun Keptra. Seems that you may yet redeem yourself. Rise."

"My Queen, we know the exact coordinate, exact speed, and exact trajectory for which Longspear entered The Void. I propose you allow me to test this hypothesis. I suggest at least two days testing, under my care, if you will?"

Her eyes popped wide open as her voice erupted. "Two days? Two days? I give you one. In one day, you will return to me and report your findings. Dismissed!"

At the end of that one day, she again sat herself among her servants in her berthing quarters and waited for that knock on the door. To the minute, it did sound. Exactly the same as the day before, the three officers entered, marched in according to rank, and presented themselves to her.

Again, she rose from among her servants. Walking like a great cat with her eyes fixed to his; straight up to him she walked. Studying his eyes as she approached, and she saw no fear in him. "My Queen, we launched empty torpedoes at The Void in a matrix of coordinates. We tested multiple combinations of coordinate, trajectory, and speed. All of them discharged and repelled. Then we tested the exact coordinate, trajectory, and speed used by Longspear. It discharged, but did not repel. It would appear there is indeed something special about this place."

A smile drew to her face, more like a sneer. "So....one coordinate, one trajectory, and one speed. But, where does Longspear think she will go? Where does she think she can hide?"

The First Officer then spoke "My Queen, maybe Longspear wasn't fleeing from us at all."

Her curiosity shone through. "What do you mean? Maybe she intends to lure us into a trap of sorts?"

"My Queen, this coordinate, it's almost directly across The Void from Nefera. Maybe she knows something we do not? Maybe, Longspear is planning to attack Nefera?"

The Queen's eyes stirred back and forth as he continued. "If Longspear did find a way to our world, she would arrive long before anyone would expect. My Queen, there would be little to stop her!"

Now, that aged dreadnaught put the fear into them once again. With it, the Queens mission took on more urgency and she sensed that there would be an even greater glory awaiting her, a far greater glory. She dismissed them, all except for her brother, Sun Anniz. "We will give chase! We must give chase! Think of it my brother. The High Queen so full of herself, so confident in her victory. What will she be when they find that she has let the Wolf sneak in?"

Sun Anniz relished in the opportunity. "My Queen, surely even one sighting of Longspear within the Neferan star system will expose her incompetence. The High Queen will lose all credibility."

"Think of it my brother...I will meet Longspear head on and save them. Then, they will gladly place their confidence in me. They will finally give me what I deserve...My throne!"

Circling him, running her fingers along his chest, round his shoulders and across his back "Commander of Ground-Swarm....my beautiful brother, bring me into this Void. Find me this Longspear, and make me your High Queen!"

"Yes, My Queen."

The five Neferan carriers lined up one after the other: the Hamunaph, the Ranakan, the Serapheses, the Arunmose, and lastly her flag ship, the Anak Re Sun. Slowly they accelerated until they were at one quarter thrust. They would pass into The Void same as Longspear and its Pack. Encountering the same sporadic disruptions, the same energy disturbance and finally the same system failures. The critical decision to switch to analog instrumentation and then to power down came too late for the Hamunaph. She suffered a series of system failures that ultimately led to fires. Fires which raged out of control and eventually buckled her hull. She depressurized within seconds and drifted dead. The remaining ships did switch to Analog and then powered down, and survived. Damaged and operating on auxiliary power, but they did emerge on the other side of The Void.

First Officer, Sun Keptra, was already tracking Longspear. "My Queen, even on auxiliary power, the jump traces are picking-up something; something big. That must mean Longspear jumped from here, right here, just hours ago. A half day at the most. We need to restore full power immediately if we are to run full jump traces."

She smiled. "Very good. Very good indeed First Officer. Put all hands to work on restoring full power. I want those jump cores active at any costs. Do you understand me?"

"My Queen, what about the Hamunaph? There must be some survivors in sealed compartments."

Without a care in her heart she replied. "Unless we need the Hamunaph for spare parts, she is of no use to me. I will not divert the resources. We need full power immediately."

The Queens order was passed throughout the ship by word of mouth. Runners darted from room to room and compartment to compartment. Even before the fires were extinguished and ventilated, power cables were being strung along her decks. The crew working like mindless drones; working frantically, taking any and all risks as if they were so easily disposed and replaced. Come the end of the sixth hour, and a cost of twelve crewmen, power had been restored.

Her trusted First Officer, Sun Keptra, quickly grabbed the heavy manuals off the shelf and dropped it onto his desk. Turning to the reboot sequence, he began calling out the instructions. Each instruction bringing the jump cores one step closer to operational. The lights on the core boxes began to illuminate and flash until every last one of them was stabilized. The jump trace executed and as expected, it produced volumes of data that only a human being could interpret. The First Officer guided his teams through the reams of data. Demonstrating his highly refined organizational skills time and again. Finally, "My Queen, we have it, we know where Longspear has jumped to!"

Before the chase could begin, several more hours were lost as the four ships completed repairs. From his console, the First Officer coordinated the triage session across all four ships orchestrating repair after repair, Commanding people and resources as priorities dictated. Then suddenly, the last of the four ships were ready. Having preprogrammed the jump coordinates into all four ships, the jump command immediately followed.

"Where is Longspear? Why do I not see her again?" The Queen's frustration could not be restrained.

"My Queen, jump traces are already running and it appears Longspear was here."

Again the First Officer reconvened the tech teams to analyze the jump trace. Hours passed as the tech teams sifted through the reams of trace data. Same as before, they reached a conclusion and a new jump commenced. Again, they arrived at a star that held nothing but a trace of Longspear. Like dogs tracking a scent, they continued to jump and trace, trace and jump. They grew tired and ill from the jump sequences, pushing through exhaustion and losing confidence in the First Officer and this new jump trace technology. Fear settled in as they began to lose track of how far they had come, a sense that they were becoming lost.

They emerged from yet another jump dazed and sluggish. Most of them too exhausted and disillusioned to even lift their eyes. Even the Queen was slow to look upon her screens. "Mm...my Queen,
There she is!
Longspear, dead ahead!"

CHAPTER 9: DIVIDE AND CONQUER

In their disbelief, their eyes were fixed to the monitors, not a sound among them. Queen Anak Re Sun rose up and stepped closer to the display monitors above. Holding onto the console with both hands as if her mind were miles ahead of her body. Moments passed in silence and then the First Officer, Sun Keptra regained his senses "Battle Stations!"

The Queen snapped around. "Yes... sound the alarm....prepare for battle!!" And then a voice from the outer rim of the bridge was heard. "So blue, that planet, it is so blue."

It grabbed the Queens attention. "Magnify that image" she ordered. "Blue...so much water...This is not Nefera...what world is this? Where are we?"

First Officer, Sun Keptra joined in, "Operations, what world is this? We cannot attack until we know what world this is." In moments, the Operations Officer responded "My Queen, of all the worlds, none are as blue as this, and so green. My Queen, this world...it is uncharted."

From the First Officer, yet another surprise. "My Queen, sensors indicate two hot spots likely from Magnesium Thermocells."

Then, the warning alarms sounded. They had detected incoming fighters. Fighters from Longspear were lofting and forming ranks. Fighters from the planet's surface were launching and rising fast.

In so little time, the planet had made many such preparations. Fighters from every nation put aside their differences and allied. Together, they presented a most formidable front. The planet prepared by evacuating the cities as best they could. Prepared for fire, rescue, and combat if it would come to that. Above all, the planet prepared by establishing the shared language to which the Neferan language would be easily assimilated. At the first sign of Neferan ships, the satellite transmissions rang out on every frequency, voice and image, all carrying the same message in the Neferan language. "Cease aggression. This is an uncharted world."

From deep within the mountain, the Earth's teams were again called to station and focused on the display monitors, scanning for a response. Captain Helforn was the first to assess the situation. "There are only four ships...I thought there would be more."

Chel responded "Commander, these few ships may just be scouting or hunting Longspear. Assume more will follow. You must engage them while you have fair odds. Attack now!"

Helforn responded sternly. "I am under orders not to engage in a war between Lycera and Nefera. My orders are to quell this dispute and to gather intelligence on both of you people."

Chel did her best to convince Helforn. "Captain, I assure you, they will attack! You must engage!"

He responded with caution. "That is yet to be seen. So far, I have no reason to believe any of your story. For all I know, you attacked them. After all, you attacked Earth…didn't you?"

Chel fell silent. There was nothing left to say. There was no evidence that she could muster to convince otherwise. A voice rang out, "Sir, still no response from the Neferan ships." Time would pass, maybe a minute or less, but an eternity nonetheless.

Onboard the Anak Re Sun, the technicians were equally scurrying to assess the capacity of the oncoming fighters. "My Queen, Longspear has launched seventy-five fighters and the planet has launched an additional six hundred. They will have us outnumbered." Seeing her chance slip away, her chance to capture that dreadnaught, she boiled deeply with anger. Thrashing about and pacing back and forth as she toiled over losing Longspear yet again.

"My Queen, should we recall the fighters and make jump preparations?"

The thought of retreating sickened her even more. She closed her eyes and stood motionless, relaxing as she had been taught from a young age. Letting her thoughts gather and assess this unexpected situation. But, she was a Queen, and a higher instinct took over. Her eyes popped open with renewed confidence. "No…no. We will not retreat! Look at that world brother and what do you see?"

The great Sun Anniz, Ground-Swarm Commander, stood there blankly with no response…for he was not a Queen. "I tell you brother, what I see is a blue world, a green world, a most beautiful world…MY WORLD!"

That voice rippled through the bridge like a crack of thunder. Everyone's eyes tilted up in shock from her intentions. Sun Anniz responded in confusion. "My Queen, I don't understand, they have us outnumbered, and we cannot win."

She walked around him in a circle, watching his every move. "Ahhh...two cities burn below, no doubt from Lycerene Thermocells. And, look there on the display monitors, do you notice that they do not join forces. Longspear's fighters and the planets fighters approach, but they do not approach together. They are weary of each other. Yes...yes...I can see it."

To that, she spun around quickly for all her subordinates to hear. "Hear me all of you. Here is what I will do. I will divide them and conquer them. First, I will plant the seeds of distrust, then I will bring them to fight each other...and when their armies are reduced in numbers, I will release my Swarm!"

She paused for her final thoughts and then gave her orders. "Communications Officer, respond to that message. Tell them that the great Queen, Anak Re Sun, requests audience with the planet below."

"Fighter Control, recall your fighters. Let my newfound friends think that we intend to comply. Let them see exactly what they want to see."

CHAPTER 10: FRIEND FROM FOE

Queen Anak Re Sun descended in all her glory, a show of Neferan strength. Three Neferan shuttles touched down and fifty of the Queen's finest ground troops rushed out in formation. Each of them bearing her banner that waived from a short staff rising from behind the neck to just above their heads. The banners fluttered in the wind, like buzzing bees.

They formed a semi-circle where her imperial shuttle would land. As it touched the ground, she gave her orders "Communications Officer, in my absence, collect the relevant intelligence details. I want to know everything about their planetary defenses."

Then she turned to Sun Anniz, "My brother, you will walk ahead of me wherever I go. Soon, I will set you to your business."

She then turned to First Officer Sun Keptra, "The same of you…at my side."

Then the landing doors dropped open and her compliment of elite imperial guards ran to their positions about the ramp. First, Sun Anniz, Ground-Swarm Commander, walked down the ramp straight and tall. In his full body armor, he was an imposing giant. Moments later, she made her grand entrance. Slowly stepping down the ramp in her armor, unlike any armor among all the worlds. A form fitted armor that accentuated her perfect body and distinguished her as a Queen of Swarm. The armor was a brilliant black embossed with gold markings about the head and neck and upon her back were lightly engraved images of her enemies, conquered or vanquished. She walked slowly, feeling the ground beneath her feet, as if she were marking her territory.

At the bottom of the ramp, her troops formed ranks on either side of her with Sun Anniz just steps before her and Sun Keptra at her side. Together, they marched to the entrance of the hangar building. The entrance was guarded by hundreds of Captain Helforn's troops all positioned shoulder to shoulder so as to guide the Neferan into the expected entrance.

Into the entrance they marched slowly with weapons at the ready on both sides. Quickly, the Queen and her elite guards were ushered into sanitary stations where they would be cleansed by the sterilizing lights so that they might be able to remove their armor and negotiate face to face. Then, they were escorted to the hastily assembled negotiation chambers.

Three chambers each sealed air tight located center of the hangar bay. All about them were technicians and linguists with their computers ready to interpret. The Neferan and Lycerene were seated at the same time and awaited the planetary representatives.

Minutes later, the planetary representatives entered. Not wearing body armor or even military uniforms. They were dressed in attire suited to politicians. They marched in and took their seats. Now, amid the resounding silence, the three peoples looked upon each other. Then, the man designated as the planetary leader spoke. "We will begin with introductions. I am President Stillwell. I have been appointed to represent all of the nations of Earth. To my right is my Vice President Zadan. To my left are my Joint Chiefs of Staff."

He then motioned for the Lycerene to do the same. Among them were Reza, Chel, Nava, and the Executive Officer of Longspear. Finally, he motioned for the Neferan. "I am Queen Anak Re Sun of the Neferan Empire. To my left, my First Officer Sun Keptra and to my right, my Commander of Ground-Swarm, Sun Anniz."

It was then back to President Stillwell who delivered his first message to both the Neferan and Lycerene. "On this day, you have delivered an unprovoked attack against the people of Earth. Thousands of my people are dead and suffering out there in those smoldering cities. I assure you, we are more than prepared to defend ourselves now. Let there be no doubt that all of the nations of Earth are united and prepared to send you back to wherever you came from. Our expectations are that you will leave and leave soon."

Moments passed before the linguists confirmed that they had translated the message and passed it forward to their representatives who read it slowly. It was the Lycerene who responded first. "Good Sir, the people of Lycera are quick to abide by your expectations except for that which we know will surely follow. The Neferan will attack Earth as part of their racial cleansing. Your planet is an abomination to them."

Quickly, President Stillwell responded. "It was you, the Lycerene who attacked...you who brought this war to Earth. I have no trust of you. I've heard about this war from the Lycerene perspective, I think it's time we heard from the Neferan. What does the Neferan Queen have to say of this war?"

The Queen raised her head slowly and looked directly at President Stillwell. "It is true that the Neferan and Lycerene are engaged in a war that is ages old. It's also true that the Neferan have decisively won that war. But, do not let the blame of this war fall upon the Neferan, as I'm sure you have been told. It was the Lycerene who first became exclusionist…in their cultist beliefs. They set about the first attacks to which the Neferan have planned long and hard to overcome. Surely, we are justified in defending ourselves."

Reza could see the expressions on the faces of the President and Vice President and he knew it was a condemnation. Having read the translated response, he and Chel both objected immediately. "There's no way to know that! Nobody knows who started the war. What we can know is that we had a war of maintenance for generations; a balance of power until the Neferan attacked in mass. Good Sir, you cannot believe them. If you send Longspear away now, the Neferan will surely attack Earth!"

The Queen had expected a rebuttal and had planned for it. Before the translation was even completed, she interjected. Now her plan was about to unfold. First to confuse by setting seeds of distrust, then to conquer. "You have my word as Queen. The people of Neferan have come for Longspear, not Earth. Look about you. Have we attacked you? No. Have we complied with all your expectations? Yes."

To that, she could see the seeds had taken. She so cleverly now maneuvered her agenda further. "I see you still have Lycerene Thermocells burning in your cities. We sympathize with the suffering from that weapon and I offer you the assistance of my technicians. They are well experienced and suitably equipped to extinguish the

Thermocells. I will place fifty of my finest technicians at your disposal."

Initially, President Stillwell declined, but Vice President Zadan persuaded him to accept. Her plan was steeped in deceit. Her intent was more than the misdirection of trust. Underneath it all, her real intent was to position as many of her troops on the ground as possible. If she could position several hundred of her troops and attack key defense posts and assassinate key planetary officials, she could set about confusion and chaos. To which, she was more confident than ever that she could blame the Lycerene and set the people of Earth and the people of Lycera forever against each other.

She sat silently now and watched the expressions around the room. But there was one more item to her agenda. "President Stillwell, there is one more thing...I trust by now that you have heard mention of the outer worlds and The Void that separates them. The Void has been impassable for as long as history records. In our journey to Earth, we learned that The Void is not a void at all. It is more of a barrier comprised of an unrecognizable energy. Even more surprising is that an extremely isolated thread of that same energy is emitting from The Void to this Earth. It is what led us here."

She paused for a moment as she knew they would all need to absorb this new fact. "If the Neferan and the Lycerene found Earth, then so can any of the Puratist Worlds. My ships have identified the approximate location of the energy source and we think it advisable to investigate."

Again, President Stillwell declined, but the Vice President was a persuasive man. A dislikeable man that most people would shy away from except for his vast knowledge which made him invaluable, especially to President Stillwell. A bitter, elderly man, imprisoned by his lifelong ailments that kept him to the crutch on most days, but to his wheelchair on the worst of days.

The Queen watched the exchange and waited for the slightest hint that Zadan had persuaded Stillwell. "I will send for a small company of my technicians who are uniquely trained and equipped to find the energy signal. I trust that you will allow me to designate ten of my bodyguards to assure their protection."

The Lycerene were taken aback by this new fact, but they quickly realized they had to accompany this expedition. It may be a chance to regain trust as well as to learn more about this energy signal. Reza could not afford to let the opportunity pass by. "Even if the Lycerene are telling the truth, if they can find the energy signal, they won't be able to tell you anything about it. It was I who translated the ancient scrolls. Star maps, symbols, glyphs, all from ancient Neferan artifacts. You will need me...and my team as well."

To this, all was agreed. The expedition would be comprised of twenty Neferan troops, twenty Lycerene troops, and sixty of Earth's own. They assembled out on the landing field in preparation to load onto the five VTECs (Versatile Transport and Evacuation Craft). Troops and air crews were scurrying in all directions and suddenly, Reza and Prowler found themselves crossing paths, and they slowed as if readying for another fight. But, they were disrupted by a familiar voice, Commander Helforn, for he had been given command of the expedition. Helforn's voice rang out loud as he called for three of his own troops. "You, you, and you, front and center! Keep these two apart. I don't want them within ten paces of each other ... and don't turn your backs on them. Not for one second. Am I clear?"

"Sir, yes Sir."

As Prowler, Stalker, Scout, and their comrades turned about to board their VTEC, they were met face to face with a sight that startled them. There she stood, in her full body armor watching them, as she had always done, to assess their readiness. Her shoulders were turned slightly perpendicular to them as she leaned her bodyweight back against her cane. As she had done so many times before, she caught them by surprise and they stood in dumb silence. But, she had been recognized by another. "Good day, Commander Atera. Most assuring to see you here." Then he paused for a moment. "Why may I ask are you suited in full battle armor?"

"Captain Helforn, it is good to see you as well. Full armor as you ask? Why, I will be joining this expedition of yours. After all, these pilots that you have here…they belong to me."

Confused, Helforn checked and re-checked the deployment roster to confirm that Atera was not scheduled to deploy. "Commander Atera, you are not on my roster, you are not scheduled to deploy."

When he looked up, her gaze was still fixed on him, never moving, not even when she blinked. Knowing her as he did, he knew that she would not change her mind, so he simply added her to the roster and motioned for the troops to load into the VTECs.

But, Atera had yet another order of business. She motioned Prowler to step aside to a clearing in between the VTECs. As always, she leaning against her cane while she stared directly at Prowler. Stomping her cane into the ground and twisting it a few more times while she drew her thoughts. "I gave you a squadron to lead and you abandon them."

Prowler immediately responded in defense of his actions. "They couldn't get through the Pack's turrets! I had to do it!"

But, she snapped right back. "They are your squadron and you are their Lead. Leadership is not your right and it's not a privilege...it's a responsibility."

He thought for a moment, wanted to defend himself, but conceded that the best thing to do, the only thing to do, was to agree. "Sir, yes Sir. Next time I will."

She interrupted him once more. "Next time? Next time? Let us hope you survive the day before you talk of 'next time'. Rest assured, you will learn that their lives are your responsibility. Let us hope you learn it before you get one of them killed." With that, she stomped her cane to the ground and twisted it deeply and then reluctantly, she used it to motion Prowler to rejoin the troops.

They loaded into the VTECs as they were accustomed, by team. Atera and her pilots loaded into the first VTEC. Then, Sun Anniz with all his Neferan Technicians and Troops loaded into second VTEC. Next, Reza, Chel, Nava, and the Lycerene Pack loaded into the third VTEC. Finally, Helforn's troops filled two more VTECs. Even as they were loading, Nava couldn't take his eyes off of Atera, and to this Reza had to question. "Nava, what are you staring at?"

With thoughts half collected, Nava replied. "I don't know. Did you see her? The one with the walking cane."

Reza responded. "Certainly, I saw her. What of it?"

Slowly, Nava collected his feelings and converted them into some-meaningful thoughts. "There is something different about her. Did you see her eyes? The way that she stared at those pilots? Did you see how she swayed that Captain…without a single word?"

Before Reza could respond, the VTEC engines roared as they rose slowly off the ground and headed off to find the mysterious energy signal. Immediately, Neferan technicians began to work their equipment triangulating the position of the signal and then running search grids until they were sure that they had located the site. The VTECs swooped down over the island and hovered there while Captain Helforn awaited identification from his Navigator. From up high, they could see a cluster of old buildings, maybe ruins. To the north were the cliffs that dropped into the ocean. On the other three sides were peaceful fields of rolling hills and flowing green grasslands. A long driveway cut through the southern field all the way out to a main roadway.

After a few minutes, the Navigator grew frustrated and called back to Captain Helforn. "Sir, this island, it's not on any of the maps. It's uncharted!" Helforn looked quickly at his wristwatch and then again at the sun which was setting low on the horizon and realized that time was running out. "Down, down… put us down on that grassy patch at the end of the main roadway."

Just as soon as the landing skids hit the ground, the doors popped open and troopers rushed down the ramps. As they gathered in the grassy clearing, Captain Helforn shouted his orders. "Time is running out people! We've got to find that energy signal. It's either underground or it's in those old ruins on the hilltop. We'll split up so we can search faster."

He pulled Sgt. Anil close to him. "You know what to do. Get the Neferan equipment unloaded and run the search grids. I'll take another team to the hilltop." With his rifle in one hand, he began running backwards as he gave his final order. "Keep the Neferan and the Lycerene apart...don't let them anywhere near each other!

Helforn's troopers scrambled to catch up with him as he ran across the two hundred meters towards the ruins on the hilltop. They stopped about twenty paces away from the entrance which was sealed by a heavy wooden door with old iron braces. Captain Helforn, realized that the buildings were not ruins at all. They were old and in disrepair, but occupied nonetheless. He approached the entrance along with two troopers at his sides. He knocked on the old wooden door and waited. Minutes passed and they knocked again. No answer, not so much as a footstep could be heard.

Atera and her pilots had stood by their VTEC and watch intently as Captain Helforn paced back and forth. The wait gave Atera time to recognize some odd features about the compound and the surrounding landscape. Despite Helforn's orders, she headed off towards the compound, alone.

Her young pilots took advantage of her absence. Prowler turned to Scout and Stalker raising the odd question. "Did you notice that Commander Atera and Captain Helforn knew each other?" Scout and Stalker simply shook their heads and shrugged their shoulders.

Stalker amused himself a bit. "No surprise. Atera's been around long enough to know everyone in this army."

Prowler joked in return. "Right...if it's military, then Atera knows it. If she could find an ancient military manual, she would read it...and take notes."

Stalker smiled a bit and then responded. "Well, for sure we will catch an *'I told you so'* when this little expedition is over. She won't let us live this one down."

Prowler shook his head in disagreement. "I'm not so sure about that. This is Commander Atera we are talking about. It's not what she says that worries me…it's what she doesn't say that I'm afraid of."

With a brief pause, Scout took the conversation in a different direction. "That Neferan, the one named Sun Anniz? I don't like him."

Stalker responded as if he had the same thought. "I don't like any one of them."

Ignoring Stalker's joke, Scout continued with her concern. "Not what I meant. This guy is a killer. I think he's the kind that enjoys it."

Prowler turned slowly to look at Sun Anniz and study him for a moment. "Right, he gives me the creeps. Keep an eye on him, but keep your distance."

Before they could continue further, their conversation was interrupted. Commander Atera was signaling for Scout to join her. By then, Scout had to run half way to the compound, to a small rocky ledge to join Atera. No sooner had Scout arrived when Atera used her walking cane to point out the features of the land. "Odd, this compound is. These walls, they could easily have been a fortress long ago. Look at the way the building sits on the highest point. Look how the hills roll, they would force an attacker into low lands and the valleys, and look at the tree line."

At that point, Scout raised her view scope and scanned the grounds, as overgrown and eroded as the landmarks were, they were visible just as Atera had said. But, then suddenly Scout noticed something that Atera had not. "We've got movement out on the tree line. Guards maybe?"

From their rocky ledge, Atera could see that Helforn was talking with what appeared to be a Monk, wearing a grey robe and hooded. Immediately, she made her way towards Helforn and the interesting Monk. As she approached them, she called forward. "Monk, if this is a house of worship, then what need have you of guards?"

Brother Sarrow suddenly stood straighter and turned about. His old and weakened voice now a bit clearer. "What do you mean guards? Where?"

Brother Sarrow motioned for two of his lesser Monks to investigate. They rounded the corner of the old monastery and stood directly behind Atera. Immediately, Scout handed a view scope to the monks that they might see the silhouettes off in the distance, under the trees, but the monks ignored her. Moments later, they turned back to Brother Sarrow. No words, but clearly something was happening.

Clapping his hands twice to get their attention, Sarrow's voice resonated with some concern. "My friends, the time has come for you to depart. Come, come, I will see you to your airships." Motioning with his hands to encourage them to move along.

Scout ran to the East and gave a loud shout. "More of these guys to the East. I'd say maybe ten or twelve...and they are armed!"

Stepping directly in front of Brother Sarrow, Captain Helforn stood sternly and demanded an answer. "What is going on here? Who are they?"

Brother Sarrow seemed to struggle to raise his words. He stood there looking to the East and then to the West. Twice and three times he scanned the horizons and each time the concern drew heavier on his face until he turned sharply to Helforn and stared him directly in the eyes. His old and bent body suddenly stood straighter and his words came through loud and clear, "My friends, I urge you to leave." Suddenly, the air rang aloud with the sounds of mortars ricketing overhead.

All eyes turned upwards as if they might see the incoming mortars, but the sun blinded their eyes. As the sounds drew imminently closer, they dropped to the ground, all of them except for Brother Sarrow. He stood alone, staring intently at the silhouettes that scurried among the tree line as the first volley of mortars erupted. Mortars like no other with their searing white flashes followed immediately by deafening blasts that mimicked the crack of thunder. Even though they wore advanced armor, their vision was temporarily black spotted by the flashes and their ears were deafened by the blasts.

The ground rumbled as the mortars struck the soft soil to either side of the roadway, and still, Brother Sarrow stood there. With no regard for the bright flashes or the thunderous concussions, he stood there motionless, as if his body were made of solid lead. Standing straight, barely flinching as the wind whipped at his robe and the dirt sprayed his face. Just a quick twist of his head to shake the dirt free from his face before he again shouted at Helforn. "Get up! Get to the monastery!"

Mortars rained down again and again destroying the VTEC's and decimating troopers that were caught out in the open. Anyone able to run did so. They followed Sarrow to the Monastery. Within the monastery walls, they were safe, but only for a few minutes as the hoard of silhouettes raced across the open fields with little defenses to stop their advance. Sarrow quickly realized that they would be overrun and called for a retreat to the most defensible position with the monastery. A round building constructed of large stone blocks with a dome shaped roof; the library.

Once inside, Helforn shoved his way through the troops until he stood face to face with Sarrow. "What the hell are those things? Don't give me this crap that you don't know!"

Just then, above the sounds of battle, a new sound rose in the distance. Not the sound of mortars and not the screams of wounded men, but a sound that made the skin crawl.

Immediately, the Monks froze still and began to mumble something, like a prayer, as if protecting themselves from the unclean sound. As the sound intensified, so too had their prayer unto the point where they were nearly unresponsive. Shuffling and stumbling about in odd fits.

The sound moved like rolling thunder and when it had passed them, the Monks slowly returned to their senses. Simultaneously, they all rushed to Brother Sarrow's side. Without opening his eyes, Sarrow looked upward, and then slowly, the words escaped his lips.
"He has found us."

Again, the sound rose up from the distance. One of the lesser Monks called to Sarrow.
"He calls…to us."
He and his legions!"

This time the sound was louder, much louder. It rolled forward with more intensity and then seemed to pause directly over them. As the sound hung there, the Monks returned to their prayers, slipping deeper and deeper into meditation. It was then that Helforn and his troops felt it for the first time. Even with their advanced armor, the sound crept in, slipping in through the ears and crawling down the spine, as if it were a living creature. In a fit of twitching and scratching, Helforn grabbed Sarrow "What is it?"

But, Sarrow could not respond. He was lost in prayer, mumbling things, speaking words that Helforn did not recognize; words from ancient languages. But, there were two words that Helforn did recognize. And just two words said it all.

The Secret…

CHAPTER 11: THE CHODUGON

There was a pause, a moment in time where everyone was fixated on Brother Sarrow who was lost in a million thoughts. But, when his eyes next opened, they were fixated on one thing. The black armor of the Neferan soldiers. Eyeing them deeply as if he could see their faces beneath their armored helmets. Then, slowly, he turned to look at the Lycerene warriors.

Immediately, a rush of voices erupted as everyone tried to speak at once, but Sarrow hushed them to keep quiet and then he spoke clearly, slowly, and with his thick accent. "We hold here for now. This library is the old Castle Keep and it is well fortified. If we cannot defend the outer walls, then the only escape is to the cliffs. My Brothers and I...we will protect you."

Captain Helforn spat back "What the hell do you mean...protect us? You, and a handful of old Monks...against those things?"

Brother Sarrow directed Helforn to look out through the small window across the courtyard to see dozens of Monks rising up from an underground staircases and pouring into the courtyard. "See, even now, my brothers wake."

Helforn gasped and stepped backwards, "Brothers? Those aren't your brothers, those are the same things, those dead things!"

It was then that Brother Sarrow gave the nod to a lesser Monk named Silas. Not a downward nod, but a commanding upward nod, directing Silas to tell the secret. While Sarrow turned his attention to the battle outside, Silas began to speak. "The time has come for mankind to relearn that which he has lost."

Brother Sarrow stayed by the heavy door, turning his shoulder to the door and squatting down low. Waiting there with his hood covering most of his face and his head tilted down, listening to the sounds of battle outside the door. While he did so, the Monk named Silas continued, "My brothers and I are Chodugon Kai. That which you fear are Chodugon Kon."

A voice from somewhere in the room called forward. "What the hell is the difference?"

Silas continued, hurriedly. "In the beginning, The Chodugon Kai and Chodugon Kon were one and the same. Created to defend the people of Earth from the Puratist invasion during the first great era of mankind."

Brother Sarrow hushed them quickly. He turned his head to the left and then to right listening intently and then he concluded that the sounds had changed. "Hear now….the mortars have stopped. The Kon are now upon the outer walls."

Helforn waited for Sarrow to finish before continuing. "You said that the Kon and the Kai were once one and the same. What does that mean?"

Silas leaned in and spoke quietly so as not to disturb Brother Sarrow. "In the beginning, all Chodugon were the same, but then half of the Chodugon...they became corrupt and turned against mankind. Since that day, Kon and Kai have hunted each other."

"Corrupt...Corrupt from what?" Asked Helforn.

Again, Brother Sarrow interrupted them and hushed them down. Turning to listen again to the sounds of the battle that had changed once more. "Hear now the sounds of sword and axe. The Kon have breached the outer walls. They are now inside the compound."

The Monk named Silas sensed the urgency to finish. "Corrupt, twisted, evil of the unspeakable kind. It's not just the warring and the killing, but the way they hunt and trap their prey...humans." Silas paused a moment and looked across the faces who were still so unbelieving. "In time, they became the creatures born of your nightmares."

Just then, Brother Sarrow hushed them sternly. Listening intently as something approached. He reached under his cloak with his right hand and pulled downward revealing his sword. Waiting as the sounds of the locks on the door clicked and clattered. Then the door burst open and a messenger shouted through, "Brother Sarrow, their numbers are too great. We cannot hold the Kon for much longer!"

Then Brother Sarrow returned his attention to the crowd. "Now listen carefully. We cannot stay here. We must escape to the cliffs. There is a hidden door along the North wall." Again, Sarrow gave that familiar commanding nod to Silas and then Sarrow turned his gaze outside while Silas told them what they needed to know. "Follow us. To get there, we'll need to cross the courtyard and climb the North Tower. Then, we cross over the archway that leads to the

North Wall. Once we make it through the North Tower, we must seal it. We cannot let them catch us on the open ground."

For the first time, one of Sun Anniz's men spoke. It was his most trusted, Sun Set'ti. "We must have twenty, maybe thirty soldiers here. I say we join the Kai and fight the Kon."

Instantly, Brother Sarrow shut the door and snapped his head around. His voice now sharp and clear as thunder. "You know nothing! Chodugon have the speed of horse, the strength of five men, and if the Kon catch you...what they will do to you! No. No. You are not ready with a lifetime of training."

Sun Set'ti spoke again. "The Nefera are soldiers, born to fight and..."

Suddenly Sarrow slammed his hand on a desk. "Do not think your weapons will protect you. Your swords are mere metal and your guns will do more harm than good inside these stone walls. Listen to me. The Kon are not like the Kai. The Kon are pure evil, thousands of years of killing has twisted their minds."

No sooner than Sarrow had finished, then they heard the chorus of the howling shrieks that resonated in the air. It was the very first time they had heard the Kon battle-cry.

Brother Sarrow took command and gave his order. "We can wait no longer. We must move now. Know this...The Kon battle-cry is paralyzing and their charge shakes the ground. Be ever on your guard for they will trap you...and bait you with your own kind. Whatever you do, do not break ranks! Stay together!" He paused one more moment, looked across them and gave his final warning. "On this day, you would do better to run than to fight. Run and do not stop!"

Quickly, Brother Sarrow stepped out into the hallway to make sure it was clear, then he waived them to follow. They moved quietly trying not to attract attention. The sounds of the battle could be heard all around them. Above them, the sounds of gun blasts and grenades. In the courtyard, the sounds of sword and axe. But all around, the Kon battle-cry could be heard. That shrieking, howling scream that was loud enough to rattle the mind.

Then, the sound of something following them. The clicking sound of footprints creeping closer. Corner after corner they ran and as they drew closer to the exit at the South corridor, those footprints drew closer to them. Nearly at the exit, when Silas sensed that the footprints were too close. He pushed the troops into the dark shadows and side corridors.

It came around the corner slowly, clicking and crawling. A Kon most disfigured, with its limbs broken and twisted so that it moved like a wounded spider. Its skeletal body was covered only with tattered rags and chunks of flesh. Occasionally, it stopped and made a hissing sound as if it could smell them. Turning its body back and forth to look down the South corridor, and then slowly continuing on by.

Quickly, Silas guided them to the doorway at the end of the South corridor. A narrow door that but one man could pass through. Quietly Silas turned the old door knob and pushed carefully until it opened just a crack. When he was sure that it was unlocked, he shoved it open to make a run, but the door smacked something. The thud was loud and echoed down the stone passageway. It was immediately followed by that hissing sound. Instinctively, every trooper turned around and ran to the shadows hoping that the Kon would pass them by once again. Moments ticked past and nothing, but then that clicking and crawling sound drew closer.

The spider-like Kon slowly crawled to a bench at the far end of the corridor and propped itself up that it might turn about. It leaned as far forward as it dared and then focused its damaged eyes in their direction. Like a dog on a scent, it moved its head ever so slightly from side to side. Slowly, it appeared to open its mouth wider and wider until its lower jaw protruded forward as it took a long and deep breath. Then it bellowed a shrieking scream while pointing its stubbed arm directly at them. An inhuman scream that sounded like the voices of many calling out in torment and the sound hung in the air endlessly. The scream echoed and reverberated down the stone corridors alerting and drawing more of its own kind. At first, one Kon, then two and finally a handful had gathered to its side.

Troops kicked and banged at the door, but it would not open, and then the Kon charged at them. With no escape, Sarrow and his Kai raced backwards through the troops to meet the oncoming Kon in a thunderous clash. The Kon were menacing with their spinning blades so fast and powerful. The Kai moved as one, twisting and spinning among each other, fast and masterful. But, the Kai were outnumbered and precious meters closed as the Kon pressed the Kai back against the troops. Back until the Kon could reach in with those long and pointed fingers snatching at the troops. Reaching and grabbing over and over until they snatched one man and dragged him back to a clearing.

Two Kon held the man down while the spider like Kon pounded his chest over and over, pausing in between each blow to see if the man had stopped fighting. As if beating a dog into submission, the spider like Kon reveled in its dominance over the dazed man. When the man gave in and could fight no more, the spider Kon straddled his body and pressed him to the ground to hold him still. Then it ripped off the man's neck collar and then tore away his outer faceplate. Underneath, nothing but the clear faceplate to protect him and with its long and pointed fingers, the spider Kon cracked it open. With one hand, the Kon reached in and twisted the man's head to the side just enough to expose his temple region, but not so far that the man could not see what they were about to do to him. Just as Brother Sarrow had warned, the Kon would make a spectacle of the man's torture so to terrorize the other troops; to bait them.

The spider Kon took a moment to look back over its shoulder at the other troops who were crowded up against the back wall. When it saw that the fear had set in, the spider Kon took its long and pointed index finger and slowly inserted it into the man's temple until it touched the delicate bone. The man's screams bellowed down the hallway and his body convulsed in agony. With its finger still in the man's head, the spider Kon twitched with excitement. Again and again, it wiggled its finger and with each scream, it riled with more excitement. Then, the Kon shoved its pointed finger in deeper, slowly passing through bone with a crackling sound and finally buried its finger deep into the brain. Instantly, the man's screams stopped and his body settled still. As the Kon pulled his finger out, it paused for a moment looking upward as it shrieked in ecstasy while the other two Kon unexpectedly raised the man to his feet and shoved him towards the Troops.

No sooner did Silas shout "Trap! Trap! Stay back!", when two more of Helforn's Troops raced forward to help the man. As they neared, they could see the blood trickling down from his temple and worse, they could see his eyes. Eyes that were wide open and frozen still, like a dead man walking. Too late, the Kon had baited them and the trap now sprung. The Kon lunged forward faster than any human could imagine and snatched the two men. Same as before, the Kon dragged the men far away from the other troops, kicking and screaming.

Trapped in the corridor, there was nothing that they could do but watch. Most turned their eyes away, but others were paralyzed by their fear, watching and feeling every blow. Seeing how the Kon held the men down and pulled open their armor, like crabs. Reaching inside with their long and pointed fingers, scraping away at the flesh. Feeling every piece of meat that was torn out and cast aside.

Like a crack of lightening, the corridor flashed with a brilliant white light as a mortar landed between the Kon and the troops, knocking them all to the ground. Their ears rung loud from the blast and the smoke hung in the air so dense that it was more like falling ash. Scattered and alone in the darkness, the survivors rolled about trying to stand, but not Prowler.

He lay there dazed and confused from the concussion and before he had come to his senses, one of the Kon had found him. At first, he could feel the Kon clawing at his ankles and slowly working its way up to his legs and then onto his chest. Suddenly, its head peered through the smoke. It was the disfigured Kon, the one with the broken and twisted limbs that moved like a spider. Still half aware of his condition, Prowler squirmed backwards kicking and clawing but he soon found himself pressed against the remnants of the stone walls. Then, the spider Kon straddled itself upon Prowler pressing its weight against him to hold him still.

From underneath, the sensation of being subdued struck a vile nerve within Prowler. The horrific sensation of being powerless, the sensation of being weak. The thought of being overpowered and defiled sparked a panic within him. Twisting and thrashing about, Prowler managed to free one arm and used it to jab at the spider Kon's unprotected ribs.

With no arm to defend itself, the Kon took to the only weapon it had. It snapped its head down to within inches of Prowler's face and blasted a horrific shriek directly into his ear. The shriek had exploded from the spider Kon's blackened mouth as its spine arched high and its jaw protruded forward showing its filthy teeth. The sound erupted with such force that the Kon's head wavered back and forth bellowing its scream. Even with an armored helmet, the shriek was so loud and penetrating that it nearly paralyzed Prowler's thoughts.

Then the Kon pounded down on Prowler's chest-plate again and again checking each time to see if Prowler had given in. Prowler's eyes nearly rolled backwards from the beating and from the harmonizing shriek that penetrated deep into his brain. Sensing the moment, the spider Kon tapped its pointed finger to Prowler's temple. Reminding of Prowler of what would come next.

Prowler's hand fumbled around searching for his sidearm and when he tried to pull it free, the Kon twisted its head down again and shrieked once more. A shriek that was unending and mind twisting. This time, it scraped at Prowler's faceplate like a rabid dog. Scratching and clawing up under the chin trying to pry the faceplate off. Prowler arched his back and kicked his legs twisting and thrashing about trying to get free, but he could not. The Kon was too heavy, too strong, and to ferocious. Prowler gave in to the exhaustion and when he did, the Kon peered down almost reveling in its dominance until Prowler screamed right back in its face and then thrashed upwards smashing his armored helmet against the Kon's protruding jaw.

Prowler's human battle-cry was not nearly as loud as the Kon's, nor as long as the Kon's, but enough to distract that thing while Prowler raised the sidearm and fired into its hips. As the Kon's body rocked backwards, Prowler fired another shot into its ribs, then into its chest. As the spider Kon's head snapped down and shrieked once again, Prowler jammed the sidearm directly up under its chin and blew the jaw apart. The spider Kon's head waivered and before it could regain its senses, Prowler grabbed it by the throat with his left hand and stuck his sidearm up into its mouth and fired again. Instantly, Prowler was covered in the spider Kon's blood...Hot, black, and oily.

It collapsed on him and before he could get free, more shadowy figures had emerged through the thick smoke. At first they grabbed Prowler, but then they saw the disabled spider Kon with its blood still pouring out. The sight of the blood drove them to frenzy for they thirsted of it. Like wild animals, they pounced on it, fighting each other for every drop of that oily blood and when finished, they peered back at Prowler and shrieked.

As they charged, Prowler opened fire. Squeezing the trigger again and again until he could fire no more as he felt something grab him, something with hands as strong as steel. Snatching him off the ground with such force that it snapped his head back and he was flung straight up into the air. Up and over the broken stone walls and out into the courtyard where he crashed down. This time, those powerful hands had been friendly Kai and not the ferocious Kon.

Looking back at the smoldering wall, Prowler could see that the walls were broken and the roof had collapsed. He knew somewhere hidden within the columns of fire and clouds of smoke, that a fierce battle between Kai and Kon was raging on. With his ears ringing and his head swirling, Prowler could but lay there trembling in fear of what would emerge from it, Kon or Kai.

The first of the Kon shattered through a broken doorway, careening directly at Prowler. It crashed to the ground with a sword sticking out of its neck. Another fumbled backwards through the doorway missing an arm. And then Brother Sarrow and one other Kai leapt out from the smoky hole and came down upon the Kon.

Before Sarrow had a chance to turn around, a third Kon jumped clear through the doorway and caught Sarrow from behind. Ready for the kill, the Kon had raised its sword high above Sarrow's head and brought the sword straight down. Bullets rippled within inches of Sarrow's face and the Kon was hurled backwards. To Sarrow's amazement, Prowler had managed to shoot the Kon before crumbling in pain. Quickly Sarrow raised Prowler to his feet knowing that his ears had been deafened by the Kon battle-cry.

By then, the Kai had pulled the surviving troops out of the rubble and into the courtyard. All around them, on the rooftops, along the walls, and about the courtyard, Kon and Kai were embattled. Dust clouds and smoke filled the courtyard as troops gathered their wounded. Unsure which way to run, the troops hesitated until Silas pushed them in the right direction. With Brother Sarrow at the point and Silas at the rear, they began crossing the courtyard.

And then they saw him. One single Kon walking slowly across the rooftop, black robed and hooded. He had the ancient markings painted upon his shoulders and he was watching them as they crossed the courtyard. A Kon feared above all others for he was different, more advanced, and built of special purpose. His body moved like no other Kon and his gaze was piercing, especially the way he stared at Brother Sarrow. Recognizing Sarrow from a forgotten era and more importantly, recognizing where Sarrow was leading the troops; to the North Tower.

While pointing his sword straight at them, the black robed Kon crouched down and let loose a shriek that echoed within the stone walls of the courtyard. A sudden redirection of every Kon in the courtyard as they rained down from the rooftops and walls. More Kon burst through windows and doorways, down onto the courtyard.

And now the troops were penned in by the courtyard itself as the Kon began to form ranks at the South corner while at the same time, the Kai began to form ranks at the North corner. Protecting the hidden door for it was their last chance to escape.

With their backs to the North corner, the Kai were well protected on the flanks standing shoulder to shoulder in a semi-circle, two and three ranks deep. Even before the Kon had massed their full ranks, the Kon charge quickened. The first few Kon to reach the fleeing troops snatched at the wounded, dragging them off and then tearing at them like wild dogs until they were suitable bait.

Other Kon drove headlong at the rear of the fleeing troops to separate out individuals and to take those who had lagged behind. The lucky troops were already making their way into the safety of the Kai front line, just as the Kon accelerated their charge and crashed upon the wall of Kai. The momentum drove into the second rank of Kai and then into the third. Feet dug deep into the soft soil and knees buckled. If not for the strength of the wall at their flanks, the Kai would have toppled over.

The pressure between the lines built and as it did, the Kai threw grenades up and behind the Kon and then the Kai heaved forward in unison. A force so great that it simply buckled the first row of Kon who fell and instantly, the air was filled with sounds of swords and axe.

Then the one they feared most, the black robed Kon, dropped down from the rooftops and charged directly at

Brother Sarrow. Like a bull, it raced across the courtyard with vengeance in its eyes.

The Kai seized the moment and shoved Brother Sarrow into the North Tower with as many troops and Kai as possible. Then they closed the gate leaving a precious few Kai behind. So few Kai against so many Kon that within seconds, the Kon were hacking at the North Gate, breaking pieces away. Silas reached the top first and turned to help pull the other troops through. When he was sure that there were no more, he turned to cross the archway, but it was then that he heard a muffled call for help. As Silas leapt downward into the stairwell, he saw a wounded man. No sooner did Silas lift the wounded man than he could hear the sound of the North Gate give way and tear open.

Kon flooded in below them while Silas and the wounded man scrambled to reach the top. Together they crossed the archway with Kon just steps behind them. Silas yelled "Now! Now! Blow it now!" And the North Tower erupted behind them. Too late for Silas as two Kon had leapt across the archway. They grabbed him by his thick grey robe and pulled him over backwards.

Together, the two Kon thrashed about, shrieking and hissing as they raked at Silas' face with those pointed steely fingers, trying to blind him. Silas found himself alone with no ally except for the wounded man who somehow found it within himself to lunge at one of the Kon and tilt it off balance.

Without the strength to defend himself, the two Kon grabbed the man by his arms and ripped them off. Then they flung him off the archway to the hoard of Kon below. Silas was still scrambling to his feet and trying to clear his eyes when the two Kon charged him. Outnumbered and cornered, he braced for the charge and from the depths of his lungs, he shouted one word and he shouted it over and over. 'Sarrow!'

The Kon pinned him to the walls and pounded at his midsection. At best, Silas could only try to lock their arms and delay the inevitable. As his legs buckled, he screamed one last time for Sarrow. He screamed so loudly that he could not hear the sound of Sarrow's blade piercing one of the Kon straight through its neck. Silas' legs gave out and he fell to his knees as Sarrow grabbed the arm of the second Kon and slashed it off at the wrist. Before the Kon could rebalance itself, Sarrow pierced it in one shoulder socket and then again in the other. Now defenseless, Sarrow kicked the Kon off the archway.

Brother Sarrow descended the stairs holding Silas from under the arm. The stairs led outside the North Wall and there Sarrow found the troops and Kai shaking off their aches and pains. Confounded, he mustered the one word he could think of and shouted it as loud as any Kon battle-cry. "RUN!"

CHAPTER 12: BATTLE-CRY OF THE KON

A distance of five hundred meters of open grassland to cross before reaching the safety of the cliffs. Taking fire from the walls that now clearly resembled the ramparts of some forgotten fortress.

Midway across the grassland, the first of the Kon descended the wall. It hesitated there, waiting while more of its kind dropped by ones and twos. Then handful after handful until the Kon poured down from the walls. Reza was the first to see them. He turned just in time to see the black robe drop to the ground and burst into a sprint without missing a step. Immediately, the lesser Kon charged forward, like a stampede barreling straight at them. Some sprinting ahead while others ran on all fours, like wild hounds.

Reza shouted forward. "Here they come!" Simply on hearing his voice, the Pack turned about and dropped to their knees with rifles at the ready. Firing down field, they struck the Kon who crashed to the ground rolling and squealing. On the first volley, it seemed a good decision to fight. But, after the second volley, they realized that they should have heeded Sarrow's warning, and run.

It was then, when on their knees, that they felt it...just as Sarrow had said. The ground began to tremble from the Kon charge and the vibration weakened their knees. Then the Kon let loose their battle-cry, their gunfire, and their mortars.

Down went the Lycerene Pack. All of them bore the burn marks of bullets and shrapnel upon their armor. All of them had fallen at least once, some never to rise. Brave as the Lycerene were, they turned, and they ran.

Ran, stumbled, and crawled towards the cliffs, carrying and dragging each other. Mortar blasts filled the sky with waves of dirt and debris such that the cliffs were obscured. But even so, they could see the others leaping from the cliffs, Kai, Neferan, and Earth's own alike. With the Kon racing in fast and ferocious, the Lycerene finally reached the cliffs, dragging the wounded over the edge as they plummeted to the water below. Every one of them carrying another including Reza who had not yet reached the cliffs.

Try as he might, Reza couldn't carry Nava any further. Reza carried him and then dragged him near to the cliffs, pulling and pulling until the blood on his hands slipped in his grip. Exhausted and gasping for air, Reza looked at the cliffs knowing it was his last chance, but he refused to leave Nava behind. Instead of jumping forward to safety, Reza jumped backward over Nava and got down on hands and knees and pushed. His feet and knees scraping across the ground and with one final shove, Nava rolled off the cliff. Then a hand was upon Reza whipping him off the ground.

It wasn't one of the lesser Kon, the kind that ran like wild dogs. This time, it was the very hands of the black robbed Kon. It lifted him up with one hand by the neck, face to face. The thing leaned in twisting and turning its head looking for an opening, some way to get at the man inside. As if it would take a bite from him. It laughed at him first, and then it spoke, "Just what little man hides in here? What foolish man thinks he can stand against me?" It held Reza out dangling him in front of the lesser Kon like fresh meat. "And what sound will this little man make when my Kon rip him apart?"

It was an evil sensation that ran through Reza as he saw its eyes; crazed. He could tell that this Kon had put a terrible suffering into so many. Suddenly, that thing whipped Reza about, casting him across the field. When Reza rolled to a stop he saw that the lesser Kon were surrounding him, like wild animals. He understood the Pack mentality well and he knew they would rush in on him and tear him to pieces. That put the fear evermore into him and the adrenaline flooded his bloodstream. His shoulders readied, his thighs crouched, and his breathing slowed. Then the jolt happened.

Reza's legs burst forward and charged headlong at the black robed Kon. Staring it straight in the eyes until the last few steps when he lunged to the left; spinning and hurling his whole body towards the cliffs and hoping that his momentum would carry him over. But it grabbed Reza by the wrist and together they skidded to the cliff's edge.

Barely balanced, teetering on the edge, Reza pounded against its steely grip while the black robed Kon scrambled to find footing. The soil was made of dry sand and loose rock that crumbled easily, bringing both of them closer to the edge. Even so, it wanted Reza. It tried to hold steady by raising its free hand and slamming it into the ground, digging those long pointed fingers into the soft soil. Slowly, carefully, it began to raise Reza up almost eye to eye again when more rocks crumbled, just a few, but Reza noticed.

Instinctively, Reza began punching and kicking the cliff's edge, loosening the soil and causing the black robed Kon to slip. It kicked and scrambled, but the ground gave way faster. Again, it raised its hand and slammed it into the soft soil, digging its fingers in deeper, but by now, the ground was loose dust. Reza could feel those eyes upon him and he knew what that meant. Bracing his feet against the cliff, Reza pulled the black robed Kon towards the edge until one of its feet skidded off.

Reza pulled again and as its second foot skidded off the edge, forcing the Kon to release its steely grip. Snapping its long and pointed fingers wide open, infuriated and enraged. Suddenly, Reza felt light as air. Backwards he fell, as they stared at each other, all the way down. In the moment before Reza heard the whoosh of the water, he saw the look in its eyes and he knew it would never forget him.

CHAPTER 13: THE NUMBER OF THE BEAST

The waves hit hard and Reza sank straight down like a rock. Down below the frothy waves and into the clear water where he could see it. It was old, very old and encrusted from setting there so long. A design that he had never seen, but for sure, it was a ship, one that could move beneath the waves.

As Reza sank down towards the submersible ship, he could see that it had a sizeable depression on the top near to the stern. In the center of the depression was a large hatch that had been secured wide open. There, he could see two Kai crew members bringing Nava into the ship and a third Kai headed straight towards himself.

Once inside, the Kai crew sealed the hatch and in a few minutes, the water had been pumped out. Immediately, Kai crew opened the forward hatch and assisted the troops forward into a large machine room. Troops fell about the decking exhausted. Too exhausted to get up and move to a more suitable room.

Looking about themselves, they realized that they were in a terrible state having lost over half their troops on the South field during the first mortar attacks. They had lost a dozen more in the courtyard. Yet again, they lost many more crossing the open field to the cliffs. Last among them was

Reza who could barely walk on his own. Before he crashed down, he could see that Chel was already rendering first aid to Nava. Quickly she turned to Reza.

"No blood.

He's breathing.

Good pulse.

Concussion for sure, but I think he'll be alright."

Reza finally settled back fatigued and exhausted.

At the same time, Prowler was scrambling to pull off his neck collar and then his helmet. Pressing his palms tightly against his ears for they pained him so from the screeching of the spider Kon. In concern, Sarrow approached Prowler and put a hand on his arm, "It is the Kon battle-cry. It will subside and your hearing will return in good time." Prowler snatched his arm away in frustration. "You said their battle-cry was paralyzing...you didn't say it was a weapon...a God damn sonic-weapon!"

Sarrow stepped back a moment and then continued. "I had little time to tell you, but for sure, the Kon battle-cry is a sonic-weapon, as you say. The pitch and oscillation will create just the right harmonic frequency to vibrate the human eardrum. The longer they hold their cry, the more deeply it penetrates into the brain."

Now the nausea struck Prowler as he doubled over trying desperately to hold in his stomach contents. He groaned aloud. "What the hell are those things? I saw them eating each other!"

Sarrow kept a hand on Prowler's back to ease him. "As Silas had said, the Chodugon Kai and Chodugon Kon were once one and the same. A mechanized army built during the first great Era of mankind."

Stalker caught on first, "Mechanized? Mechanized? You mean those things are machines....robots?"

"Yes. Chodugon are machines. A skeletal body made of composites and flesh grown of a genetically engineered fungus. A blood made of hydraulic oil...most precious in its making."

Stalker, as always, had to know more. "The first great Era of mankind. How long ago is that? One hundred years...maybe two hundred years?"

"No. Chodugon are older than that. They..." Silas had tried to answer, but Stalker, and Scout interrupted him and hurriedly conversed on the idea.

"What's that....like a thousand years old?"
"No, no, gotta be more like three thousand years."
"Some tombs are at least five thousand years old."
"Wait, what's beyond that? Nothing right?"
"Just the last ice age."

Another Monk named Ishman pointed directly at Scout, "As you have said, it is close to the last ice age. In fact, there have been three Era of mankind. One for each of the last three ice ages. The Chodugon are nearly thirty-six thousand years old."

Scout responded in disbelief, "Thirty-six thousand years? That can't be. Humans were throwing sticks and stones back then, not building machines."

"Sticks and stones as you say? No, not true at all. In terms of evolution, your species has been relatively unchanged for almost one hundred thousand years. When you first became civilized, nobody knows."

Scout rebuked Ishman: "How then is there no such evidence? There is nothing from the last ice age back one hundred thousand years. Haven't you ever heard of the Missing Link?"

Silas intervened, "Do not expect the Earth to show you of these ancient civilizations. Metal rusts, wood rots, and even stone erodes. And then there are the Glaciers. Each Era separated by the ice, some twelve thousand years in between the coldest ages. The Glaciers run deep and scrape the land clean. Crush anything in their path and carry any fragments with them out over the oceans. Mountains raised, valleys carved, and lakes filled…all to start like new. But above all else, the Earth itself rotates on its axis once for every two ice ages. The Era from whence the Chodugon came is now buried under the polar caps."

Helforn grew impatient and disrupted the conversation. "Enough of this history lecture. Where are we?"

Silas offered, "You are aboard the submarine Valiant. She was once the flagship of the Chodugon Subsurface fleet."

Helforn fired another question. "What will you do with us now?"

Silas responded. "We will return you to your kind. You should be safely in the hands of your President Stillwell by tomorrow."

"But we got wounded here. They won't last that long!" Helforn objected with utmost concern.

Silas motioned to one of the Kai medics. "The Kai medics will tend to the wounded in the triage center. Take them there now and remove their armor."

With the wounded now routed to the triage center, all eyes turned back to Silas. A voice from the back of the room called forward. "What now?" A very simple response from Silas, "It would be wise for you to take your rest. The nearest landfall is at least half a day's time."

The exhaustion settled over them and they lay back on the deck plates, workbenches, and some even on the machinery. Ever vigilant, Silas and Ishman stood watch over them.

Hours passed and they began to wake. By ones and twos, they gathered themselves to their feet and followed Silas to a larger room where they could talk. They gathered around. Sun Anniz and Reza stepping forward so the on screen translators were sure to capture everything. Helforn opened with the questions. "So what happens now? You drop us off somewhere and the Kai disappear into history again?"

Silas thought for a moment before speaking. "This time it's different. It's more complicated. Far more complicated."

"What do you mean?" Atera had to know.

"If this were any other base, the attack would be of little concern. They happen from time to time. But, this base was a Signal Station, and more, it was the very last one."

The signal is what they had come for and Atera needed to know more. "You mean that signal that we were searching for? You had something to do with it?"

"Yes. The Kai have guarded The Signal Stations since they were created, hiding them from the Kon. Now, the Kon have them, every last one of them…Thanks to you."

Stalker blurted out, "What? What do you mean thanks to us?"

Brother Sarrow stepped forward. "They followed you here. Somewhere among you, there is a spy."

Helforn grew defensive. "But who? None of us even knew where we were heading. We just traced the energy source from the Signal Generator?"

Silas attempted to clarify. "Did you not notice that the Kon were not fully regenerated? Their flesh appeared dead and rotted as it has not had time enough to grow. That can mean only one thing, they were only recently waken from their hibernation. They did not have adequate exposure to sunlight enough to regenerate their flesh. Awakened very recently and set to follow you. Maybe not one among you, but surely, someone who knew of your mission."

Then it occurred to Brother Sarrow, "I surmise that it was the travelers from the outer worlds that informed you of The Signal and its purpose?"

Helforn responded, "All we know is that there is some Void...or barrier that separates many worlds. It's comprised of some unknown energy and some thread of that energy is being transmitted here...here to Earth."

Sarrow turned his head sharply as he recognized a flaw in Helforn's understanding, a critical flaw. "The Void and The Signal are one and the same, and they are both of this Earth. But, you speak of The Signal as though it were transmitting from The Void to the Earth. The truth is quite to the contrary. The Signal is a message sent from Earth, from these Signal Stations. As long as The Signal is active, so too will the Void. Both of them in our keeping, until now. The

Kon will undoubtedly find it and shut it down as they have done with all of the other Signal Stations."

Helforn drew concerned. "But Why? What is this signal for?"

Sarrow paused a moment and then resumed. "To protect the Earth, to hide it until it be lost and forgotten all together." And then Brother Sarrow turned sharply towards the Neferan and Lycerene. "Ask them. The children of the Puratists." Sarrow paused a moment and then continued with discontent. "I see your war of righteousness still consumes you."

Prowler and Scout talked quickly between themselves.
"How did you know about their war?"
"We just found out ourselves."
"Are you saying this war has happened before?"
"I think he is saying this war never ended."
"But now it's back...here...to Earth."

Silas stepped in. "At the height of the first great Era, man traveled freely among the stars. In those days, there were thirteen worlds. Each world self-governed, with no Empire or Federation to bind them. So far away from each other that they became isolated. Their generations progressed without diversity and so became narrow of blood and even narrower of mind. They became self-absorbed; some to their ideologies and therefore had become self-righteous. Others to their religions and therefore had become cultists; 'holier than thou' as you might say. But most to the color of their skin and therefore had become racist. Collectively they became known as the Puratists. Each of them embodying the belief that they are better than all others. Unto the point of believing that they are a Chosen People, a First People, or even a First World."

Again Prowler and Scout resumed their quick chat.
"What about Earth?"
"Right, we are a mix of races."
"We got every kind of religion and ideology."
"What happened?"

Silas paced for a moment thinking. "The Earth was a place that existed between the Puratist worlds. In their eyes, Earth was the lowest of places. A place where the impure melded be they of any type. Refugees, cast-outs, fugitives, and prisoners. But, most of all, they were slaves, bought and sold in their youth and later abandon in their old age ...by the Puratists."

Stalker arrived at the conclusion, "So Earth was always a mix...they must have been oppressed....they must have rejected the Puratist ways....sooner or later, they would have revolted."

"Yes. Exactly that," said Silas.

Stalker absorbing all this new information looked directly to Sarrow and came quick to the question, "So why do the Kon want to shut down the Signal Station if it protects the Earth? Didn't you say that the Kai and the Kon were once one and the same?"

Silas responded quickly. "True. The Kai and the Kon were once simply known as Chodugon. A mechanized army built to defend Earth from the Puratists. An army of fifty thousand Chodugon and we were fully equipped with the machines of land, sea, air, and atmospheric. All built special for us, special for our purpose. Even so, there was a flaw."

Prowler then joined in "Wait...wait. Did you just say there are fifty thousand Chodugon? How the hell are we going to fight that?"

Silas responded, "Brother Sarrow did indeed say there were fifty thousand Chodugon, but not anymore. There have been many conflicts and catastrophes since then. And, lest you forget, the Kai and the Kon are at war. We hunt each other, always hunting each other with each passing day. By my best account, the Kon number forty-five hundred strong and the Kai number just under four thousand."

Stalker returned to his original question. "But why are the Kai and the Kon at war? What started it?"

The question was for Sarrow to answer "As I said, for all the advanced technology, there was still a flaw in the Chodugon. The Chodugon are machines....we can take orders, but we cannot give orders. We simply were not built to think independently or to make decisions. Inevitably, upon the field of combat, one must adjust and adapt. As a result, our initial battles against the Puratists were marred by failure. Jaromad was forced to make the very decision he opposed."

"Who is Jaromad? What decision?" Stalker insisted on an answer.

Sarrow continued. "Jaromad was the great architect of it all. The architect of everything...the Chodugon, the equipment, the Signal Stations, the Void, everything. His knowledge transcended all men during his time and ever since."

Stalker immediately sensed the danger. "Ok...Ok, but what decision? What did he do?

Silas paced back and forth a bit, hesitant to provide further details. But, he was asked by a human and so he had to respond. "He was pressured hard by the suffering of his day. The politicians, the elders, everyone begged him to fix the Chodugon. To save the people from annihilation! To deliver them from the Puratists."

Stalker's impatience shone clearly now. "But what did he do?"

Again, Silas found it difficult to continue. "They wanted him to fix the Chodugon so that they could adjust and adapt as needed, to make their own decisions."

Stalker had figured out what that meant. "You mean they wanted the Chodugon to think for themselves....to be self-aware? Is that what he did?"

Silas then continued, "Yes. Against his better judgment, he engineered a single prototype. Jaromad recognized that such a Chodugon would need more than just the software to think...it had to control and control is not a thought....it's an emotion."

Silas paused while thinking. "In addition to the core Chodugon Scripts, the Black Robed Kon has a unique emotion processor chip that gives him the instinct to control. The never ending urge to control. They work together you see. The Chodugon need someone to control them, and with the emotion processor chip, he is that control."

Sarrow stepped forward to continue the story. "Before they realized what had happened, the Control prototype had turned against mankind and taken more than half the Chodugon under his control. Hence the name Kon. We on the other hand, are the Kai which is short for Kon-ai. It means *outside of control*."

"So how is it that the Kai are not under his control?" Asked Helforn.

Sarrow continued. "It was one of Jaromad's assistants who saved us. Her name was Miravan. Under Jaromad himself, she was next in charge of both the Chodugon project as well as the Control project. She knew the prototypes call codes and she also knew how the Chodugon cognitive processor worked. She modified a maintenance script that was used to purge unnecessary memories. Essentially, as soon as we hear his calls, it is erased from our memory. You have seen firsthand how it works…you saw what happened to us when he called to us."

Stalker again sensed the warning. "And what happens if he ever figures this out and decides to modify those call codes?"

Sarrow replied almost regrettably. "Then you had better hope by that time that you have relearned The Common Language, the language of our Scripts. That you may re-code them, change them such that he not know."

To that Atera nodded to one of her technical experts, Hunter. He understood what Atera wanted and would set about deciphering the scripts as soon as he could.

Again Stalker inquired, "So, how do we know which one is the Control prototype?"

Sarrow continued, "He is out there somewhere, always and never will he hibernate. It is his control and he keeps it that way by ensuring that mankind never again achieves a level of knowledge equal to the creator, Jaromad. He is there to suppress your technology by any means. When you see hate, when you see oppression, when you see war, it is likely he or his Agents. Such are his ways."

Stalker wanted a more direct answer to his question. "But how can you tell this one Chodugon from all the rest?"

Sarrow's voice turned sharp and clear again.
"You saw him...did you not?
Even more... You felt him, didn't you? Hmm?
Black robed and hooded.
Moving more like an animal than a man. In combat he always wears the ancient markings upon his shoulders. Those markings put there by Jaromad to signify that he is the appointed one, the one that all Chodugon should follow. But, he mixes well among men and so he dresses to hide when among them. A wolf in sheep's clothing... as you say. But you will know him by his number as all Chodugon bear the number of their inventory."

Pulling back the hairline to reveal a number coded upon his own head, Sarrow spoke the unthinkable. "You will know his number my friend because you already know his number. For he is that which keeps mankind from becoming... and his number is zero-zero-zero-six-six-six."

Stalker jumped right in, "Wait, wait, six-six-six, The Beast you say? The Devil, Satan! Are we talking about the same entity?" Before anybody could answer, Sun Anniz interrupted, "The Neferan legends also account of such a creature that bears the number six-six-six."

Prowler stepped forward thinking aloud, "Six-six-six, The Beast, that explains that horrific screeching...those things move more like Demons than robots. The Kai do not move like that."

Sarrow spoke softly now, almost shamefully. "With so many thousands of years hunting and killing, the Kon have evolved into something different. You see...every Chodugon shares the same operational scripts which are written in The Common Language. Call them instincts if you will. At the core of the Chodugon instinct is the command to form ranks, to fight in the Phalanx formation, for there is strength in numbers. But, individuals are weak. The Kon have evolved beyond that basic instinct. Using it and twisting it to divide their enemy ranks...for the kill. That means terror tactics of the unspeakable kind."

Having seen the torture, the baiting, and the trapping, everyone fell silent. They had witnessed that thing, seen how it moved, heard its demonic shriek, every bit evil. And then a voice called from the back of the room. "Where did they learn such things?"

Sarrow almost laughed. "You taught them! Humans...sitting around the campfires telling of your nightmares. Talking of your Devils and your Demons and other hideous things. The Kon watched, they listened, and then...they became. They became every bit the Demons that terrify you, such that you could not tell the difference."

Still shaking off the pain in his ears, Prowler disagreed. "Nightmare? I never had a nightmare like that. One of those things pinned me to the ground...screeching in my face...tried to rip off my face plate. That's no robot...more like the Hounds of Hell."

Reza hesitated, knowing how much Prowler hated him, but he had to speak. "It had me up on the cliffs...that black robed Kon. I saw its eyes. They were wide open, bulging, darting back and forth. Control...it is crazed for control! Absolutely insatiable!"

But, Stalker needed to know more. "The black robed Kon, the Control prototype, he wants to shut-down the

Signal Stations. He wants war...bloodshed...death? Is that what he is after?"

Silas returned to the conversation. "You underestimate him for he is not so simple minded. He keeps mankind under his control and by seizing the Signal Stations, he intends to bring the Puratists back to Earth, that he might control them as well, that they never challenge his dominance. If the ages should tell you one thing for sure, he is a conqueror, he is a deceiver, and he is a manipulator. Again, these are his ways, and in that, he is the master."

Then Atera, who had sat silently asked, "Whatever became of Jaromad? Why didn't he stop the Kon?"

Silas spoke with an almost human sadness. "It was a great weight to bear...in those most horrible of days. To have seen that the fall of Earth was brought about by the very Chodugon that he had built to protect it. He was found dead, by his own hand. Shame, sorrow, or grief...no matter, for it was more than he could bear. It was left to Miravan to deploy The Void which Jaromad had designed. As you can testify yourselves, it was a masterful success. For that, the people still loved him so. They mourned of him for many days and nights. Then buried him in a grand tomb."

Lost in thought, Atera hadn't even realized she had spoken aloud. "Buried him? In a tomb? What tomb?"

Silas seemed a bit confused, but he explained. "If we knew where the tomb was located, then the war between Kon and Kai would have ended long ago."

Troops looked at him oddly not understanding how a tomb, eloquent as it may have been, could stop the Chodugon War. "They didn't just bury Jaromad, they buried his knowledge. The knowledge behind the Chodugon, the

Signal Stations, and The Void. His tomb is his library and it would take a thousand scientists a thousand years to relearn it all."

Silas watched them mull around thinking over this most unbelievable story. But they had seen that thing and felt it. Somehow, they knew it was true and they eventually looked back to Silas. He continued on. "My friends. There is one more thing you should know. There is a legend of another."

CHAPTER 14: THE GOD OF COMPASSION

Sarrow looked sharply at Silas, something between them was in disagreement. Something that Sarrow did not want to share; "I see no worth in this legend. It is but a waste of time." He looked to the humans and said, "My brother Silas has a curious interest in this legend. He has followed every last trace of evidence since the beginning. Still, nothing to prove its worth."

Silas continued. "But, we are here with time on our hands." To that, Sarrow simply turned his attention elsewhere while Silas resumed. "There is a legend of another Chodugon equal, but opposite to that of the Control prototype. Another Chodugon who is self-thinking and driven by the same emotion processor. They are identical with the exception of emotion. One of Control, and the other of Compassion."

Prowler couldn't contain his agitation. "You mean we got another robot out there that's just full of love? Maybe his name is Cupid?"

"No. No. I did not say 'love'. What I said was Compassion. Think of it like this. On the one hand, Control is the root of all evil human emotions. Fear and jealousy, greed and hate. They are all emotions that stem from a need to Control. On the other hand, Compassion is the root of all good human emotion. Even love, true love, stems from Compassion."

Captain Helforn interrupted Silas, "Common sense will tell you that love is the root of all good human emotions. Just ask any human."

Silas quickly retorted. "Let me state it another way....If you have love without the ability to feel for another person's wants and needs, then you don't have true love at all. In that case, what you have is merely the need to control the person of your desire."

Helforn insisted, "So how do we find this Compassionate prototype?"

"Like I said, it is but a legend. The Compassionate One does not walk with either Kai or Kon, he walks alone. Nobody has ever identified the Compassionate One.

Sharply interrupted by Sarrow "If he exists at all! I tell you again, there is no worth in this legend."

Helforn didn't see the concern. "So why would we care about a Chodugon who is full of Compassion? He poses no threat to us."

Again, Silas paced a bit. "Because the legend says that he is the opposite of the Control prototype. Where the Control prototype is the undoing of man, the Compassionate One rebuilds and reeducates man. He walks in the shadows working through populations to find the few men who can be encouraged or enlightened, the few men brave enough to spur on the rebirth cycle of technology."

At that point, Prowler asked, "But why would Jaromad create two Chodugons with different emotions?"

Silas sat down slowly. "Again, it's not so simple. Jaromad was an old man by the time of the Chodugon wars. The legend says that Jaromad had built the first emotion processor inside a mainframe merely as a game...a toy if you like, and he did so when he was a young man. He built it for entertainment and never intended it for any other purpose, but the war and suffering pressured Jaromad and so he re-used his original emotion processor in the Control Unit."

Stalker had pieced it together. "That explains how the Control Unit came about, but what about the Compassionate One. I thought you said Jaromad committed suicide?"

Silas perked up. "Ah, observant you are! After Jaromad's death, Miravan was assigned to carry on his works or to destroy them. While she was in the mainframe destroying his old files, Miravan found the original emotion prototype. It awoke and spoke to her, same as it had done with Jaromad when he was a young man. It would say, 'My Jaromad, may we play the question game today?'

Miravan realized that the emotion prototype had learned much from Jaromad. Most importantly, that it grieved for Jaromad, same as herself. She was so awed by its awareness that she couldn't bring herself to destroy it. She decided to upload it into a Chodugon. From there, she furthered its training all the days of her life. She gave it the knowledge to survive among men, but most importantly, she gave it the task...to protect mankind. To serve mankind rather than to control it."

"So how would you know this one Chodugon from all the rest? Does it have a number, or a name?" Asked Stalker.

"If he had a number, it was lost with Miravan. But, Chodugon can recognize Chodugon nevertheless. They cannot hide from each other. In the same way humans can recognize other humans by the way they walk or the way they talk, so to can Chodugon recognize Chodugon. Every Chodugon is built identical aside from the flesh which may take on many variations. Being the same, their body movements are all the same. In short, all Chodugon share the same body language. It is like a signature."

And then, as always, it was Helforn who brought their focus back to the threat at hand, "It's nice to know there will be somebody around to clean up the mess if we fail, but I ain't counting on it. How much time do we have? When will the Kon shut down that Signal Station?"

Sarrow was the only Kai who knew exactly where the Signal Generator was hidden and so he replied. "The Signal Generator is dug deep into the Earth, encased in bluestone. Ten hours…. maybe twelve."

"Damn it!" snapped Helforn.
"That's hardly enough time to mount a counter offensive, even if we radio ahead. Where is your transmitter room?"

"As I said before, this ship is old. The transmitter equipment has long since fallen into disrepair. Only the essential mechanics remain."

Helforn looked to his own troopers. "What about our transmitters? We had several of them. Where are they?"

Hunter grumbled, "All of the transmitters were on the VTECs when they went down."

Stalker had already considered the personal transmitters located within their armor. "And of course, the transmitters in our armor are too weak for that distance." He looked at Sun Anniz and Reza who nodded the same. None among them would work.

Helforn turned to Sarrow. "What about this old ship of yours? How fast can she make?"

"Sir, we are running eighteen knots. I dare not push her beyond twenty."

"Then do it. Bring her to twenty knots. Get us to the nearest air base."

"Yes Captain Helforn," said Silas. "I will deliver your order to the bridge myself."

Then Silas reminded them of the inevitable. "I'm sure this goes without saying, but soon, the Chodugon will awake....all of them. The Kon will certainly have the lead on us, they hold the advantage."

As always, Prowler could not hold back the frustration within. "And we are stuck here! Stuck in this rusted old hulk with no radar, no radio, and we are crawling along like some slug!"

Helforn knew Prowler was right. He knew there was absolutely nothing to do; not just yet. "You're right. We're here with nothing but time on our hands so you better use it. Rack out and get some sleep till we make landfall. It's wise to assume we will be back on that island for a counter offensive."

They settled back in preparation for their sleep. Only troopers native to Earth were afforded the comfort of removing their helmets. Prowler had already removed his helmet and so he was the first to find a resting place and squat down. Chel, so tired that she settled back with her eyes still open. She unknowingly set her gaze upon Prowler and could not help but notice that the strain on his face persisted. She could feel the loss and the rage inside him. For some reason, his eyes darted right to hers and she was shaken by the hate in his eyes. She turned her head downward away from his sight. They slept. All of them.

CHAPTER 15: THE CHODUGON MAP

With a thud and a screeching sound, the Valiant had beached herself. Just as promised, they were at the nearest air base and fortunate for them, it bordered the sea. Any other ship would dread such a beaching, but not the Valiant, she was built special. With a double bow meant for rapid deploy of troops and equipment directly onto a beachhead. Straight in she went and up the beach. The outer bow doors swung down and dug into the beach sand to both anchor the ship to shore, as well as to act as ramps for troop deployment.

The troops knew it was time to head out even without anyone having to state so. Standing up was the hardest part for most of them, but eventually, they were up and heading toward the ramps. Along the way, they saw more of the great ship. Had they seen how deteriorated she was, they would have reconsidered pushing her to full speed.

But, the sun shined ahead of them and that's where they headed. Passing through its halls so decorated with carved and engraved metalwork, images older than they could know. Amid the clamoring, Reza found himself staring at one wall. Half of it was covered by some images and the other half was a large patch welded into what had clearly been battle damage. It was Silas again who would pass on that bit of history. "As I said when you arrived, this ship had once been the flagship of the Chodugon Subsurface fleet.

But, in the first days of the Chodugon war, before we knew not to trust our own kind, she was rammed in this very spot. Had she sank in deeper water, we could not have salvaged her. A secret she remains. The Kon not knowing."

But, Reza was deep into thought and hardly heard what Silas had said. "Huh...I...I figured she had gone down from that hole." Reza then motioned to the part of the image that had not been destroyed. "What is this here? This looks like a kind of blueprint, or something like a three dimensional map."

Silas reached forward touching it and said, "That is the map of the continent Adlaria. Somewhere there is the tomb of Jaromad, lost under the polar caps. With all the damage to the map, we will never know."

Reza thought to himself just how right Silas was. He nodded to Silas so that they might catch up with the rest of the troops. From the beach, they looked back and watched the bow doors rise and then quietly, Valiant slipped backwards under the waves from whence she came.

Once on the airbase, Helforn quickly radioed their location and was granted new VTECs to shuttle them back to the hangar where they would assemble yet again. As they did before, the troops were loaded onto the VTECs by team; Reza and his Lycerene Pack, Sun Anniz and his Neferan Swarm, Atera and her pilots. This time they would be accompanied by Brothers Sarrow, Silas, and a handful of Kai.

Their armor weighed heavy on them by now. As advanced as it were, the armor could only be worn for short periods of time or the body would fatigue. It had to come off and thankfully the receiving party was prepared for them. Hurried right off the VTECs and into the Hangar building where the troop's armor was removed and each man was cleaned. Wounds were tended while fluids and electrolytes were administered along with medicine. From there, they passed directly through the sealed door and into the familiar negotiation rooms. There they gathered once again. Three chambers for three worlds. The linguists, the technicians, President Stillwell, Vice President Zadan, the representatives from Longspear, Queen Anak Re Sun, and many more.

With people still scrambling into the chambers, President Stillwell resumed his lead. The hangar bay was silent and tense, except for Reza as he moved to sit side by side with one of his technicians, hoping to connect to Longspear and look again at Chief Cree's files, the ancient scrolls.

President Stillwell opened the mission debrief. "Captain Helforn, what the hell happened out there? We had a truce, an agreement that there would be no conflict among us and yet, less than half of the troops have returned. We know there was a firefight. What we don't know is just which of you started it."

Helforn rose slowly, still trying to find the words to communicate such an event. He knew he had to respond to their questions and their questions only, but minutes mounted. "Sir, there was a firefight, but it wasn't any of us that started it."

Vice President Zadan almost reprimanded Helforn. "Do I need to remind you of what's at stake here? It is for us to decide who we trust, not you."

Again, Helforn paused to think about the passing time, worried that these questions could go on for hours or worse, days. But, he answered as was expected. "Sir, as I stated, it was none of us. We did indeed…"

He was cutoff abruptly by Vice President Zadan. "Then who were you fighting?"

Reza used the distraction to his advantage, motioning for his technician to bring up Chief Cree's files during which, President Stillwell asserted himself over Zadan's questions. "I want to know about this signal. Did you find anything?"

Again, Helforn felt the time passing, but at least Stillwell's question was somewhat in the right direction.

"Sir, we did indeed identify the location of The Signal. We also learned that The Signal is not being sent to Earth, rather, it's being sent from Earth. The Signal is a message that activates The Void. They are both of this Earth."

Puzzled, Stillwell looked to Queen Anak Re Sun and spoke in an untrusting voice, "I thought you said that signal was being sent to Earth?"

She replied slowly and persuasively, "Yes. That is as I have said. But, as I also stated, we have never encountered this type of energy before. We knew little of The Signal and it must amount to nothing more than our lack of understanding."

Zadan dragged the questions again. "Just what type of energy are we dealing with here?"

An unimportant question that could only serve to waste precious time. Helforn sensed pressure mounting as the time passed yet again. He had to do it and so he stood straight up, "Sir, I need you to hold your questions. I need to…"

"What you need to do is answer my questions. Are we clear?" snapped Zadan frustrated that Helforn would dare to take control of the agenda.

The room went silent. For as much as Stillwell needed Zadan, he felt the need to restrain him. He motioned with his hand for Zadan to settle back and let Helforn speak freely. Zadan's face showed his frustration as his eyes squinted and his jaw twitched. Then his expression went blank while slowly settling back into his wheelchair.

Queen as she was, she took note of the rift between Stillwell and Zadan. Again, Reza took advantage of this second distraction, motioning subtly with his fingers for his technician to page further into Cree's ancient files.

"Sir, what we have now is a problem bigger than the Lycerene and it's bigger than the Neferan. That signal was meant to defend Earth from the outer worlds; there are twelve of them. It works with The Void, a barrier...to hide Earth from the Puratist worlds. Until today, that signal was secure, but somebody followed us to The Signal Station. There is your firefight...The Signal and The Void are compromised. We have only hours left to mount a counter offensive."

Stillwell leaned in slowly and fearfully, his years showed clearly on him now. "I'm trying real hard to understand you. Who exactly followed you to The Signal source? Who exactly did you fight?"

Helforn lost his cool and snapped "And I'm trying real hard to tell you what happened. Damn it... I was there and I don't believe it myself!"

The hangar bay fell silent as Helforn paused a bit realizing what he had done. Where to start such a story? He ran his hands through his hair as the sweat began to shine on his face "You wanna know what happened out there. Alright then, here it is...and don't any of you interrupt me again. Got it?"

He looked around the hangar and realized that he had their silent acceptance.

"I'll take that as a yes." And then he began. The words just flowed. "Alright...alright...alright....Them there, the Lycerene, they told us of the outer worlds, all twelve of them. They told us about the war among those worlds. Fighting over race, religion, anything so self-righteous."

Stillwell blurted out "A Race war...a Jihad, lasting thousands of years? You can't be serious?"

Helforn quickly resumed before he could be sidetracked further. "What they didn't know is that Earth had been a party to those wars...thousands of years ago. It was The Signal and The Void that were built to protect Earth. To hide it away from the Puratist worlds until Earth be forgotten."

Pausing briefly while he ran his hands through his sweaty hair again and again. "President Stillwell, the same architect who built The Void and The Signal also built an army of robots called the Chodugon, some fifty thousand strong and fully equipped with their own weapons. But these robots, they were losing the war. They couldn't think for themselves on the battlefield. So, the architect, Jaromad....he made one of these Chodugon more advanced, more intelligent...to give him control over all of the Chodugon. He made one of them...self-aware."

By now, Helforn broke into an all-out sweat and had that look of full defeat "Eh...you're gonna love this next bit......That thing turned against the humans and took half the Chodugon with it. So, even though The Void had protected Earth from the Puratist wars, the Chodugon started a second war, their own war."

Helforn paused yet again needing a drink for his throat had drawn dry and tight. "It was the Chodugon War that brought about the collapse of an entire era. So, you ask just who we were fighting out there. We were fighting the Chodugon. Now, that thing has The Signal Station and as soon as he finds the Signal Generator, he's gonna shut it down along with The Void. Sir, Earth will be exposed to the Puratist worlds...all twelve of them."

The stares returned and Helforn could tell that they questioned his very sanity. "Don't believe me huh? I told you ... I don't believe it myself, but I saw that....that thing. Look around they will all tell you, they saw it too!" The eyes moved back and forth across the room and heads nodded. Still they could not accept it. Helforn looked directly at Stalker, "Bring the Kai forward! Bring them here right now!"

Stalker promptly escorted Sarrow and Silas closer to Helforn. Sarrow with his hood covering part of his face once again and Silas at his side. "They're not much for believing our story. So, we're gonna show them what you're made of." Helforn motioned for a Sentry. "Give the hooded one your blade!"

To that, Sarrow rolled up his sleeve and pressed the knife against his forearm. He looked just like any man and so they squirmed at the sight of Sarrow pressing the blade into his flesh until it hit the bone. Then, he scraped it forward until a chunk of the flesh separated and plopped to the ground. He held his arm high enough for everyone to see what lay beneath. Not a bone, but a shiny metallic composite skeleton.

Stillwell exploded as his Sentries scrambled to protect him. "You brought one of those things here? What the hell has gotten into you?"

Sarrow then spoke and again, the air resonated with silence. "As your brave Captain has said, half of the Chodugon turned against mankind. They are known as the Kon and they serve the one called the Control Unit. The other half of the Chodugon are known as the Kai. We are the guardians of The Signal Generator and we still serve mankind."

During the discussions, Reza had been paging through Chief Cree's ancient scrolls until he saw what he was looking for. It had been a faint memory, but now the image so clearly matched his suspicion that he could not hide his expression. Queen as she was, she took notice. "You there! What are you doing?"

She rose from her seat and walked swiftly towards him pointing her finger at the computer. She stopped at the wall that separated the two chambers, trying to catch a glimpse of his screen.

Reza was surprised that anybody had noticed as he paged through the files and he was unprepared for it. He knew she was trying to see the image and so he motioned for the technician to close the file. "I'm logging my wounded and dead. That is all."

The Queen erupted, "Liar...Liar...I saw symbols. I saw the images...ancient things!"

Maybe Reza could have convinced them otherwise, but he did not know that the chambers were full of audio and visual equipment, recording everything. Zadan looked to his technicians. "Replay it! All of it!"

The technicians quickly turned their monitors around so the replay was visible to all. At first, nothing unusual. Just Reza and his technician logging into Longspear's network, and traversing directories and files. Then, they saw as Reza had opened the first file and paged through the ancient scrolls. Images of old relics, ancient writings, images of symbols, artifacts, and then the image of the ancient box which had brought them through The Void.

Silas recognized something of it and stepped closer. He began to formulate the question, "Where did you get...?" and before he could finish, the replay cast the final image. The one image in all the universe that could possibly be of such value, the map to Jaromad's tomb. The same map that Reza had seen on Valiant, only full and complete.

By the looks on Sarrow and Silas faces, President Stillwell could tell it was important. "What is that?

Silas looked to Reza "You knew of this... We spoke of this... and yet, you did not tell me?"

Again, Stillwell interrupted, "What does it mean?"

Reza and Silas were ignoring Stillwell. "I could not be sure. I had only recently come into possession of these files when my predecessor was killed in battle."

Sun Anniz jumped in, "We have warned you not to trust the Lycerene. How much more do you need to see?"

Silas nearly scolded Reza, "But you knew of this? You knew it meant we had another option and still you said nothing of it."

Finally, President Stillwell had enough of being left confused. The old soldier in him broke out and his voice changed.
"At ease People!
I want to know what this thing is.

I want to know exactly what the options are."

He looked directly at Silas for an answer. "It…It is your trooper, Captain Helforn, he mentioned an architect named Jaromad. He was the architect of the Chodugon, the Signal, and The Void. He was the architect of everything. When he died, he was buried in a grand tomb with a library containing all of his knowledge, preserved for future generations. With it, we could reconstruct the Signal Generators rather than fighting the Kon."

Stillwell replied, "So why didn't you do this before?"

"Because, the location of the tomb was lost during the first Chodugon War. For thousands of years, both the Kon and the Kai have searched for its location. All we had to guide us was a map that was mostly destroyed. The Lycerene named Reza had seen the map onboard Valiant. He should have told me there was another copy in his keeping. Precious hours are lost now."

Helforn asked the obvious, "But, we have armies and weapons that could flatten that island. I say we attack now!"

Sarrow interrupted with the grim news. "I assure you that by now, the Kon have already fortified in preparation for just such an attack. Even now, they draw their forces together. Chodugon, equipment, and machines of war, the likes of which you have never seen. All that and more for The Signal Generator is a precision instrument, delicate in its making. If you attack with heavy weapons, you yourselves will disable it."

Helforn knew the might of his armies. "We could have thousands, maybe ten thousand there within hours. I've seen those things. We don't have time for a treasure hunt!"

"Yes, but the Kon only need to hold out long enough to unearth The Signal Generator and then they can disable it themselves."

Stillwell sat silent. Thinking to himself. He was not known as a decisive man and it showed. After a long pause, "I agree with Captain Helforn." He turned to his subordinates. "Make preparations for a counter offensive."

But Zadan saw differently. "My President Stillwell, I would suggest otherwise. What if the Kai are right? Then we will need to rebuild The Signal Generator."

Stillwell felt the pressure and he rejected with agitation. "There is no way to know that anything remains in that tomb but dust. I can't risk it. I say we stick with what's tangible and what's tangible is The Signal Generator, we know it's on the island, so let's take it!"

But, Zadan was ever clearer and he proved himself once again. "Surely, we have men enough for such a mission. Why would we not cover both of our options? We could send one force to the island and send another, say... these few men here...to the tomb. I am confident we can spare as much."

Stillwell thought. "This I can agree to." He turned again to his subordinates and did his best to portray himself the commander. "The counter-offensive is in your hands. Prepare the necessary." The hanger came alive as numbers of subordinates rushed out of the exits fully understanding the urgency at hand.

Then he turned to his trusted captain. "Captain Helforn, you've earned yourself another expedition. I'm sure you'll need fresh troops and equipment. Whatever you need, just sound-off and my staff will assist."

Just as folks began to stir, as if the meeting were over, Reza realized he had to be there. He turned his head back and forth as if looking for some reason he could voice up. "If you are going to search for this tomb, then you need me there."

Without skipping an opportunity, the Queen snapped out "You? Lycerene, you above everyone else are the least to be trusted! You have proven that yourself."

Zadan spoke forward, "We have learned much of you and your kind. We will do without you this time."

Reza was no match for a Queen. No match for her wit, so he spoke directly to Silas. "What you have is a fuzzy little image of a map. Is it clear enough for you to find the tomb? No. No, because it's a three dimensioned map that contains markers which indicate the place as well as the time, a star-date, as you and I had discussed back on Valiant."

Silas nodded. "True. This is very true. We will need a copy of the map from your files."

Reza snapped. "Why would the Lycerene give you a copy of that map if we are enemies? Who may I ask will give you all of the symbols and interpret it for you? And lastly, you speak of trust, it was the Lycerene who fought the Kon on the open grassland so that the rest of you may escape to the cliffs! Tell me again that the Lycerene are not to be trusted!"

Silas' head moved a bit as he thought. "I'll say this of it. Few humans have ever stood against the Kon. Fewer still have survived."

The Queen could see that Reza's words had sway to them and she sensed that the decision would be turned backwards. She did not know what, if anything would be in that tomb, but whatever it was, she wanted it. "If these Lycerene refuse to cooperate, if they leave you with no other option, then as before, I offer you my technicians and their equipment, at your command."

Helforn and Stillwell looked at each other. They knew what the other was thinking. Again, Helforn was in charge of the expedition and so it would be for him to speak the orders. "After the last expedition, it would be advisable to have more troops. I request forty Lycerene, forty Neferan, and one hundred of our own…and I'll take the Kai as well." Quick to clarify one more inclusion. "I expect Commander Atera and her pilots will be on board."

Just as discussions settled out, another technician on the other side of the room stood and spoke directly to President Stillwell. "Sir, at this time, we are tracking a category three storm. In fact, the outer front of that storm will be touching down here within the next ninety minutes. We will be launching directly into the path of the storm. If we miss that deadline, the next launch window will be plus three hours."

Stillwell looked to Helforn. "It's your mission Commander. Can you make the launch window?"

Helforn took some time to think it through. "Sir, we'll make it alright." He looked around the hangar. "Ok People. Let's pull this thing together proper! First, any incoming troops from Longspear and the Neferan fleet need be ferried down immediately. Second, we need a staging area out of the weather. Can we get Hangar Bay Two cleared out?"

The responses were positive. "We will have Hangar Bay Two fit and ready in thirty minutes."

"Good. Good. Troops and their equipment should be ready for assembly in plus thirty-five minutes. We make equipment checks and final briefing there." Then Helforn looked to the Queen and the senior officials from Longspear, "You may accompany your troops through the briefing. You have only that much time to spend with them. For now, we'll have some meals served so we get these troops ready to go." To that, the meeting was over.

CHAPTER 16: THE SECOND COMING

Amongst themselves, each to their own kind, they talked. They shared everything that they had seen. They spoke of Chodugon and their equipment, the waking of Chodugon across the globe, and the anticipation of skirmishes wherever the Kai and Kon would meet. They even spoke of the legend of the Compassionate Chodugon. But most of all, they spoke of the Puratists and their wars. The very war that they were born into and the very war that they were on the edge of finishing.

Sun Anniz shared it with his Queen. "This world, it became a place where the dregs from every race collected. It was a penal colony and a slave trade." It made sense to her now and she immediately understood why this world was such a mix of races. Like an infestation, but then she saw something she could use of it. "So, there are some of our own kind here. Maybe they can be persuaded….maybe they can be turned if given the right motivation. Yes. I dare say that there will come a time when they will find the alternative unbearable. Trust me my brother, the pieces are aligning just as I have said."

Having eaten and filled their stomachs, their thirty-five minutes had passed. It was time to move to Hangar Bay Two.

The small squadrons of Neferan, Lycerene, and Earth troops passed quickly and entered Hangar Bay Two. As they did, they could see the gathering clouds, the storm was coming.

Along the way, the path was guarded by Sentries each having a guard dog. In all the commotion, they had not yet been given direction to their specific places. They simply followed the Sentries into the middle of the hangar bay up to the last Sentry. There, they gathered round, team by team.

As could be expected, the Lycerene found themselves in awe of those creatures, those guard dogs. Sentries struggled hard to keep them under control and without their armor, the Lycerene were unsteadied. Sun Anniz found humor at it and nudged one of his men to stir a confrontation. Sun Kefer stepped forward. "Ha! They worship the creatures for thousands of years and when they finally see one, they cower! And look, it's just a plain old dog. I'd love to see their faces when they meet a real wolf."

The words sparked tensions as the Neferan and Lycerene banded amongst themselves and formed lines. But, for the swiftness of Scout, they might have erupted. She looked directly to Chel and spoke delicately. "You mean you've never seen a dog before?"

Chel spoke rather softly. "No. On our world, the canine have been extinct for a thousand years. We know of them only by our legends that tell of their ferocity, and of their loyalty." Chel hesitated amid all the dogs growling, but eventually she concluded. "And stories of their playfulness."

Scout felt something familiar. "Yes, they are all of that and much more." She turned to the Sentry. "He is a gallant one. What is his name?"

The Sentry pulled back hard on the leash, "Sir, his name is Atlas. I suggest you stay back. He's the alpha male and he is stressing hard. Not to mention that he was the one who pounced on the Lycerene in the forest. Atlas remembers the Lycerene all too well."

"Yes. He is certainly stressing." Scout circled around the dog staring at him curiously. "I was raised on the Plains, on a farm with many livestock and many dogs to guard them. I've seen these guys stand their ground even against the wolf. I've even known a couple to battle it out against the wolf and come home torn up. I have a way with them. Watch."

Scout knelt down a couple meters away from Atlas. She called to him. "Good boy. That's a good boy." Over and over until his jumping and scratching turned to pacing. "Now, you see he is curious." She put out her hand, palm up with her fingers closed. Then, she mimicked the dog's nature by lifting her head as if she was sniffing for his scent.

The dogs tone changed somewhat. "Now, you see he acknowledges that I am no threat." She sat still waiting for the dog to settle down. "Bring him slowly. Let him come at his own pace." Atlas moved backwards and forwards, circling around, over and over. Amid her continued calls, "Good boy, come to me my good boy," Atlas crept closer and close. In the last few feet, she kept totally still and peacefully quiet. Atlas moved around her, sniffing and then eventually brushing his sides against her. At last, he put his head to her hand and she gave him a warm and soothing stroke. They were friends and now they played for a moment.

Turning around, Scout saw Chel kneeling just like herself, captivated, like a child waiting to play with the dog. As far as Scout knew, Chel was an unprovoked killer who dropped the bombs on Earth's cities, but now Scout saw a different side of Chel, the Lycerene. Scout understood now how such a longing that had lasted generation after generation become something more.

A second passed before Prowler and his rage intervened, "Don't forget that Bitch and her Pack bombed two cities; because I guarantee you....I won't forget." And just that quickly, hatred was in the air. The three teams separated once again and formed lines between them.

Helforn came through the door along with the Queen and senior officials from Longspear. There before them was the mob on the verge of a brawl.
"Attention!
Neferan, form ranks to the left!
Lycerene, to the right!
Earth own, to the rear!
Clear the center! I say again...clear the center!"

They were interrupted as doors burst open. Infrastructure teams brought in pallets full of armor and equipment. Helforn shouted his commands. "Rack that armor up against the outer walls. Keep the center clear. We got fresh troops coming any minute!"

Some of the equipment was odd, including several pieces that were far too large for a soldier to carry. Stalker, true to his ways, needed to know exactly what it was. He walked over to one of the technicians who was busily preparing the equipment. "What have you got here? This doesn't look like any field equipment we're trained to handle. This stuff... it looks like it belongs on a ship."

The technician simply replied, "Where you're going, you will need everything from a temporary shelter to ground penetrating radar, and an ice drill...a real big ice drill!" Then the technician chuckled and walked away busied once more.

By now, the doors were secured open as people and equipment moved in and out nonstop. Amid all the activity, the fresh troops started to trickle in. They were Earth's own and they were clearly confused and unsure where to go. They simply started walking across the center as a disorganized crowd. They were in the way and more importantly, they looked sloppy. Like second rate troops and Helforn knew what the Neferan and Lycerene would think.

"Halt! This is a staging area people, not a schoolyard. Back it up... form ranks along that forward bulkhead. Look alive people. Move...Move...Move!"

Once Helforn's troops had formed ranks, he marched them along the outer perimeter. He marched them right past the Neferan who were unimpressed. He then brought them around the rear corner to join Atera and her pilots. Even before his troops joined ranks with Atera's, he could hear Reza bark the same orders to the incoming Lycerene troops. Only, they were far more disciplined and entered two-by-two in lock step. Clearly, these troops were among the Lycerene very best. These troops were sharp and they looked it. A single Master-At-Arms walked forward of them. All Reza need do was point the location where they would muster and his Master-At-Arms did the rest.

Just the moment that the Lycerene troops were steadied, new sounds filled the air. This time, the marching was so loud it could be heard from outside the hangar. The technicians had little time to react and found themselves fleeing or pressing themselves hard against the walls. Anything to avoid being overrun by the oncoming Swarm. The Neferan troops came through the doors in double-time march, three abreast. Each and every one of them was massive, and so nearly identical.

As the Neferan troops made their way down the left-hand side of the hangar bay, the Queen made her way across the front wall to where Vice President Zadan was sitting. A small table setup for him and his wheelchair. She spoke in an almost submissive voice, "They are excellent troops Vice President Zadan. Wouldn't you agree?"

He stirred for a moment collecting his thoughts delicately. "Indeed, Queen Anak Re Sun. I dare say that their marching skills are among the very best. My compliments."

She bowed her head most nobly. "Thank you. My troops will be honored to hear they have impressed you so. As for my technicians who are still working out there in the cities…they report that they are nearly finished extinguishing the Lycerene Thermocells. I am hearing that both your technicians and my technicians are working hand-in-hand and therefore expect to finish ahead of schedule. I would say that is quite an accomplishment."

Zadan replied in kind. "We are receiving similar reports. Due credits have been given to your technicians. My people on the ground are most impressed with the knowledge and perseverance of your team. The Lycerene Thermocells are a most horrific weapon and I fear it will take decades to rebuild these cities. If ever."

She edged a smile and then blinked her delicately painted eyes. "Well, let us hope we have the same collaborative teamwork on our next expedition. The more I think on it, the more I believe your suggestion to pursue both options is the wiser decision. That is why I give you the very best of my troops. I entrust them to your command now Sir. They have explicit instructions to respect you and your Commanders as if they were your own."

Taking a moment to respond, Zadan sought to maintain their partnership. "That is most reassuring, Queen Anak Re Sun."

To that, she bowed her head again and then made her way across to her troops. She had been brief, to the point, and planted her seed just as she had planned. Even so, she was not exactly finished. She took advantage of the audience; that it could be used to her advantage. She marched along the perimeter of the hangar like a cat on the prowl, every eye was on her as she had planned. Her armor accentuated every curve of her body and her body movements so fluid as to mesmerize Earth's men. She used every opportunity to cast her eyes towards the troops of Earth, making eye contact with as many of them as possible. She could sway their devotion with nothing more than those eyes.

Chel would be first to comment, "Look at her. She'll stop at nothing to gain their favor."

Reza joined in, "For sure, we are in a bad spot. We are losing their trust while the Neferan are gaining it."

Nava couldn't hold his concerns back. "We've got to do something. Sooner or later, those Neferan carriers are going to attack Longspear. I say we have Longspear attack them first!"

Reza thought about it. "No my friend, there has to be another way. We need the people of Earth and they need us."

Nava pushed back. "Longspear is outnumbered. If we strike first, we got half a chance. But if the Neferan put a jump on Longspear, we're done for."

Reza stared at Nava sternly. "No my friend. We know what the Neferan are up to even if the people of Earth do not. We know sooner or later, the Neferan will make their move."

Chel voiced her thoughts, "I agree with Nava. Longspear stands a better chance with the Queen and her brother down here. I say the second they put those rifles in our hands we take them out while Longspear takes first strike. This may be our only chance!"

Reza leaned forward and spoke sternly. "And what if we fail? Did you think of that? If Longspear is destroyed then so is every last Lycerene!"

Still the pallets of equipment rushed in as people of every kind moved in and out of the hangar. Technicians floated back and forth preparing the equipment. The hangar was loud, too loud for the briefing to begin, but now the mission planners had arrived. Helforn called for attention. "Before I begin the briefing of our upcoming mission, let me update you on a few developments:

First, Neferan and Earth technicians are ahead of schedule extinguishing the Magnesium Thermocells.

Second, a full scale offensive to retake The Signal Station will be under way in plus one hour.

Third, as we feared, the Chodugon are waking across the globe. Reports from every continent indicate we have skirmishes and clashes. It's already widespread. For now, each nation to its own, at least until we have a centralized communication center.

Fourth, as if I gotta say the obvious....that sound you hear is the coming storm. We are down to the minute people. We make it or break it in the next forty-five minutes."

Distracted for a moment as more pallets of armor rolled in, he paused. "I don't like repeating myself so listen up. Here's how our timetable breaks down.

In Plus two minutes, troops will begin suiting-up body armor.

In Plus fifteen minutes, troops will begin weapons checks.

In Plus thirty-five minutes, begin loading troops onto the VTECs.

VTECs are marked as follows. Red tipped wings for the Neferan. Yellow tipped wings for the Lycerene. Blue tipped for Earth's own. The Kai will load up with Atera's troops. Don't mix em up people, these VTECs have been special fitted for your respective armor feeds. It's going to be a long trip and you'll need to be jacked-in.

The winds are near hurricane force, and it's gonna get worse. VTECs are on tie-down with release crews at the ready. Load-on, jack-in, and buckle-up. When we lift off, I suggest you hold on...and I do mean hold on. This is going to be the worst launch of your life!"

Turning about to make sure that everyone was still listening, he gave his closing orders. "Time waits for no man people. I mean that literally. Anyone falling behind gets cut from the mission.
If you got questions...
If you got delays....
If you got problems...
Then bring em up here to the mission planners.

That's it!
Turn to soldiers work!
Turn to people!"

It was an old saying *Turn to*. It was short speak for *Return to soldiers work* and it was often accompanied by a hand gesture. Holding two fingers up and turning the wrist. Prowler had his own version and he didn't hesitate to let it past his lips. "Turn to people....turn and burn!"

Immediately, the first whistle sounded. The Neferan and Lycerene were unfamiliar with the gesture, but they saw how Earths troops responded, quickly they got the point. They turned directly to the work of suiting-up their armor. Troops all about the hangars ran to and from gathering their armor and suiting themselves, suiting each other. Mission planners paced about the floor looking for signs of issues and delays. Directing techs and assistants to wherever they were needed. The clock ran down fast as troops scurried into formation one by one. More than a handful on each team were late, but they signaled that they were still good.

While troops suited-up their armor, Sarrow and Silas crossed the hangar bay headed directly towards Helforn. "Captain Helforn. A moment of your time, if we may."

Helforn was busy and hardly up for a distraction "All you Kai got to do is board up with Earth's own. Just follow us and we'll get you loaded up."

"Captain Helforn. There is a more pressing matter."

Helforn motioned with his hand for Sarrow to wait just a moment while he finished with the mission planners. Starting his second conversation before he had completed his first; but seamlessly, "Whatcha got?"

"In your briefing, you stated that the Chodugon are awakening…and that Kai and Kon are already clashing."

Helforn gave a quick response. "Yes. Sarrow, you said that would happen…right?"

"Yes, Captain Helforn. The Kai and Kon will always hunt each other, but this time he seeks the collapse of your civilization. Same as he has done so many times before."

Helforn stood there thinking it through. Before he could speak, Silas joined in, "Captain Helforn, his methods are always the same. First, he knows that he can't kill everyone, so he will seek to destroy your infrastructure…energy, transportation, communications. Then, he will hunt and kill your leaders, and your scientists, physicians, anyone who is of the learned kind. Without them, your technology will collapse all on its own. Starvation and disease will finish his work."

Shaking his head in disbelief, Helforn asked, "Won't the Kai be able to stop them…or at least slow the Kon?"

"The Kai can only slow the Kon down. Remember, as I said onboard Valiant, he has his agents and entire lineages at his ready. Those are real humans, same as you. They are lineages that are generations in the making. Soon, they will carry out his sabotage and his assassinations. Wealthy beyond your knowing…wealthy enough to have private armies. Even armies within your army. In the coming days, even your own kind will turn on you. You will not know just who will attack or when it will occur."

In disbelief, Helforn questioned. "You are saying that humans will fight for him? I just can't believe these people could hold a grudge for thousands of years."

Sir, it is not a grudge. They believe they are the keepers of an eternal secret. They are something of a cult and believe that it is their task to prepare and receive…the second coming."

Helforn ran his hands through his hair again. "You're kidding me, right?
The second coming of what?
Some messiah?
Some God?"

"No Sir. They do not believe in messiahs or Gods. What they believe in is the second coming of the Master Architect. They believe they hold the secret knowledge to resurrect Jaromad. He is their cult, he is their religion, and he is their purpose. They will kill anyone or anything including themselves for that purpose."

For the first time, Helforn shuddered.
"Fanaticism! I get your point. I'll forward your comments to President Stillwell right away. He'll assign a task force. They'll get extra troops where they need em."

"Captain Helforn, He will move fast. I fear he already knows exactly who to target. If you have any chance at all, you have got to evacuate your most valued people. Move them to safe havens. Hidden places, fortified places. Keep moving them if you have to. Please pass this strategy to President Stillwell."

The second whistle sounded and the doors again burst open with pallets of weapons and ammunition. The pallets were delivered to their respective teams and the troops hurried over. Grabbing their weapons and ammunition and quickly returning to their designated positions to clip their ammunition to their armor and check their weapons. Drawing their bolts, setting their sights, and testing their recoils. Anything they could check short of a full lock and load. Even with explicit orders not to lock and load, every man kept an eye on the other and a trigger finger at the ready.

The third whistle sounded and the enormous hangar doors were unlocked with a loud bang. The doors then screeched as they separated. Instantly, the wind caused a sudden shift of air pressure throughout the hangar as the air was sucked outside in a great whistling. By the time the doors were separated ten feet, the wind was whipping around inside the hangar. Techs and troops alike were swayed by the gusts. Anyone not engaged in the first run knelt down to steady against the winds.

The fourth whistle sounded and Helforn was now standing in the center of the hangar doors. Per his mission plan, he called the troops out. Not a long distance by any means, but with the wind to their faces, they made a struggle of it. Pulling and pushing each other through the gusts.

Just as Helforn ordered, they loaded on, jacked-in, and buckled-up. Anyone forgetting to hold on was quickly reminded as the wind gusts slammed into the VTECs rocking and rolling them. If not for the tie down straps, they would have been strewn about. Wind whistled throughout the cabin as the changing air movements pressurized and depressurized the cabin. Doors closed, engines ignited and power was vectored. They would launch into the wind. Every VTEC having lost control at one moment or another, but every VTEC was up and headed north.

CHAPTER 17: INTO THE STORM

They headed into the blackness of the oncoming storm. What was a storm cloud and what was smoke from the smoldering cities could not be discerned. If one good thing of the rains, it would help extinguish the fires that still raged. But that was of little concern to the men being bounced around and they knew the worst was yet to come.

As they approached the storm front, they made little headway. The VTECs were powering full thrust, and yet it seemed as though they were hovering still while the storm front came upon them. The best Helforn could do was to order the VTECs spread out far and wide so as not to collide. It came with all its wind, the torrents of rain, and the blinding clouds. The storm struck like a wall of water and the VTECs shuddered and bounced.

Twisting and turning, the VTECs disappeared into the blackness. Even radar could not penetrate through the density of the clouds. Radios crackled with communications from everywhere. From the bases on the ground, from the Neferan fleet, and from Longspear, but mostly, from the VTECs themselves. Radio chatter so heavy it would match even the worst of combat. Pilots struggled frantically to keep their noses pointed to the wind. Like balancing a stick upon ones finger, the VTECs teetered and tethered left and right. All while rising and falling as the storm winds whipped around. Copilots kept to the task of managing alerts and extinguishing electrical shortages.

Then the wind shear hit and the VTECs floundered. Thunder cracked amid a blinding white light and when their eyes could see once again, they saw one of their VTECs roll under and nosedive straight down. It disappeared from sight and it vanished from radar. The VTEC had been Helforn's, and now the mission would proceed without his lead.

The hours passed and as suddenly as the storm front had come, so too had it passed. The sun shined so bright on the other side that it watered their eyes, but a welcoming sight nonetheless. The VTECs emerged on the other side and quickly, they regrouped. Immediately, the call came to assemble the squad leaders from every VTEC on a single frequency.

Vice President Zadan had been appointed to lead the overall mission from the ground since it was his proposal. He opened the discussion, "All our sensors indicate that Captain Helforn's VTEC was brought down in the storm. Search and Rescue crews are already deployed and running search grids. Although we haven't found any wreckage, we expect a total loss of life. Having said that, our first decision is whether to proceed, or to abort the mission."

Over half the squad leaders voted to abort the mission as it had little promise to begin with. They would rather be dropped right down on the island and make their stand against the Kon. Then Atera spoke. "The Kai said it was the Architect's library. That his knowledge had been buried with him. If that is true, then somebody is going to find that tomb. If the Kon do have spies as Brother Sarrow has stated, then it will only be a matter of time before they hear about the Lycerene map. I say it is better that we find the tomb before the Kon does."

Zadan took the initiative and closed the decision. "We proceed then. Our next order of business is to determine a suitable replacement for Captain Helforn."

The communication channel grew silent as the decision could lean to any team. Reza was first to take advantage of the opportunity. "As I've said before, I am the one who has studied the artifacts and the ancient symbols. I am confident that I can take the lead from here."

Quickly Sun Anniz objected as expected. Offering his own brand of leadership. "Vice President Zadan, what you have here is an army of distrust. Captain Helforn was a respectable commander, but what we need now is strength. Someone strong enough to keep the distrust under control. The Neferan are fully pledged to your order Sir and by that order, I am already in your service."

Zadan responded favorably, "Commander Sun Anniz, thank you for reminding me so. I will give it my consideration."

But, Atera trusted neither Reza nor Sun Anniz and she spoke, "Sir. I will lead the mission." Zadan responded abruptly, "Commander Atera. Is that you?"

"Sir. Yes. Sir."

Zadan continued. "Commander Atera, frankly speaking...your injuries...you are in no shape to assume the lead here. In fact, if it were not for your association to Captain Helforn, you wouldn't be on this mission!"

She responded cleverly, "Sir, then you have already proven my point. Captain Helforn himself would cast his vote in my favor."

Zadan was taken aback. As much as he knew of her reputation, her young years, he had heard of them well enough. "And just what would you be capable of doing if the troops clash? How do you propose to defend even yourself?"

She spoke slyly. "Sir, I have my pilots…and I have my ways. Surely you have heard of my ways?"

Moments passed and finally Zadan concluded that at least Atera was one of Earth's own, he knew he could trust her. "So be it Commander Atera. You and your troops will assume the lead. From this point forward, the mission is in your hands. We resume radio silence for now and regroup upon your final approach." The radio went silent.

Immediately, Reza set to his work. His special task of translating the three dimensional map that would pinpoint the location of Jaromad's tomb. He had promised to have his solution in two hours, but now he lost a third of that time. Atera texted across to Reza:

From Atera: Status on the coordinates?
From Reza: In progress.
From Atera: Identify the issues of your delay.
From Reza: No issues aside from the storm.
From Atera: In plus three, we reach the ice shelf.
From Reza: I am tracking no risks at this time. I expect to have solution in hand by then.

More hours passed and Atera texted across for another status check. Reza double checked and triple checked his solution. He was ready.

From Atera: Status on the coordinates?
From Reza: Solution complete.

From Atera: Confidence level?
From Reza: High confidence.
From Atera: Transmit now.

Reza transmitted the coordinates to Atera. With the exact coordinates in hand, Atera calculated the new course and revised her ETA for touchdown. Less than sixty minutes in flight remaining. It started out as a quiet sixty minutes.

Then, Hunter took a break from his task, that of learning the Chodugon Call Scripts. He pulled himself away from his personal computer and stretched backwards. His thoughts slipped out. "Ahh! Can't be. Just can't be."

Prowler responded, "What can't be? What are you talking about?"

Hunter had the look of doubt on his face. "That thing. The Compassionate One. I just don't think it can be real."

Prowler seemed to have no doubt that it did exist. "Well, that Control Unit, I saw that thing and it's real enough for me."

Hunter made a joke of it. "Yea, but I am not buying this legend that some robot floats around for thousands of years spurring on technology. Sooner or later, this thing would get noticed. The Kon and the Kai have been looking for this one and they never found a single clue...not one single clue."

Prowler just ignored the joke. "Well, did you notice the inventory number of the Control unit? It's zero-zero-zero-six-six-six. It doesn't take a priest to figure out that one. This thing...it fits the description perfectly. It's deceptive, it's manipulative, and it's controlling. This thing has been around since before recorded history. I mean it is The Beast if ever there was one."

Stalker joined in siding somewhat with Hunter, "Right, but even Sarrow said it. These Chodugon cannot hide from each other. Their body movements are a signature that they can identify. Where would this thing hide and still spur on the rebirth of so much technology?"

Prowler was unconvinced. "I don't know, but the way I see it, if that Control thing exists, then I have no reason to think the Compassionate One doesn't. The real question is 'who' is this Compassionate One? I mean, this thing may be hiding, but if it is real, then it has got to be close by, especially now."

Then Scout joined in, "The Monk Sarrow, I bet its Brother Sarrow. Didn't you notice how the lesser Kai all seem to take their direction from him? He is way ahead of the rest of them."

Stalker voiced back somewhat irritated. "Well, I got more the impression that they were like...like...communal or something like that. Like the Kai are all somewhat equal, aside from some subtle differences." His point was weak and he knew it. He resorted to his old ways, applying a bit of sarcasm. "You guys should hang out with Silas a little more often. Spend your time chasing ghosts if you like!"

Prowler poked back. "Maybe. But for sure, the Kai guarded Sarrow's escape up the North Tower. He must be important to them. They locked themselves in the courtyard to buy him seconds, no doubt they expected to be overrun. I think he knows more than he's telling us."

Hunter sensed that he had started something that would get out of control and so he injected a new idea, "What about that Lycerene...Reza? He seems to have all the answers. He knew where The Void was, how to penetrate it, and how to find Earth. He even knows where Jaromad's tomb is. Doesn't that seem a bit odd?"

Stalker laughed aloud. "Right, like the Compassionate One somehow got lost on another planet and took twelve thousand years to find his way home." He chuckled at his own joke. "Welcome home O'Compassionate One?"

Hunter didn't like being the brunt of Stalker's joke and snapped back, "I didn't mean it quite like that. What if Reza knows who it is? Or if somewhere in his ancient scrolls, Reza can find out who it is! Did you think of that, you smart ass?"

Stalker seemed interested, "Right. Either this guy knows something, or he is purely magical. I don't trust him, I mean this guy expects us to believe he figured all this out, all on his own? The Neferan Queen caught the guy keeping secrets about Jaromad's tomb. I don't trust that guy at all."

Hunter responded more eager now, "The Lycerene had those artifacts for thousands of years and one guy figures it out? Come on. I mean, even Atera, she loves ancient stuff, especially old military stuff, and I bet she couldn't even do it."

Hunter had assumed Atera had not been listening. But, as always, she had. She peered back over her shoulder just enough to see them. "I wouldn't be quick to say so, but maybe you are right."

Before anybody could respond to her, the pilot called back for Atera. It was time for the VTECs to make their final approach, time to radio back to Zadan.

Scout took the conversation in a slightly different direction. She looked at Stalker and Hunter, "I know you don't trust Reza, nobody does. But, I've been thinking about these people, the Lycerene. Did you see how they responded to a simple dog?"

Stalker turned to her. "Yea, the one named Chel, she said there were no canine on her world. Been extinct for a thousand years."

Chel had a distant look about her. "Right. But, there is something familiar about them. I was raised on the Plains. If there is one thing I know, it's that the people of the Plains are unlike any other. Their ancestors were trackers and hunters. They also live...like the Wolf."

Stalker interrupted her. "What are you getting at?"

She continued, "I think these people are similar. I mean their ways, it's as if I was home again, except for one thing. They are a people of the Pack, yet they know no Wolf."

Stalker didn't see her point, "What of it? What's your point?"

"Well, the people of the Plain are like the Wolf, they believe in its purity and they live like it. That means...they never lie."

Stalker stirred a bit, "You heard Zadan, didn't you? It's his job to decide who to trust, not ours."

The cabin lights changed from green to red followed by a sudden rush of the engine thrusters. It gave them a good stir and immediately, they knew it was touchdown time. Memories of their takeoff were still fresh in their minds causing them to set back and hold on with both hands.

Soon, the windows were white with the snow that was kicked up from the thrusters. Finally, the clunk and whoosh as hydraulic systems powered down. As soon as the cabin lights turned back to green, they eagerly popped their belts and unjacked. They stood up shaking off the stiffness that had set in from the long voyage. Radios crackled as Atera gave the orders to unload. Everyone and everything.

CHAPTER 18: TO WAKE THE DEAD

With a soft thud, the cabin doors dropped open onto the snow. They marched forward into the brilliant light that was cast down by the sun and then again cast up by the snow. Outside they could see the landscape. It was white, pure white, with a crystal blue sky as far as the eye could see. No mountains or cliffs. Few if any flat spots. Just rolling drifts like sand dunes and the constantly whisping snow that was kicked up by the arctic winds. Looking around, they could see that all of the VTECs had touched down in the same formation as that from which they had launched. Two rows to protect the troops from the winds. They marched down into that space between the VTECs where everyone was gathering.

Atera stood at the center surrounded by the Techs who were discussing the procedures for unloading and configuring the equipment. Troops gathered around and as the last few straggled in, Sun Anniz shouted aloud, "What are we waiting for?"

Atera called them to gather round; "Without Captain Helforn's VTEC, we have lost some of our Techs and our backup drill. According to Reza's coordinates, the tomb depth is deep, but we should still make it with the two remaining drills. However, we don't have enough Techs to

176

get them into position and setup, so we will need to use troops to do the heavy work."

She pointed at one of the Techs who bore markings upon his snowsuit indicating he was the senior lead, his name tag read Dreyden. "For the time being, Troops will take their orders from this Tech Lead, Warrant Officer Dreyden." She knew the Troops wouldn't like that bit of news since Troops and Techs didn't mix well. So, she forewarned the Troops. "I expect you will be on your best behavior!" With her cane, she motioned the Tech Lead forward and then she stepped aside.

Dreyden described the task. "The drills are stored in the cargo bays of VTECs six and seven. With this packed snow, each drill will need a team of ten men to lift it into position. If I were you, I'd allocate twenty per drill and rotate them to avoid fatigue."

Reza and a handful of technicians were already some fifty meters behind the VTECs marking positions in the snow. Dreyden continued as he pointed to them. "Turn to your rear and notice the technicians marking our entry points. That's where we setup the drills. Got any questions?"

Stalker voiced first, "Yea. How far down is this tomb?"

Dreyden replied, "According to the Lycerene, it is fifty meters down."

Stalker continued, "And how are you going to get us down there?"

Dreyden realized that Stalker was toying with him and responded in similar fashion, "Well, my first plan was to drill straight down and let you free fall, but Commander Atera didn't like that plan." After waiting for the chuckles to settle down, he resumed, "My second plan is to drill on an angle so you can walk down. After all, you will want to come back up sooner or later...I assume."

Stalker was silent by now. It was Prowler who continued with the questions. "Walk down? On Ice? Maybe you Techs can walk in your puffy snowsuits, but we are wearing armor. I assume you know that Armor and ice don't mix well?"

"Right. My original plan called for three ice drills so the angle was minimized to fifteen degrees slope. Now, we are down to two drills which puts us at a twenty degree slope. Anything over twenty degrees and you'll reach the tomb on your back, your belly, or your ass...if you are lucky."

Prowler had one final question. "What do we do with the other sixty troops in the meantime?"

Dreyden replied, "I suggest they return to the safety of their VTECs. It's gonna be at least forty-five minutes before we move again."

Stalker thought it odd that they would need to move the VTECs again. "What do you mean move again?"

Dreyden amused himself with his response. "Well, those ice drills are the most violent machine you're ever gonna see. I don't want the troops or the VTECs anywhere near them when they start ejecting debris. Let me tell you people, those things are gonna rattle your bones." Dreyden had a good roll with his first jokes and felt confident enough for one more. "Trust me when I say those drills are enough to wake the dead."

He could tell by the sudden stiffness of the troops that he had said something they did not like. Stalker was quick to give it back to Dreyden. "You may be right. Let's hope not. It's best that you Techs leave that part to us."

Dreyden recognized that they had come to an understanding. He nodded and then barked his final "That's it gentlemen. We've got the sun on our side so let's not waste it."

VTEC one lifted up and circled around apparently dropping a marker exactly above the tomb. VTECs six and seven lifted up and backed as close to the entry points as possible. Troops formed lifting teams and trudged thru the snow with the heavy ice drills leaving them exactly where Dreyden wanted them.

The troops were quick to return to the warmth of their VTECs, leaving only the Techs to assemble the drills. Troops watched through the windows for what seemed like an eternity as the Techs ran back and forth with tools and schematics. Parts and pieces were assembled and adjusted. From a distance, it looked like Earth's Techs were just as sloppy as its troops. Amid all the commotion, Dreyden positioned himself into that space between the two drills. Suddenly, the sloppy scurrying ceased. Using his hands, he gave the signal to his Techs to evacuate the area except for a select handful. Then he signaled them to set the drill angle to twenty degrees. Clip on the fuel cells, and test fire the engines. He turned about to face the VTECs and signaled for them to lift off. He caught them by surprise, and he seemed to enjoy it.

Hovering at around one thousand feet, the troops could look out the windows of the VTECs and see the action below. The few techs that remained on the ground ran to the temporary bunkers. Only Dreyden remained exposed, meticulously adjusting his controls to engage the drill engines one at a time. Then he moved the drills forward. As their forward most edges impacted the snow, the howling sound of the drill's jet engines echoed across the landscape. Two drills harmonizing so loudly that they could be heard even above the engines of the VTECs.

Small puffs of debris were ejected out the back and were carried off by the winds. The drills progressed slowly at first, but then the full face of the drill bit buried itself into the ice. Grinding and scraping sounds shrieked across the landscape. More violent than before, the drill suddenly pulled itself down into the ice. The debris now erupted out the back and shot straight across the sky for one hundred meters or more, arching up and over like a giant white rainbow. Rocks, Ice, and snow gushed out and began to pile up exactly where the VTECs had originally touched down.

By now, the sound was utterly deafening. It echoed off for miles. An echo that seemed like it was crisscrossing the skies. Even the snow drifts began to tremble and wisps of snow rose off of them to be carried off by the winds. Anything that Dreyden had said didn't measure up to the utter violence of these drills. Surely, if the dead were buried below, they were awake by now.

The drills quickly buried themselves into the ice and out of sight. For the first fifty meters, they bore side by side. Beyond that, the drills bore in sequence. In this configuration, debris from the first drill would be passed back to the second drill, which would extend the total ejection distance. Together, they would just about clear the two hundred meter distance.

Looking out his window, Stalker tried to gauge the speed of the drills against the marker that was dropped directly over the tomb. He surmised that they could reach the tomb in as little as two hours.

As the drills passed the ten meter mark, the 'all clear' was given for the VTECs to touchdown again, but this time with a seventy-five meter clearance between the drills and the VTECs.

Immediately, Techs dispatched once again. This time carrying sensitive equipment that would be used to draw a picture of what lay beneath the ground. The vibrations created by the drills would pass through the ice in frequencies and resonate off of anything solid beneath the ice. With the resonating waves, their computers might construct a picture of what lay beneath the ice. Sensing that this new equipment would prove interesting, some of the troops gathered about the Techs, watching and speculating as to their purpose. At first the images represented nothing recognizable, just the streaking lines that looked like the scribble of a child

Then, the image was refined and refined again. The image began to take shape. Still it was unrecognizable by the troops, but the Techs could make sense of it. Densities indicting rock, ice, and then something else. They worked to refine it further.

All at once, the image refreshed and something caught their attention. Beneath them, lay a mountain ridge and at the very peak, something clearly man made; something that stood up above the ridge, like a tower. Suddenly, the Techs raced back and forth with excitement making it apparent to everyone that something had been found. Having waited so many thousands of years to find this piece of the legend, Silas joined the crowd. Even upon the first of the images, he was captivated. For that, Scout poked a bit of fun at him, "Brother Silas, I do believe you have a thing for these legends."

He turned to face Scout, not fully understanding her brand of humor. "The tomb was not part of the legend. It was known to exist, but after searching for so many years, both Kai and Kon had given up."

Still looking for clues as to the identity of the Compassionate One, Scout probed more questions. "So the only part that is legend...is the Compassionate One?"

"Sir, Yes, Sir"

Scout began to wonder if Silas might be the Compassionate One and began to probe him with questions. "Brother Silas, just why is it that you are the only Chodugon who has an interest in this legend? It would seem that maybe you have the ability to think beyond the average Chodugon?"

"Sir, the legend is born of mankind and not of the Chodugon. Of mankind, there are so many legends, Gods, demons, and deities of all kinds. In the beginning, mankind referred to the Compassionate One as a God, not a Chodugon. Even unto this day, mankind holds the Compassionate One among its pantheon of Gods. There was no reason for me to think that the God of Compassion was of my kind, a Chodugon. But then came a day when I encountered something that made me accept the legend as something physical, a Chodugon. To state it more precisely, I saw something that can be explained in no other way."

Stalker snapped in disbelief, "What? You met the Compassionate One and yet you said that nobody has ever identified him? Which is it?"

"Sir, I did not say I met him, I said that I had an encounter with him. It was in the midst of a battle, one of the greatest battles in all of history. The battle occurred during the collapse of the first Era, when mankind grew hungry. On one single day, nearly one hundred and fifty thousand men met in open battle. Both Kai and Kon were there on that day.

At dusk, a wave of men struck us from the rear and I was swept apart from my squad. It was dark by the time I had returned and when I found my squad, they had all been cut down, every last one of them. Lying about them were the bodies of hundreds, maybe a thousand men and one of them called to me. He told me of the battle and then suddenly, he pointed to something up on the rooftop. I saw it, crouched down and silhouetted against the night sky. It saw me, I know it did. With a single leap, it crossed overhead to another rooftop and disappeared."

By now, even Atera was listening to Silas' account. "Brother Silas, how can you be so sure that what you saw was the Compassionate One? Maybe it was just another Chodugon?"

"Sir, I am sure of it Sir. I ran about the fallen Chodugon and jacked-into their memory. I could see that it fought like no human, like no Chodugon. It had a fighting style the likes I had never seen. I replayed the memory back further and further until the time just before the attack occurred. My squad had come upon him unexpectedly and with his full body armor, they did not recognize him as a Chodugon. They gave chase and eventually cornered him.

As the legend goes, the Compassionate One only attacks to defend himself. The legend also says, "*Upon the dance and the song of his sabers, the God of Compassion will be undone; with his many arms, he will smite thy eyes, friend or foe.*"

That legend made no sense until I saw it…I saw what he did before he attacked. You see, Chodugon are all identical and hold their shield in their left hand and their sword in the right. But, the Compassionate One has two sabers, for he is a two handed swordsman. I saw him prepare for combat. He settled down with his knees bent deeply and feet pointing outwards. Then, he stomped his feet one at a time. Next, he unsheathed his swords. It was right then that I understood the legend, *"song of his sabers."* Two swords whipping in the air…making a howling sound. And in that same motion, I understood, *"With his many arms."* Two arms moving fast, beyond the speed of any man. Beyond that of even the best Chodugon. It gave the visual illusion that he had four arms, maybe six."

"Interesting Brother Silas, all this and you did not identify the Compassionate One?"

"Sir, no Sir. As I said, he wore full body armor."

Scout saw one more oddity in Silas account, "But, if this God….or Chodugon is supposedly so Compassionate, then why the bit about, *"smite thy eyes?"* Doesn't that mean this Compassionate One also kills?"

"Sir, yes Sir. I assume to protect himself or to hide his identity. But, the legend also says, *"The God of Compassion will be undone."* I take that to mean that in times of danger, the Compassionate One may lose his 'compassion', become a true Chodugon, a killer, as it was built for."

"Where then did all that talk about Miravan and the mainframe prototype come from?" Asked Scout.

"Over the years, I have pieced the clues together. From my encounter, from stories and lore, from artifacts and archives. From these clues, I have made my assumptions."

Atera then smiled and gave her final conviction. "That's a lot of assumptions Brother Silas. Still sounds like a lot of fantasy to me. I understand now just why Brother Sarrow sees no worth in it all."

Techs raced back and forth and one of them returned with Dreyden. Amazed they were with the find below the ice, truly the archaeological discovery of the millennia. But, he took no time to marvel. He needed to use the image to double-check the drills angle of descent. To his amazement, the drills were right on track, exactly on track. But for sure, a change in plans was necessary for the vibration of the drills would likely damage the structure. Dreyden ordered that the drills approach as far as twenty five meters from the structure and then stop. They would melt the ice and pump out the water for the final stretch.

As the drills made their final approach, the techs snapped more images. Images to the left of the tomb, to the right and directly above it. The images were now much clearer and distinct architectural elements of the structure could be discerned. For starters, it was constructed atop a sheer cliff face. There was no way from the ground to the tower without climbing straight up several hundred feet. That made little difference now that the entire valley and mountain were covered beneath thousands of years of ice. Furthermore, it was constructed of something denser than the granite rock from which it stood upon. And, it ran deep into the mountain. An entire complex had been bored into the top of that mountain. The very last images appeared to have identified the depression directly where Reza's coordinates predicted; an entrance to the structure.

As the sun was noticeably lower in the sky, the chill increased along with the wind. Small vehicles on ice tracks were loaded with equipment and hoses. They raced into the tunnel and soon thereafter, water began spurting out the hoses. It froze in the air and blew away in the wind. All this time, the troops had stood behind the Techs watching over their shoulder. Waiting quietly, waiting patiently, but now they stirred a bit.

Dreyden suddenly turned about and approached Commander Atera. "Sir, we've reached the structure. It's truly amazing. See for yourself. There are writings and symbols all about the entrance. I gather those symbols are gonna mean something to you folks so we're going to take an extra thirty minutes and clear the entire wall."

The troops knew that meant it was time to return to their meeting place in that space between the VTECs.

Atera was ready to give her orders. "Our Tech Lead, Dreyden, has confirmed that we have reached the tomb. That the mission is now back in our hands. We'll send the Kai down first. I expect they will sniff the area for booby-traps and the like. I also expect the Kai will take first attempt at interpreting those symbols. The Kai will descend in plus five minutes and we will descend in plus fifteen. We will burn through our thermal packs in short time down there so we will work in shifts, sixty minutes to a shift, twenty-five troops to a crew. Let's pack it light people…shields, swords, and side arms only."

The Techs motioned for the Kai to line up at the mouth of the tunnel. Techs had setup a lifeline that ran center of the ice tunnel from top to bottom. Each of the Kai were lined up and clipped to the lifeline. They attempted their first few steps on the ice and found the footing unstable, but soon, they were out of sight.

Atera readied her first crew. She did so by walking the length of their ranks and hand selecting them. Moving as if she already knew each and every one of them; and indeed, she had. She studied them as expected. She sought them out and pointed at them with her cane. One by one, they dropped any unnecessary equipment and ran to the mouth of the tunnel.

She only paused a moment when she had to choose her leads. She chose Reza, for he had proven skillful with the ancient artifacts thus far. She also chose Chel, Prowler, and Scout. She knew pairing Sun Anniz and Reza was a risk and she knew to leave Stalker behind to guard the rear. All twenty-five of her choosing now clipped on and awaited her final orders. She stood before them and spoke with perfect clarity. "You've got two priorities. First, secure the entrance. I mean nothing going in and nothing coming out. Second, find us a way into that tomb. Let me be perfectly clear on this one. Find us a way in, but do not enter that tomb under any circumstances. You do not enter that tomb until I'm there with reinforcements. Are we clear?"

"Sir, yes Sir!" Stepping aside, she used that word again. That familiar word that her team had come to despise. "Begin."

Twenty degrees sounded easy and standing at the top of the tunnel, it looked easy. But, like the Kai before them, they found it to be anything but easy. Now, they understood just what Dreyden meant when he said they might arrive at the tomb ... "on their ass."

They trudged down into the darkness. The tunnel that started out the width of two drills merged into one and from there on was a dizzying tube that went on endlessly. Illuminated every so often by a glow-stick, but otherwise near blackness at some points. Even the extra lights positioned at the tomb entrance did little more than to paint a white dot at the end of the tunnel. Holding on to each other at times but mostly holding on to the lifeline. Each time someone lost footing, the lifeline would jerk and pull the whole crew with it.

At midway point, they took a slip that brought a handful of them to their knees, so Reza used it as an opportunity to pause for a rest and also to survey their progress. Looking backwards, nothing but a spiraling tunnel with a blue dot at the center, the sky. Looking forwards, nothing but a spiraling tunnel with a white dot at the center, the tomb. Regardless of the length of the tunnel, it felt small, it felt pressing, it felt tight. At that point, they realized that if anything were to go wrong, there was no way out. Upon reaching the tomb, with the extra clearing, they breathed a bit easier.

CHAPTER 19: SYMBOLS AND SECRETS

One by one, they emerged from the darkness of the tunnel, unclipped, and stepped forward onto the safety of flat ground. An ice cavern that had to be twenty feet high and thirty feet across with just as much depth. Bewildered, as they stared at the massive wall towering before them. As the last of the troops unclipped, Scout reminded them of their orders. "Let's get busy people. We got orders to secure this position. Give me five guards to the left and five to the right. Everyone else take up positions in the tunnel."

Reza approached the wall and touched it with his armored hand. It looked like stone, black and greenish, wet and dripping, with no seams, or cracks. Brother Sarrow approached Reza. "Sir, the area appears to be clear of any traps. All we have here is ice and stone."

Reza nodded, "Aye."

Brother Sarrow continued. "Sir, the symbols on the wall, most of them are unreadable with age. It will take more time and even then, I cannot be sure that enough remain to interpret anything useful."

Reza was unprepared for that possibility. "But, this is it! This must be it...right?"

Brother Sarrow pointed to a circle that seemed to bind the two doors together. "Sir, Yes. Sir. The tomb was hidden away here, in secret for thirty six thousand years. Look here, you see… the seal is unbroken. The tomb has never been opened."

Still, Reza could not pull his eyes away from the wall. "Amazing! It must have been beautiful in its day." And then it occurred to Reza "But, how do we get in?"

Brother Sarrow shed the bad news. "Sir, the symbols are eroded. Without the symbols, we do not know how to open the seal."

Suddenly, the awe inspired Reza realized the urgency of the matter. "What? We can't get in?"

Prowler was listening and now hastened his way over. "Well, we certainly didn't come all this way for nothing, we'll just blast our way in!"

Brother Sarrow spoke with total confidence. "Sir that will do you no good."

"And why not?" Prowler snapped.

Sarrow continued. "Sir, these walls are made of the Composite and it must be a foot thick, at least. No Sir, this wall will not give to any amount of blast."

Prowler would not give up. "So, what next? How about a torch? What about a drill?"

"Sir, no torch and no drill will penetrate, our only chance is to interpret the symbols. They are the key to opening the seal."

The Kai and Reza set immediately to interpreting the symbols starting with the few that were clear. Most of them appeared eroded or washed out, but every so often, they could interpret a symbol. They went over the symbols again and again, each time, they could identify a bit more, but not enough. After a while, they began to accept the obvious, that the symbols were lost to time. The disappointment of it began to show on them, all of them, but for Prowler, it was worse. The strain of it bringing his mind back to thoughts of his home, a city that was but smoldering ambers by now. He put his back to the wall and slid down in defeat.

It was Scout who first came to him, knowing his temper, sensing that he was losing focus. She knew that sooner or later, they would need Prowler back, just the way he had been. Putting her back to the wall, she slid down right next to Prowler and steadied him with light talk. But on the other side of the cavern, someone watched. He must have felt her eyes upon him and his skin crawled at the thought of it.

"What are you staring at?" He shouted to Chel.

Suddenly, everyone stopped, they turned and saw Prowler staring at Chel. She made quickly to turn away, but Reza saw it. He had seen the way Chel looked at Prowler before, but this time, he knew instantly what it meant. He had known her since their earliest days at the Academy and in all those years, never had Chel looked at any man for any purpose other than to soldier. No matter that her face was concealed by her helmet, he could tell by the way that she shy away, the only time he had ever seen Chel shy away.

Reza immediately stepped forward to disrupt the incident, forgetting that this was Prowler. Instantly, Prowler sprang to his feet and made his first step at Reza, but before he got close enough to strike, Scout raced to step in front of Prowler and would not let him pass.

"Don't do it! We're trying to stop a war here! Think about it, people are already dead and suffering. Lots more if we fail. They are going to need you Prowler...everything you've got!"

She tried to steady him with her hands, but he thrust them away wanting to hurt someone, anyone, but not Scout. Finally, he turned and walked back toward his spot against the wall, slamming his armored back against it. While the anger welled within him, he angrily tapped his helmet against the wall again and again. When he could contain it no more, he thrashed an elbow backwards smacking the wall and then slid down back to his original position.

Still they stared in his direction, not a word, speechless. Slowly, he realized they were not staring at him. Chips and chards of that black and green wall now lay about him. He picked one up and looked at it, confused and puzzled, but he knew the chips and chards had something to do with the stares. He stood slowly and turned about to look at the spot that everyone else had come to notice. The black and green had chipped away and what lay underneath ...it shined.

Instantly it became evident that the solid and seamless wall, void of seams and cracks was actually a coating of some sort. Maybe a camouflage coating or maybe just the buildup of dirt and grime that had encrusted itself over the composite; either way, it was a thin layer. Slowly, they gathered around staring at it and without a second wasted, Prowler grabbed his sword and gouged at the wall, chips flaked off with ease.

Kai and troops alike rushed to the wall chipping and gouging, every one of them aside from the ten men ordered to secure the cavern. Reza headed straight for the symbols and just as soon as he cleared the first one, he looked at

Sarrow to see if Sarrow recognized it. "Sir, yes Sir. I recognize the symbol, but we need more, many more."

Soon, the chips became debris and the debris became a pile. They made short work of it and then stood back. The details of the wall were now visible tenfold without the grime. Such architecture, such imagery, such delicacy that it commanded ones deepest attention. No tomb had ever said so much about the man inside.

Before they could regain their composure, footsteps crept up from behind them. It was Commander Atera with a fresh crew. With her, she brought Sun Anniz and his trusted, a few more of Reza's men, Dreyden and his crew, and as expected, all of her pilots. She had trained them her way and for something this important, she would have them at her side. She called across the cavern bringing everyone to attention. "Let's run status and swap out crews. Gather round!"

When they had all assembled, she began. "It looks like our Kai friends will be able to translate the symbols. If there are any Chodugon behind those doors, we will need reinforcements. Let's double the guard and have them bring more side arms down here."

Then she proceeded to tell them of the latest status message sent by Zadan. "News from Vice President Zadan is not good.

First, the task force assigned to counterattack at The Signal compound is pinned down and they have already taken heavy losses.

Second, the Kon are gaining momentum. Attacking strategic sites: communications, bridges, tunnels, airports and sea ports. The Kon know exactly what to hit, when to do it, and then they disappear.

Third, still no sign of Captain Helforn's VTEC. Storm damage is so widespread that they have suspended the search and redirected the search crews to civil support."

Reza asked the obvious question. "Are they recalling us...aborting our mission?"

"President Stillwell wants to recall us, but Vice President Zadan believes our little treasure hunt is becoming more important by the minute. He has negotiated a ten hour window and then that's it. We got ten hours and then we pull out."

Reza blurted out, "Ten hours? We might not even have the doors open by then."

Atera agreed. "Right. We are already down sixty minutes so let's get on with it." With that, she concluded the status briefing and sent the crews on their way. "First crew, head topside, except for Reza, Prowler, Chel, and Scout. Everyone swap out your thermal packs."

Impervious to the cold, unending in their endurance, the Kai would remain with them for the duration. Before the first crew was even out of their way, Sarrow and Silas resumed the task of interpreting the symbols. One by one, they were able to form the old language. They compared and conversed regarding the symbols for they had the words, yet not the meaning. "We recognize the symbols, but they are not letters like your alphabets. They are more like hieroglyphics and there were several hundred of them in their day. It's not just about meaning, it's about position and context." Motioning with his hands to different patches of symbols. "This paragraph here, it is fairly translated. It says...

Herein lies The Master Architect.
Master of all sciences.
Teacher of all spirituality.
Scholar of all disciplines.
Passed on in body upon the great upheaval.
Set to rest upon the mount of gratitude…or….in gratitude
Preserved in mastery for future sake."

"But here, this paragraph is much more difficult and it is the one we need; it speaks to the entry of the tomb. Here is the closest we can translate:

To he who passes of the All Seeing Eye,
    Access shall be granted.
Present thyself upon the Stone of His Master
    And submit Thy Design."

In his technical background, Hunter had worked with many an architect and he passed a quick joke of it, "Submit thy design? That sure sounds like an Architect to me. You probably have it translated perfectly…only an Architect can understand another Architect."

As he had solved so many of the riddles, Reza stepped forward and began to run through his thought processes:

"Passes of the All Seeing Eye? Maybe this means some type of God?"

Sarrow responded, "As I have said before, there are lineages that embody the elements of his legend. Throughout time they have preserved these symbols. Even today, they are everywhere and are easily identifiable if you know what to look for. One of their symbols is the All Seeing Eye. It has many meanings; it can mean an all seeing God, it can mean spiritual sight, or higher knowledge. But, here, before this tomb, I take it to mean that 'something' is watching us… 'something' is going to determine if we are granted access or not."

Immediately, Atera sensed the danger. She called to her guards, "Be on your ready!"

Nodding slowly, Reza then proceeded, "Stone of His Master?" Is this also some symbol of those lineages?"

"Sir, No Sir. There are many symbols, but none that make reference to any stone."

Thinking back to all the artifacts in the ancient scrolls and all of the forgotten symbols, Reza thought aloud, "Is it a key or an object we are supposed to have? Maybe the tomb and the key work like a … transmitter\receiver?"

"Sir, I cannot say with any certainty." Said Sarrow.

Reza and Sarrow worked back and forth across the wall, searching for a symbol that represented The Stone of His Master. After many attempts, they conceded to failure and joined Atera who had been standing quietly, staring at the passage. "Commander Atera, what are you thinking?"
"It is like a riddle of sorts. It first draws your attention to one subject *Present thyself*. Then, it draws your attention to another subject *The Stone of His Master*. In doing so, it takes your attention away from the most important part. *thyself upon the stone*."

Looking around, they realized there were no stones to stand upon, just ice. It was then that Dreyden joined in. "The images we snapped indicate solid ground just a meter or so below where we are now. Once we saw the doors, we didn't think to clear down any lower. If you move your troops back into the tunnels, my Techs will clear the ground in twenty minutes."

With her cane in hand, she gave direction. "Clear the cavern people, back it up into the tunnel." The few Techs on hand resumed their work melting the ice and pumping out the water. As promised, melting down and down and then slowly, the ground beneath came into view. Not to waste a minute, Atera, Reza, and Sarrow paced in and around the Techs as they worked, trying to catch a glimpse of what lay below. As the ground cleared, more troops joined in. To their disappointment, there were many stones and many more symbols that lay beneath, far too many to easily determine which stone was the Stone of His Master. Pacing up and down the stones, Sarrow and his Kai searched for just such a symbol while troops scurried on hand and knee to scrape the grime off of the symbols. Then a shout from Reza at the far side. "This one, I've seen this one before. It was everywhere, scrolls, artifacts, even the ancient box that I used to decrypt The Void. What does this one mean?"

Sarrow and his Kai came quickly to Reza's side. "Sir, it is an image that persists even today, for all the thousands of years the meaning is still unchanged. The Compass and the Square are both tools of the Architect, this symbol given its meaning in memory of him. This symbol is one with the Master Architect, Jaromad."

Reza stared in amazement "So this is it? This must be it! This is the Stone of His Master." Checking his clock, he realized that they had lost nearly two more hours. Moving quickly, he stepped on it and turned about to face the wall. Instantly, lights sparkled across his chest and the ground vibrated lightly followed by a loud clang and then suddenly the ground shuddered and dropped straight out swallowing Techs and Troops alike.

Anyone lucky enough to be on solid ground ran for the safety of the ice tunnel, but not Chel, she ran forward to the wall where Prowler hung on struggling to pull himself up. Again, she had her eye on him even before the ground gave way. Leaping towards him on her belly, to hold her bodyweight against the Earth, she reached for him. Amid all the scrambling and shouting, nobody had noticed that both of them had now rolled off the edge and into the pit. Some five or six meters down into a larger basin.

As the dust settled, the troops above were ordered to stay in the ice tunnel out of fear that more ground might give way while those troops down in the pit called to each other and gathered around the injured. Alone, Atera stepped forward and called out in all her urgency, "Sound off down there! Give me names and status!"

Names called off one by one, twelve in all including Chel and Prowler. For the first time, Reza realized that Chel was down there so he cautiously stepped forward with Atera. To their ease, no serious injuries were reported. Atera pointed across the broken ground. "See there? Trap doors! This tomb has defenses."

Reza replied, "Most definitely, and no telling how many more traps we will hit. We gotta get them out…now!"

Down inside the pit, their eyes adjusted to the dim light and they could see that the pit was more like a sewer or a dungeon. Ice crystals clung to the walls and more ice hung down from the ceiling. Amid the ice were other objects that slowly became recognizable. Frozen bodies of animal, human, and Chodugon, but strewn about and dismembered. It was clear that the tomb had indeed been found by others and it was also clear that none had ever gained access.

The obvious question arose in their minds, 'Why in parts? Why strewn about?' And then an awful sound arose from the darkness, the creaking sound of twisting metal, like a giant spring recoiling. When the sound reached ear piercing levels, something flashed across the pit and struck one of the troops. Striking with such an impact that it shattered the man and cast the body parts in all directions. The blood itself splattered into a hazy cloud that hung momentarily in the air.

Troops clamored at the walls, but they could not gain a foothold or a grip. As Atera and Reza stepped closer and closer, that sound began to build for a second time. Again, the screeching sound passed through the darkness and another trooper was shattered. Immediately, that sound rose again and although they did not know what it was, they knew it came from the shadows, far back from the deepest parts of the pit where they could not see. They searched, they ran, and they climbed at the walls, but the blood on their armor made them slip and crash back down.

Atera called for more troops who rushed to the ledge with hoses and tools, anything they could find. Then, that sound shot across the pit and a third trooper was snatched. In the pit, Reza could now see Chel, blackened by the blood. Together their eyes met and he knew that there was no way to get them out.

Reza looked up at the symbols upon the wall and then back down into the pit as that sound mounted again and with it came the screams. Cupping his hands to his ears to drown them out, he looked at the symbols again and then over to the Stone of the Master, bringing images of scrolls and artifacts to mind. Pushing the screams out of his mind to make room for the symbols, the images, and the riddle.

The Stone of the Master.
The All Seeing Eye
The Lights.
Submit Thy Design.

The final bit of the riddle. He needed to solve the last bit of the riddle. *"Submit Thy Design."* He called to Sarrow and Atera, "Submit Thy Design....What does it mean?"

Together they understood that the only way to rescue their troops was to solve the riddle. They gathered at the Stone of His Master. Reza shouted above the screams. "I stood here....right here....and then there were lights."

Atera joined in, "The All Seeing Eye, it's got to be a scanner! It's got to be scanning for something!"

"What? What are we supposed to have?" He turned to Sarrow "You must know. What is this thing looking for?"

That sound snapped again and yet another trooper gone.

Distracted by the horrifying sounds, Sarrow's thoughts scattered, "They buried him with his technology, for future generation's sake. The key must be something that any future generation could possess. I don't know! I cannot say!"

Reza blurted out, "It...it must be something in the riddle. The riddle itself is telling you what it needs."

"To he who passes of the All Seeing Eye,
Access shall be granted.
Present thyself upon the Stone of His Master
And submit Thy Design."

Slowly Reza moved about as if the answer was coming to him. Suddenly, he knew what he had to do. With that sound mounting again and the screams now turning to cries, he had no time to explain.

He lunged forward and grabbed Dreyden and then shoved him onto the Stone of His Master. Reza unsheathed his sword and raised it to Dreyden's neck as if to sever the head, but before he could finish, Sun Anniz had seized the moment, a perfect excuse to kill Reza.

Catching Reza totally off guard, he made easy work by smashing the sword out of Reza's hands and thrusting a knee to his midsection. Backwards Reza rolled across the stone floor, in gut wrenching pain. Before Reza could get to his knees, Sun Anniz descended upon him with his sword high above his head. As the sword whipped downward, it was broadsided by another. Scout, tiny as she was, had managed to deflect his blade, but she crumbled under its weight. She had kept her eye on Sun Anniz exactly as Prowler had told her to do.

Scout rose quickly and by the look in her eyes, she made it clear that she was second guessing the Neferan account and by the look in Sun Anniz's eyes, he made it clear that he would get her, sooner or later. Sun Anniz blurted out, "The Lycerene was trying to kill Dreyden. He would kill him if not for me!"

Reza grunted and groaned having difficulty breathing air back into his lungs. Pulling himself to his knees, he shouted the solution to Atera:

To he who passes…
Present thyself…
Submit Thy design…
It was scanning me! My design!

She understood implicitly, Reza had been wearing armor when the All Seeing Eye scanned him so the scan failed. With that sound mounting yet again, she drew her sword and sliced off Dreyden's headdress, barely nicking the skin beneath. Just as that screeching sound erupted, the blood trickled down Dreyden's neck. Lights flashed across his body and found "Thy Design," that being the blood which carried the design of his DNA. All at once, that terrifying sound ceased. A human is what it had wanted, and a human is what it had found.

Screams settled down changing to groans as the trap door began to rise up, into the light. Troops rushed from the ice tunnel to the edge, but they were staggered by what they saw. Pools of blood and splatters everywhere with bones, limbs, and organs strewn about. More than all of it, their comrades lay about blackened by blood and exhausted from fear.

As the trap door clicked into its final position, the ground shuddered with a new sound. Without ever having heard it before, they knew exactly what it was. It was the sound of metal scraping across metal as the massive deadbolts unlocked from inside the tomb. The deadbolts screeched as they were pulled free, and finally, a rush of air was sucked into the vacuum of the tomb.

The moment that Atera waited for had arrived as the doors cracked open, first one inch, then two. Atera dropped to one knee and motioned for the guards to come forward and ready their weapons. So massive the doors were, that they creaked only inches at a time. Into the darkness they stared, looking deeper and deeper into it with anticipation that Chodugon might wake from within and pour out into their cavern.

Had it been any other structure, they would have taken to the offense and rushed inside, but not into that darkness, not at the thought of Chodugon. Rather, the guards switched on the light atop their rifles and shined the beam into the darkness. Behind the doors, nothing but more composite, this time pristine, like they had never seen before. Nothing but a long passageway decorated with more symbols.

CHAPTER 20: THE PASSAGEWAY

At first, a sigh of relief passed through the troops. Then, the realization that they had not yet rendered aid to their comrades who were still crawling through the blood amid the body parts.

Unrecognizable as they were, Atera rushed to her troops and wiped away the blood looking for Prowler. Reza did the same looking for Chel. Name after name until both of them were found, shaking and trembling. It was the blood that clung to them that made them tremble so.

Not like the blood of combat and neither was the feeling it gave. It was thick, it was coagulating, and it was freezing to them. The kind of blood that is so dark that it appears miles deep. Atera knew that the blood needed to come off and she turned to Dreyden, "Get those pumps turned around and get this blood washed off!" Up from under their shoulders they were lifted and dragged to a clean spot near the tunnel entrance.

As if Dreyden could read her mind, he was already moving on her command when he shouted back, "Heads up! Here it comes!" Just a matter of pushing one lever in the opposite direction and a straight stream of water shot across the cavern. He kept the water running until the blood washed thin and pink and could no longer hold them captive in its spell.

As if she had seen it a thousand times before, she knew their minds were gone. Backwards she would take them, back to another time and she did this the only way she knew how. She reprimanded them, all of them including Reza and she did it like never before. Gone was her usual demeaning monotone and polished voice, replaced by a voice loud and thunderous, enough to command their attention. "I ought to have you people court marshaled! I told you people to clear the cavern until the Techs melted the ice. I didn't tell you to go tramping all over my cavern! And I sure as hell didn't tell you people to go stepping on traps. Next time you wait on my orders…you don't touch anything without my orders. Am I clear people?"

They barely mumbled, "Sir, yes sir."

It wasn't fitting and it wasn't humane, but she had to do it. She had to divert their attention away from the blood. Not one trooper budged, yet she could sense that their comrades were waiting for their turn to help. Turning about, she gave them her final, "Shape up people. I won't be so nice next time!"

The five survivors stood there in the pink snow still dripping. Friends of theirs rushed in and guided them to the other side of the tunnel where the ground was clean. Prowler's first words were shaky, "What a bitch. She chews us out after we been damn near chewed up! I…I couldn't see that thing. What the hell was it?"

Stalker ignored the question assuming a little humor was needed. "That bitch will never change. I don't know who is worse, the Chodugon, or Atera."

It was perfect timing. They all burst with a bit of chuckles as if the stress escaped free from their chests. Scout added a bit of her own humor. "Right, for sure, if the Chodugon don't kill us, Atera just might."

Prowler almost got a smile out of it. He was getting back to his old self. "What happened anyway? All I know is that we were looking for *The Stone of*…something, and then the ground just went out."

Stalker gave him the answer, "Reza found *The Stone of His Master* and decided to step on it, apparently, he's never heard of a booby-trap."

Scout sensed that Prowler had missed a few more key developments. "Right, but it was Reza that got you out, he figured out the riddle. In case you didn't notice, Sun Anniz put the sword to him. I told you I didn't trust that guy."

Still in disbelief, still so fixed on the Neferan account, Prowler's heart hardened more so, "That Lycerene…Reza, he deserves whatever he's got coming."

Stalker interrupted. "I got to agree with Prowler here. For all we know Sun Anniz was just trying to save Dreyden. It could have been an honest mistake."

Scout looked deeply into Prowler and she tried another angle. "Prowler, when you were hanging over that pit, was it Sun Anniz who tried to pull you out? Was it Sun Anniz who held on so tightly that he went over the edge with you?"

Still shaking, Prowler's voice was quiet. "I didn't see who tried to pull me out. It happened too fast."

Scout pointed at Chel who was now surrounded by her kind. "Look over there…surprise, surprise. When everybody else ran away from the pit, she ran in…she ran to you. I told you once before, the Lycerene are like the people of the Plains and I also told you that the people of the Plains never lie."

With a check of her clock, Atera got things moving again. "Let's move it people…Form ranks against the walls, half to the right and half to the left! We are down almost four full hours. We can't wait on a fresh crew, we go in as is!"

"Heavy Infantry to the front.
Regulars to the rear.
Everyone else in the middle.
Two-by-two in staggered formation."

She turned about and shouted her orders to the troops still hold up in the tunnel, "Once we enter, put two men forward into the entrance of the passageway. Hold there and remember, nothing goes in…and nothing comes out!"

She then turned to Dreyden. "Send a runner topside. We need a fresh crew down here. And send a message to Zadan. Tell Zadan that we have opened the tomb and it appears to be fully intact. If they know we are in, they might give us more time."

With her hand, she gave the familiar gesture. "Turn to people! Turn to Soldiers work! Move in!"

Alone she stood, facing the tomb entrance as her troops filed into the passageway from both sides. As if they had all done this before, they staggered in from the left and the right without missing a beat. Atera herself joined in, slipping right between Stalker and Prowler. The passageway glittered brightly as their lights danced along the ornate composite walls. Images adorned above, below, and on both sides in a never ending script. Glyphs and symbols raised, rather than carved into the wall so finely detailed that they could be traced with the tip of a blade. Images passed quickly, but Silas and Sarrow recognized enough of the symbols to determine that the passageway spoke of the very first Era, its civilization…and it's undoing.

A distance of fifty meters had passed quickly and without interruption, but suddenly, their radio receivers went sporadic and then simply turned to static. They could not communicate outward through the thick composite walls, they were on their own. Ahead of the dancing lights, nothing but darkness, like a veil. The veil had always been darkest just ahead of the dancing lights and they chased it along as if it kept moving along with them. Suddenly, they were enveloped by the darkness, all around them except for the passageway still illuminated to the rear. Even the sounds had changed to something cavernous. "Halt! Don't take another step!" Atera shouted.

Searching with their lights, they grew more cautious by the second. No longer did their lights dance and no longer did their lights reflect ahead of them. Nothing but blackness all about them, swallowing up their light beams as if shining into the thickest black smoke. It unnerved them a bit, at least until the Techs brought in the heavy-duty floodlights. More minutes lost.

The floodlights fired-up with a low glow of orange that quickly intensified into a brilliant white light. Too quickly for the eyes to adjust and so they turned their eyes downward for a moment. They cast a beam directly ahead of them striking an object.

The object was simply unrecognizable, it bore no resemblance to any tomb or temple. Even with the flood lights, all that they could see was some object glimmering in the center of a massive cavern and all around it was the blackness of open space.

The object appeared to be a giant column or shaft that connected up into the ceiling of the cavern. Most of it was obscured by a bridge that arc'd up and over to connect it to the ledge where they stood upon.

Immediately, troops spread out to make way for Atera, Reza, and the Kai. All things considered, the bridge was questionable, but with time running out, she ordered two infantry to cross the bridge and test it out. Back and forth they went along the bridge before they gave the 'all clear.'

Immediately, the floodlights were moved up to the arch of the bridge to illuminate the object in its entirety. Again, they shined the lights straight upward to the ceiling and then worked downward. A slight repositioning of the floodlights and for the first time, a glimpse of what lay below.

Reza called out, "That doesn't look like a tomb. It looks more like a ship."

Sarrow studied the object looking high and low, moving from side to side of the bridge as if he recognized something. He redirected the floodlights downward, into the darkness checking busily two and three times before he called upon Silas to confirm his assumption. Together they discussed the shape of the object below. Four chambers connected to the main shaft below. Each of them identical, like the arms of a cross.

"What is it Brother Sarrow?" asked Atera.

"Sir, indeed, this is the tomb of Jaromad, the very shape of the structure confirms this. It is yet again another symbol that is considered sacred by the lineages that embody his legend. Only centuries ago, they bore it upon their shields and breastplates. When they took to the sea, they would fly it on their flags and sails. Even to this day, they encode it into the very architecture of their tombs and temples. The symbol has had many names over the Eras. Today, you call it the Cross of Eight."

Prowler knew something of the symbol. "The Cross of Eight is used by a number of cults...it has many names...it can mean any number of things."

As always, Silas offered up more history. "Sir, this is true. However, there is only one cult that bears the name of its purpose. Their name is derived from the earliest form, 'Tomb Hunters'. Eventually, the name became 'Temple Hunters'. Modern history incorrectly assumes that their quest was to find the tomb of a desert king. But, what they really seek is known to them as 'First Tomb'...Jaromad's tomb. Surely, you know the cult whom I speak of?"

Before Prowler could respond, Atera interrupted them with a more relevant question, "It is such an odd shape. This cave is round so why would they make the crypt itself in the shape of a cross?"

Reza started his usual train of thought. "Did you notice that it is not connected to the cavern walls in any way? It only connects to the cavern by the shaft that runs from the top to the bottom."

Silas continued the thought. "Yes...Yes. The crypt itself does not touch the outer walls. It's almost free floating."

Atera added her thoughts. "It must have something to do with tectonic activity. It could certainly survive an earthquake."

The conversation passed back to Reza. "Or... a flood. This crypt could certainly remain here submerged if need be."

Atera called to the Techs to redirect the floodlights as far down as possible. Immediately, Sun Anniz blurted out, "Look there! There is something below the crypt! We need more lights!"

More flood lights to the left and more to the right, all shined down to the depths of the hollow. Something so massive hung there below them. Not one cross attached to the shaft, but five crosses stacked atop each other. All made of the shining composite.

What started as a single crypt now became an entire complex. They would have to enter it and navigate down through the levels to find what they had come for. They all sensed the passing time and checked their clocks, another thirty minutes had passed. Sun Anniz followed up, "Five of them? That could take hours and we only have four hours left."

Atera thought aloud for a moment, "We keep going. Let's get these people back into the same formation with Heavies to the front and Regulars to the rear. There is our entrance to the complex." She pointed to the opening in the shaft at the far end of the bridge and the troops scurried into formation and headed up the bridge, straight into the opening with their flashlights gleaming ahead of them.

While standing at the entrance to the complex, they used their flashlights to scan the staircase that led down into the shaft. Their lights met with a dizzying sight. The shaft was some five meters across and it was hollow. Looking down from inside the hollow, they could see an endless spiraling staircase that led down the entire length. Pausing once again, as one of the troops broke a light stick and dropped it. Passing down, it illuminated the shaft with a greenish glow, down it went and at the twenty meter mark, it cast its glow on a section where the spiral leveled. That being the entrance to the first Cross of Eight and upon the leveling were four doors, one leading to each chamber. The light stick continued down further to the second level and by the time it reached the third level, the glow was a blur. Without their floodlights, the bottom was an endless darkness.

Atera had resumed her position same as before, right in between Stalker and Prowler. Pausing at the top of the shaft and looking down, Stalker took to his usual ways and ran his calculations. "That's gotta be a hundred meters, maybe a hundred and fifty. Climbing stairs with armor on, we can make fifty, maybe seventy-five meters. Beyond that, we got risk brewing. Not to mention that we're gonna use up twice the oxygen and burn through our thermal packs." Sun Anniz and Reza both nodded same of their armor. Atera was aware of the risk. She gave her usual nod and raised her hand in that familiar gesture. "Turn to soldiers work." Down they went.

Along the walls of the shaft, more of the same glyphs and symbols. But this time, they were accompanied by pictures and murals. A story to be told in murals using images as simple as the most ancient of cave writings. War.

The images of a war depicting weapons, the killing, and the dead...piles of dead. These walls were the very chronicle of the Puratist wars, images spiraling downward as if moving through time in stages. They climbed down without even so much as a moment wasted to interpret the images. Nevertheless, it was easy to see him, the Master Architect, Jaromad. Represented in the many stages, always depicted in a white aura and clothed in his scholarly robe. In his one hand, a Compass and in his other hand, a Square.

Upon reaching the first level, Atera called them to pause and they gladly settled back against the stairs to rest their legs. She looked to Stalker and with a motion of her cane, directed him to approach the door of the first chamber.

Stepping his way down, between the troops, he stopped at the leveling to check himself over. To prepare himself for what may be on the other side of that door. Cautiously, he stepped towards the door with sword in hand. He called to Sarrow, "The doors...they have no handles, I see no key holes. How do we open them?"

Before Sarrow could respond, Stalkers eyes saw a familiar symbol above the door, the All Seeing Eye. He froze, but too late for he had stepped within the sensors reach. With the sound of a tremendous hiss, the door zipped open and a bluish gas burst forward enveloping him as it swirled. His legs leapt out from underneath him and he lunged backwards landing not on his feet, but on his rump.

The blue gas erupted through the door and up the shaft in a howling gush. Torrents of it were escaping in such volumes that it could only be caused by something forcing it out. Every fiber of every trooper twitched in anticipation of what would emerge amid the gas, but not so. The gas evacuated the chamber as abruptly as it had started. Slowly, Stalker repositioned himself on one knee and inched his way closer to the door with light in hand. Nothing but more darkness. Still, he hesitated to enter fearing that Chodugon would ensnare him in a trap. Rather, he called for a light stick, snapped it and tossed it into the chamber. It began to glow green and as it intensified, he could see the first glimmers in the chamber. He turned towards the troops for a moment to reassure them that the chamber was clear and when he turned back, the first silhouette emerged.

Still on one knee, but leaning backwards against the railing, Stalker gripped his sword tightly and held it out in front of himself. Then, one silhouette became two and two became three until there were many. Bracing himself for the outpouring, when a sudden flicker of lights from within the chamber had overwhelmed his eyes. Lights within the chamber had activated and were so bright that he had to turn away. With his vision blurred and spotted, he hesitated to process the scene before him. Rows of silhouettes. A second, maybe two seconds, before he had realized that the silhouettes were statues and not Chodugon. His body slumped and his sword clinked upon the ground as his senses settled into relief.

CHAPTER 21: CHAMBERS AND CRYPTS

Atera raced to Stalker as best she could while motioning for her Heavy Infantry to move forward into the doorway. She knelt down beside Stalker with her eyes and her sword-arm towards the door, never flinching until she too felt the danger abated. Looking down at him as if she could see him through his armor, she studied him as she always had, checking to assess his readiness. She could see it now, that fear was beginning to teach him what she could not. A solid slap upon the shoulder and then she grabbed him from under the arm as if she could pull him up.

Not to be outdone, Prowler offered a joke in kind, "Don't worry, your shining armor looks great...at least on the outside." Still weak in the knees and a bit shaky, Stalker finally spoke. "That's funny, but right about now, I feel like I could puke in this armor." Scout immediately laughed. "Don't do it...just don't do it."

First among them to step foot into the chamber was Brother Sarrow and his fellow Kai. They walked in delicately, moving along at a steady pace as they studied the glyphs on the walls and even more so to study the statues. Atera followed and directly behind her were Reza and Sun Anniz. Moments passed without a word between them, simply staring at the maze of glyphs that adorned the walls, floor, and ceiling of the chamber. Endless scripts each to its own frame, like the pages of a text book. Staring in amazement at one of the statues, Reza broke the silence "Who are they?"

Silas knew the history so he replied. "Look at them. Not one among them is like the other. Beyond the precious metals and stones that adorn them, what do you see?" Still more silence and so Silas continued. "Look in their hands, each of them holds a symbol." Stalker seemed to catch on. "It looks like Mathematics to me."

"Sir, you are right. This entire chamber is the library of Mathematics and these are the Scholars of Mathematics. By their names, I recognize some of them, each one of them was a genius in his own niche of Mathematics. Their lives span the thousand years leading to Jaromad's generation."

"But, where is he? Where is this Master Architect?" asked Stalker.

"Sir, he is not among them."

Confused, Stalker looked around and then looked back to Silas. "Why not? Isn't this his tomb?"

"Sir, what you see here, it is even more than what the legends have accounted for. It would appear that this is not just the library of Jaromad, it would appear this is the library of an entire Era. They must have added more levels in the years after he was entombed."

Atera interrupted them, "So, this chamber holds no mention of The Signal Generator?"

"Sir, no Sir. We need to move on to the next chamber."

They backed out onto the leveling and approached the door to the second chamber. Again the door zipped open and a torrent of bluish gas erupted. By now, they had come to assume that the bluish gas had a purpose. Put there to protect the priceless contents of each chamber from oxidation and corrosion. Moments later the lights flickered and illuminated the second chamber which was full of scripts and statues just like the first chamber. Sarrow and his Kai moved with more urgency this time. They immediately entered the second chamber and separated so they could scan both walls simultaneously, walking along searching and reading. At the far end, they met and then returned down the centerline. "Sir, this is the chamber of Physics. As it were with the first chamber, the Signal Generator is not present here."

So too of the third and fourth chambers, which were dedicated to the sciences of chemistry and astronomy. "Sir, it would appear this first level is dedicated to a select set of sciences, the ones known as the Exact Sciences. The only sciences in which the functions are truly repeatable and predictable."

Realizing that more time had slipped away, Atera checked her clock. "We are now down to three hours. We're going to have to move much faster."

Prowler took to his calculations. "Sir, even if we run through these chambers, our thermal packs won't last but two, maybe three more levels."

Atera had to make the risky decision. "Right. We'll take the Kai as far down as we can, then we'll head topside while the Kai continue down. That's the plan, so let's get moving people!"

Down the spiral they raced to the second level, there they split up into four teams and opened the doors to all four chambers simultaneously. At the same time, Atera had positioned herself at the center of the level to await status of each chamber. The second level was cleared in good time. "Sir, this level houses biology and the sciences of the healing Physicians."

Down the spiral again to the third level. Following suit with their prior run, they split up. Returning one by one to Atera, they concluded once again that this level held nothing of The Signal Generator. Having improved their pace so, they decided that they could handle one more level.

Down the spiral same as before to the fourth level, but this time, the pictures on the walls changed. It was Silas who took notice of it and grabbed a light from one of the troops. "Commander Atera! Look here, this mural…it depicts the time when the Puratist wars ended and the Chodugon war began. Somewhere in this time frame The Void was deployed." Silas used his light and traced the murals up and down the stairs. "There, it's there! That symbol would be The Void! We're getting closer now!"

Atera gave her usual nod and motioned them to continue down. Doors opened, gases burst outward, and then Kai raced inward. She waited out in the leveling, pacing and staring about the murals, taking in the images of the Chodugon wars. Checking her clock again and again, then walking over to the edge where she shined her light down into the darkness.

Still so much more to go. Then, from one of the chambers, a voice shouted out, "Commander Atera, here! It is here!" She raced in followed by Reza and Sun Anniz and the rest of her team. The images were self-evident, this chamber was dedicated fully to The Void and The Signal Generator. Pages upon pages of images and text filling every available inch, symbols and icons that would need to be translated.

Amid all their excitement, Stalker called the risk to their attention. "People, we are outta time here! We better hope they have extra thermal packs up in the cavern because we sure won't make it topside on these cans!"

Atera reluctantly agreed. "Form it up people! We go out the way we came in, except for the Kai. They will stay here and await the image-copy teams. Heavies, drop your plate armor here, no extra weight on the trip up."

Regulars assisted the Heavies with removing the extra plate armor and they simply let it rest wherever it fell. Plates, clasps, and straps littered about the decking. With the extra poundage removed, the entire team could move at the same pace. Without even an extra word to the Kai, up they went into the darkness. For the first time, they were looking up into the spiral staircase and quickly they realized that looking up was a bad thing.

Past the third level with ease, but between the third and second levels, their legs began to feel the strain. Stalker called out. "These cans got a minute or two left, then we are on empty!" Passing the second level and their legs were now burning and their lungs began to feel the ache. Stalker called it out. "That's it, the cans are empty! It's gonna get real cold, real quick!"

Up over the second level the troops began to slow as their leg muscles tightened. Atera took notice of their sudden change in pace and knew that if they kept pushing they would outpace themselves. "Slow it down! Slow it down! We're going to have to tolerate the cold here. Slow it down and pace yourselves. Just get to the cavern and we will fire up those ice torches." The slower pace helped with the cramping, but the cold set in fast. Not like regular cold. This was so cold that the heat was conducted right out of the body through the armor, as if it were being sucked out. The worst of it being the cold air that they inhaled, so cold that it burned the lungs and cutoff their breathing. Coughing and coughing, yet they trudged on.

Back they went, past level two and even slower as they passed level one. Now looking up with just one remaining spiral, they could sense that they could make it. Pushing and pulling each other until finally they had cleared the final steps of the spiral and they clamored out straight across the bridge and into the long passageway.

By now, the cold was unbearable. With the absence of heat, the evaporative system in the armored suits had failed and sweat began to accumulate. Armor now conducted cold more easily as it slipped and slid all around them. Hypothermia began to set in as muscles cramped and spasm. No longer pushing or pulling, they carried and dragged those who could not make it.

Near to the end of the passageway, they could see the lights of the two guards in the cavern, yet still too far. Some fell where they were, others trampled around them. Disoriented and confused they pressed on towards the lights, towards the guards. Finally, in the last twenty meters, the guards themselves rushed into the tunnel to drag them out to the clearing of the cavern where Dreyden already had ice torches aglow and readied his Techs with fresh Thermal Packs. Like waves of warm water, the heat circulated through the inner armor and they groaned in relief. Slowly, the trembling settled out, the sweat evaporated, and the coughing subsided.

Atera called to Dreyden and he rushed to her side, "Send a runner topside! Tell Zadan that we found it! We found The Signal Generator, schematics!" Then she ordered more, "Get your imaging team down there, on level four, the Kai await and will guide them. We need crystal clear images of everything. Be sure those images come out perfect, we won't get a second chance!"

"Sir, Yes Sir!"

Like the rest of her team, Atera settled back to take her rest while fluids and nutrient packs were passed around. They simply moved to the sidelines and watched as Dreyden took over, directing his Techs up and down the lines. Equipment moved to and fro as Troops and Tech worked together to prepare for the imaging teams to descend. Atera reclined and had just about closed her eyes when the runner returned, "Sir! Sir! We can't raise Zadan. We can't get through to anybody!"

Dreyden turned abruptly, "What do you mean you can't raise anybody?"

"Sir, there is just too much chatter. The radio is just overloaded with units calling out for help. The radio operator says for the past sixty minutes, all hell broke loose. The best he can tell, the Kon are only part of it. Citizens are panicking and rioting...police and military can't contain them."

Atera and Dreyden looked at each other and then Atera gave the orders, "Get those images ASAP, every last one of them. In the meantime, get everyone else up to the VTECs and we will take off as soon as the last image is done."

She walked about the cavern gathering them to their feet and directing them to make their way over to the lifeline where the Techs would get them clipped on. Again, twenty degrees didn't look so bad, not from where they stood, not an impossible climb, but this time, they were tired. Scout had put herself in the lead and having learned her lesson in the spiral, she made sure they paced themselves. Up and up they went, again, pausing at the midway mark. This time, mostly looking towards the light at the end of the tunnel; towards what they knew would be clear skies and clean white snow.

They continued onwards, eventually reaching the point where the two ice drills had merged into one. The tunnel now doubled in width and for the first time, they felt as if they could stand tall and stretch out. Still, fifty meters to go and they slowed just reveling in the openness. Scout thought to urge them on. "Almost there people! As soon as we get out, we go straight to the VTECs and jack-in. Then, we get some rest!"

That's as much as she had time to say before the first tremor struck. Small and barely noticeable such that Scout wasn't sure everybody sensed it. "What was that? Did you feel that?"

Voices joked from the rear, "Feel what? I'm so tired I can't feel my own teeth!"

It struck again, this time a bit louder. Loud enough that they all stopped, and looked about.

Prowler's instincts scaled up. "I think the ice is settling. We must have destabilized it."

The little bits of ice and snow that drifted downward from the ceiling lent credence to the idea. Scout looked about, still a bit unconvinced "Ok...ok I don't think it's going anywhere just yet. Let's keep moving, slow and steady!"

Upon the next step they took, the third tremor struck. Stalker knew it precisely, he had considered the ice density, considered the outside temp, the ground temp, and even considered the vibrations of the ice drills, "That's not ice settling...those are mortars!"

An all-out rush to the end of the ice tunnel where they could look out across the landscape, the drifts, and the snow that constantly wisped in the wind. Far off, they could see the VTECs with people running about, all facing to the drift line behind the VTECs. Something was happening, but as of yet, nothing to see. Then slowly, emerging from behind the drift line, a single Chodugon, black robed and hooded, marching forward with sword in hand and the sun to his back. Then, another and another.

Troops poured out of the VTECs, Neferan, Lycerene, and Earth's own and they prepared to face the oncoming charge, but not the troops emerging from the ice tunnel. Atera had ordered them to hold their positions, hold until she had sized up the threat. Six Kon, then seven and eight made their way over the drifts and closed the distance. Then, in the last fifty meters, they charged. A fearsome speed with the Kon battle-cry shrieking across the snow drifts.

Atera and her pilots watched from the ice tunnel as troops ran toward the drift line and attempted to setup a defensive perimeter. Even as the last of them was still emerging from the VTECs, the Kon were upon them. Eight Kon charging against thirty Heavies and a dozen Regulars. The line immediately gave way and became a circle with Kon hacking away at the perimeter.

Quickly, the Heavies realized their thick armor was a good match for the Kon. The fear abated and so they pushed back, a triumphant moment for them as the Kon lurched backwards in the snow. The Heavies now took to the offensive and gave chase across the drifts. Again, Atera's troops stepped forward sensing that they had the upper hand, but she ordered them to stand down. More so, she didn't like the fact that the Heavies gave chase, for she knew the Kon would never retreat, not unless they were setting a trap. On the radio, she shouted orders,

"Halt! Halt!

Do not approach the drift line!'

I say again…stay away from the drifts!'"

CHAPTER 22: UPON THE DRIFTS

Only a handful of the Heavies heard her and managed to stop short of the drift line. The others ran up to the crest of the drifts and were staggered by what they saw, another Kon trap. A most fearsome Chodugon weapon greeted them from just behind the drifts. In its day, it was known as The Skewer.

A multi-tiered cross-bow with racks and racks of six foot long metal spears. Its purpose was to devastate rank after rank of infantry. At the tip of each spear, a high density composite made for piercing armor. At the other end, a short chain that whipped about as it passed through the body, making a wound three times its original size; enough to pass a fist through.

Before they could stop and catch their balance, the blast rocked the very ground as the spears whistled through the air. The lucky ones died instantly. Sometimes skewering two and three men on a single spear. Others, lay devastated as arms and legs were carried off. But, the spears carried on through the air.

Anyone remaining out in the open ran for the only cover they could find among the drifts; that being the VTECs, and the Ice Tunnel. Another blast, another whistling, and another arching. Spears rained down all around them. Still too far away and so the spears did no harm to her troops. But out in the open, two Techs were skewered as the spears turned downward.

From the distance the black robed Kon observed and he could see that his trusted spears would cause more harm than good for he also wanted what was inside that tomb. Rather, he and his Kon turned and marched across the ice, to take the tunnel by sword.

Reza stepped forward, "He's coming for the tomb! We got nothing but small arms and swords in here! We gotta get down to the VTECs and get some rifles, maybe rockets!"

Had Reza not stood so tall and spoken so firm, Atera would have ordered him to stand down, but he was exceptional and there was simply no other option.
"Turn to….As fast as you can."

And, just that fast, Reza, and his Pack dropped their gear and raced across the drifts. Across that seventy-five meter clearance between the VTECs and the ice tunnel, staring at the oncoming Kon as they charged headlong towards each other.

Without so much as the slightest turn of her head, Atera barked another order. "Send a runner down below. Tell Dreyden we got incoming." One of the Regulars at the rear took the order without hesitation. He clipped on the lifeline, and ran full speed until his feet gave out on the ice. Down he went.

As Reza and his Pack approached the VTECs, they could see the rifles scattered all about the place; leaning against equipment, setting inside the VTEC bays, and strewn about the dead. "Grab-em! Grab everything you can get; especially that automatic rifle!"

Never in a million years did Reza consider that the black robed Kon remembered his voice; remembering Reza from the cliffs, it honed in on him. Bullets cracked all about him and shrapnel scraped across his armor.

Nava responded, "Damn, they're fast!
They are already on us!
It's…It's a trap, like the old Monk said.

Reza instantly recognized it. "We got to run for it!
Go, Go, Go!"

They ran hard, but the snow bogged them down. Step by step, the Kon closed the distance. As they began to circle around the Pack, the black robed Kon unsheathed his sword and headed straight towards Reza.

Atera reached down and grabbed her swords at her sides and hinged them over. That sound repeated throughout the ice tunnel as every trooper did the same. Suddenly, another sound arose. Something from deep inside the ice tunnel, a grinding, a rumbling, and it came up fast. Scout could feel the ice vibrate and rumble beneath her feet, a feeling that she had experienced before.

"I can't see what is coming!
It…it feels like a Kon battle charge!"

Out of the darkness it roared and scoured over them, nearly pulling them along in its wake. It burst forth out of the ice tunnel in a snow cloud and roared out into the sunlight. Dreyden's drill machine, moving so fast that it almost got airborne. As the snow cloud cleared, they could see that the machine had been stripped of the heavy drill bit and was now little more than a tank powered by a huge jet engine.

The machine roared forward kicking up snow, ice, rock and anything else that got in its way. Straight at the Kon who for the first time, were forced to retreat. The machine chased the Kon all the way back to the VTECs while Reza and his Pack ran back to the ice tunnel.

As soon as they were all safe, Dreyden turned his machine around and returned to the ice tunnel. Even before he dismounted his machine, he was already asking. "What now? We need those VTECs."

Atera thought about it "He won't give up, not now. He has waited thousands of years, he will call for reinforcements…..every Kon he can muster."

Prowler was already ahead of them, scanning the VTECs looking for the Kon. "That black robed Kon …he's up to something. I don't like the way he is moving."

By now, they were looking at the Kon, and the Kon were looking at them. With a single step, everything changed. The black robed Kon stepped forward at a confident pace and the winds that came in from afar carried a new sound. Whatever it was, it drew closer. Atera saw it first. "They are airborne, Chodugon transports!

With a sudden rush, aircraft jetted over the drift line. Five in all and they were clearly Chodugon transports. Just as the transports approached the VTECs, they took a sudden dip and released something. Round objects that fell the short distance to the ground and then bounced, skipped and rolled across the ice. Clouds of debris erupted as they chewed their way across the drifts and just as they slowed, Atera realized what they really were, Kon. Suddenly, the Kon erupted from their tightly-curled positions and burst into a run without missing a step.

"Riflemen, take up positions! Fire at will!" Shouted Sgt. Anil, the senior rifleman. Immediately, the shots rang out and Kon crashed down in a cloud of snow, squealing while their precious black blood spraying everywhere. Even so, the Kon charge accelerated. "There are too many, too fast, we can't stop them. We got to retreat....to the tunnel".

Turning to clip onto the lifeline, they found it had been chewed up by Dreyden's ice drill. It was gone. They would have to take their chances with no line to hold them steady. Hesitantly, they dropped down to ride the distance on their knees.

Moving though the blackness, they were blind, yet they could feel the rush, they could feel their bodies swerving left and right as they rode up and down the rounded walls, back and forth until they found some way to slow the descent. Some rolling on their bellies and digging elbows in, others detaching swords and gouging the hilts into the ice.

Suddenly, the darkness gave way to the lights in the cavern. Bodies zipped through the entrance, clipping some of the guards while others slid straight into the wall. Bodies began to collide and pile upon each other. Even before the last of them had reached the ice tunnel, troops were rolling and twisting about trying to get to their feet. Readying themselves in anticipation of the oncoming Kon, grabbing for rifle, sidearm, sword, anything.

Silence at first as they instinctively listened for the sounds of the oncoming Kon, but none just yet. Mumbling arose as they wondered what to do next. Stalker, as always, ran his calculations. "Five transports, each dropped ...maybe... ten Chodugon. At best, we disabled twenty...that still leaves thirty of them." He looked around and quickly counted. "And just about thirty of us."

Atera looked directly at Stalker, she didn't say anything, but Stalker knew what she was thinking. He said it for her, "Not good enough! Not nearly good enough!

Prowler's frustration surged. "What about the Kai? Can't they help?"

Chel answered, "Radio won't reach the Kai through the composite walls...and a runner won't make it down in time. Commander Atera, we don't have any Heavies...I mean, their plate armor is down there where we dropped them. Sir, we have to go down....now!"

Without a second's hesitation, Atera agreed. She spun about putting herself at the entrance to the passageway.
"Form up.
Heavies to the front!
Techs, and Pilots next.
Regulars, to the rear.
Wait on my order!

Atera hushed them with her hands. Listening to gauge the position of the oncoming Kon. Hoping there was enough time for everyone to flee; else get caught behind to face the Kon alone. All eyes on her now as they waited for that single word, the very word they used to dread. Now, they were so eager to hear it.
"Begin!" Their legs burst forward.

CHAPTER 23: THE FALL OF COMPASSION

Into the passage they went knowing this time that the distance ahead of them was at best fifty meters. Again the lights danced across the composite walls. Near to the end, they could see the glow cast by the flood lights. For a second, it seemed like they were safe, then the sounds echoed from the rear as the Kon entered the passageway, dragging their swords along the Composite walls to make a screeching sound; something to terrify their prey, to distract and slow them.

Emerging from the passageway, the troops streamed right out onto the bridge. Even as the first of the Techs entered the spiral staircase, the Regulars to the rear were opening fire. The Kon had closed the gap now to maybe twenty-five meters, not enough time to get everyone in the spiral staircase before the Kon would be upon them. Sgt. Anil called forward to Atera, "Get them inside the stairwell, we'll hold the bridge!"

Atera disagreed. "That's suicide! You and your riflemen will come with us!"

With seconds to convince her, Anil shouted. "We will trap them on the bridge. Trust me…we will trap them!"

She lowered her head to find some reason to disagree, but could find none. She turned about to listen for the Kon, to gauge their distance, and then gave a nod, more like a bow, and turned to join the fleeing troops.

Anil was setting a trap by hiding his riflemen just below the crest of the bridge, to catch as many Kon on the narrow bridge as possible. Staggering his four riflemen with the forward two on their bellies and the rear two on one knee. He powered down the flood lights and turned them about, pointing them at the Kon.

"Cease fire! Cease fire!

Queue them up on the bridge, at the narrowest point!

Hold fire until I hit the floodlights."

Everyone knew what that meant. He would blind the Kon as they entered the bridge. It might buy them a second, but seconds mattered. The sounds grew louder and louder, ten meters at best until the sound of those scraping swords and shrieking battle cries gave way to the sound of a stampeding charge.

The Kon rushed upon the bridge, two-by-two in full stride. On all fours lunging through the air as their powerful legs reared. Focusing their eyes on Atera and her troops still scrambling to get inside the spiral staircase. Intentional or not, Atera made the perfect bait while Anil and his riflemen kept silent and still.

Hiding in the blackness until the bridge was loaded with Kon and then Anil hit the switch. Kon reeled in the bright lights as the riflemen unleashed a full volley. Sparks flickered as the bullets struck Kon near and far, knocking them from the bridge and down into the darkness below.

The first wave of Kon was destroyed amid the deafening roar of gun blast. The second wave of Kon approached more cautiously. As they charged, something flew through the air, rolling and twisting as it passed overhead and landed behind the riflemen.

Anil turned, but it was already upon him, black robed and slashing. It came down on Anil's right arm, then his left. With a backhand, it threw Anil off the bridge and leapt down upon the remaining Riflemen. Now fully overrun on all sides, the riflemen were torn apart, piece by piece. But they had stood their ground. They had bought the few precious seconds. And more, they had evened the odds a bit.

By the time that thing and his Kon had reached the spiral staircase, Atera and hers had put at least two full levels between them. But, they didn't stop there, they raced down towards the Kai who were now out on the leveling of the fourth floor.

As she rounded the final leveling to the fourth floor, Atera called down to the Kai. "They are right behind us!
Ready the Heavies!
Ready the Heavies!"

As soon as the Heavies leapt off the staircase, Kai were there with plates in hand. Clip, strap, and fasten plates as fast as they could, but it was tedious. Sarrow shouted "We need more time!" to which Atera shouted right back. "Make them think we are many! Shout it out! Loud, Loud, Louder!"

In the confines of the spiral staircase, their voices were amplified. They stomped their boots to the metal decking and slammed their swords upon the railings until their battle cry roared up the stairwell causing the Kon to hesitate.

Immediately, the Kai motioned the troops as far back as possible, so they could make plans. "How many Kon?" Shouted Brother Sarrow. "What are their numbers?"

Stalker answered. "There were thirty or so to start. But our riflemen got a few of them on the bridge." Prowler blurted out "That was a hell of a firefight...got to be more than a few!"

The sounds of the Kon descending were unmistakable. Their shrieking and hissing was amplified by the echo within the spiral stairwell. At best, they had twenty or thirty seconds.

Sarrow took charge, "We hold them here at the stairs. It's the narrowest point. We'll put the Heavies and the Kai up front. Regulars to the rear." With a pause, he looked to Atera. "Techs and Pilots are no use in this fight. Get them out of the way…into the chamber. If we have to, we will retreat to the chamber…that's where we make our final stand."

The Kon descended carefully as they rounded the fourth and final leveling. They paused to count the numbers of Kai and troops; to assess their readiness. Sarrow, in return, looked across the Kon, at their eyes, and knew the very moment it would begin. Battle cries on both sides erupted so loud that the spiral staircase vibrated. And then it happened.

The first Kon charged forward, while a second Kon leapt straight out into the crowd. Without a word between them, the Kai chose their marks. Silas to the first Kon and Sarrow to the second. Silas immediately grabbed onto the charging Kon to lock it in an embrace and use it as a shield. At the same time Sarrow spun at the flying Kon and swung his sword to chop-of its arm.

More Kon funneled into the staircase pushing against the Heavies who had formed a wall at the foot of the stairs. Silas and Sarrow were right behind them spearing and slashing any Kon within reach. In a matter of moments, the black oily blood of the Kon sprayed everywhere. It formed puddles on the metal decking and eventually caused the Heavies to slip. As the first Heavy went down, he was gored by a Kon spear, the line collapsed and Kon poured in and among the Regulars. The retreat had begun.

233

Atera had put her pilots and the Techs against the back wall of the chamber. From there, they could see the battle unfold. At first, Regulars were racing thru the door, but within moments, they were tripping and falling backwards as the Kon battled their way in.

Then she saw it, the first spray of blood as the hacking began. They were defenseless like sheep in a pen; pressed so tightly together that they could not fight back. One by one, the sound of hacking, screaming, and blood spraying everywhere. The thought of her team so ill prepared repeated again and again in her mind until her hands began to tremble.

Stalker and Prowler could see the look of desperation on her, even with her helmet on. "Get behind us. There is nothing you can do!"

The thought of it struck her. Her injuries, her walking cane, her in ability to do what she was made to do. They pulled at her until she was behind them, but her mind was somewhere else. "There is something…"

Almost without thought, her legs carried her towards the door. Along the side wall, struggling to hold herself upright as the bodies slammed against her. Ahead of her were the blood spatters now dripping down the walls, but she continued onward. Halfway across the length of the chamber when suddenly, there was a sudden spray of blood so thick that it soaked her. Looking down she could see that it was Dreyden laying on the floor. Staring at the enormous hole in his chest only made her trembling worse, so she stepped forward.

Another few meters, right up to the front line, and when she turned to look, she saw Scout laying there, trampled underfoot. Her mind swirled to dizziness, just as a Kon charged her. It paused only when he saw her walking cane. Quickly, it conclude that she posed no threat and it returned to the front line.

Just a couple more steps and she rounded the corner against the front wall. She limped her way toward the doorway and then stopped to glance upward at the 'All Seeing Eye'. Rather than stepping through the doorway, she waived her hand in front of the 'All Seeing Eye' and the door zipped closed.

Then she turned around to face the Kon, stepping forward without her limp, without her trembling, and without her dizziness. Two and three steps towards the Kon and then she tipped her head down. Staring at the Kon, studying them to find their weakness, the way a predator studies a herd.

The Kon took little concern with her and turned back around to resume their hacking, but she stomped her foot. First, the right foot stomped hard to the decking, and then the left foot. She settled down deeply with her thighs almost parallel to the ground. Again, the Kon turned to look.

Reza was the first to realize what she was doing. "Chel, look at Atera. She is distracting them, she is trying to make them believe she is…that other robot…the Compassionate One." And Chel blurted out what little she could. "They won't fall for it! They'll cut her to pieces!"

Slowly, Atera let her hands settle upon the swords that were still attached to her outer thighs. A click and a pop, and she detached her swords, one in each hand. Just as fluidly, she tipped her swords forward and the blades hinged out. Her eyes peered down the length of one sword, then the same of the next, as if she were performing some kind of battle ritual.

The swords then began to swirl about her, moving as if they were the wings of a butterfly. Round and round slicing through the air. Starting slowly, as if the swords were weightless, but gradually accelerating until the air started to whistle about them. "See, she is doing exactly as Silas said, the silence, and the swords. Just like Silas told us."

She was fast, but it did not convince the Kon. Again, they turned back to resume their attack…and so she accelerated. As fast as they had ever seen any human and now the Kon were at least confused. Turning sideways to look again, unsure if it could be true.

By now, Sarrow had also realized what Atera was doing. "Silas, she buys us time. Attack now!" But, Silas just stood there ignoring Sarrow, staring at Atera.

"Silas, now, now! Silas, listen to me!" This was it, this was the moment she had bought them. With or without Silas, Sarrow raised his sword to strike the Kon down, but then the room thundered as Atera stomped her right foot again, then her left.

Her arms now moving all about her as the swords glittered in the light. She accelerated again, and then again, unto the point where her arms, like the swords, became a blur. Appearing at one moment to be two arms, then two arms became four, and four became six. The air now bristled with the sound, like a song, and then in a split second, it stopped. Atera stood there…dead still.

Kon and Kai alike knew that no human could wield a sword with such speed, they knew that no Chodugon was a two handed swordsmen, except for one. They knew it by legend only.

Immediately, the Kon formed ranks and charged at Atera with their shrieking battle-cry. But, she stomped her foot to the deck and her chest heaved as she let loose a battle-cry of her own, not a shriek, but a roar.

From her faceplate the roar burst forward twice as loud as the Kon and it resonated throughout the chamber and then slowed to a growl. When next her eyes peered forward, she was changed. Any human traits were now replaced by pure battle algorithms. As the legend said, *'the God of Compassion will be undone'* and will lose its compassion. It will become a Chodugon, a machine built of singular purpose...to kill.
"Watch now my soldiers.
Learn now...to kill the Kon!"

From her deeply crouched position with swords held high, she spun outwards. Her first thrust had pierced the neck of one Kon; its black oily blood sprayed outward. Then she whipped around and crouched low to sever the knee of another. Still, Silas and Sarrow stood there as confused as anyone, man or Chodugon.

More Kon advanced towards her, and she again took straight to the offense. Relying on speed rather than power and force. For every two or three strikes, only one was powerful enough to inflict damage. The others were designed to distract the Kon, to keep them in a defensive mode; always to keep them in a defensive mode for that is how to kill a Kon.

Blades, elbows, hilts, knees, shoulders, head-butts, anything and everything. Alone, she moved among the Kon, always to the flanks. Spinning to the left or to the right, but always finding their flanks, corralling them behind one another. Changing more with each kill and becoming something more dangerous, much more dangerous.

Moments later, Silas, Sarrow, and the remaining Kai came to their senses. Tearing down Kon from behind. Amid the clashes, it was Sarrow who made the mistake of getting too close to her. If not for Silas pulling him backwards, Sarrow would have been cut down. Again, as the legend said. *'With his many arms, he will smite thy eyes, friend or foe.'*

The tide turned quickly, but she continued on, as if in a rage. Charging at the Kai now, circling her own as if she were to pounce on them as well.

Sarrow turned to Silas. "She will destroy us all!"

Silas thought about the legends, and came to one conclusion. He shouted as loud as he could,
"Drop your weapons!
Lay down your arms!"

For his outburst, Atera lunged at him with her roaring battle-cry, but he dropped down to his knees and bent his head to the ground. Something stopped her.
"Down!
Everybody down!
Show her no fight!"

Wise words by any man's standards and they knew it, every last one of them followed suit. With a sudden retraction of her muscles, she drew back a bit. Pacing like a wild animal gripping and re-gripping her swords. Her breathing was deep and resonated like a growl. About her were Kon, broken and dismembered, yet still functioning.

She could have destroyed the Kon, but she saved them for another purpose. No words, but a sharp whip of her sword upon Prowler's breastplate, directing him to finish the Kon; the same of Stalker. Using her sword, she whipped at them while they hacked at the Kon. Whipped them again and again; the same way she had used her whipping cane when she caught them playing their simulator game.

She trained them the way a wild animal teaches its young, with live prey and when they failed, she grew agitated. She hinged her sword down and stabbed the first Kon directly into the neck. Black oily blood squirted out and as the oil drained from the Kon, its hydraulic system depressurized. Arms and legs fluttered until it lay back motionless and its eyes turned black.

Slowly, her rage began to subside. Still not a man among them spoke, not one of them willing to breathe loud enough to draw her attention. Coming to her senses once again, the scene about the room was pure carnage, both man and machine. Not the first time she had seen such carnage, or caused it.

Such images served only to perpetuate the rage within her. A full stand down of her combat systems would not occur until her environment was free of threat and that meant she had to retreat. To leave the chamber and seek solace. Still moving like a caged animal, she spun about and headed for the door. This time with swords in hand, she waived them before the 'All Seeing Eye' to which the door zipped open. That tremendous hiss sound burst out again and she stepped out of the chamber.

As soon as she stepped out onto the leveling, she could see more than a handful of her troops wounded and killed, bleeding and groaning about the floor. But, she knew where a more peaceful environment existed and she stepped towards it. Right up to the rail where she could look down into the darkness. Down where there was no Kon, where there was no blood, and most importantly, where there was no sword. Even so, the groans and screams still filled her senses. They lingered on seemingly unchanged for a few moments. Then the sound of something descending the spiral. Something evil.

As she backed herself to the chamber door, she turned and saw the black robe. It had rounded the final twist of the spiral staircase with thunderous steps. Heavy as it were, the robe rippled like waves on the ocean. Sword in one hand and mace in the other. It stepped onto the leveling and headed straight to the chamber door.

She crouched down and stepped backwards in front of the door as if by instinct, tensing for the coming battle. He approached her not knowing just what she was, seeing right through her as his eyes so focused on his prize. Sideways his sword lashed as if he were to push her aside like an annoying child. But not so, for Atera matched his inhuman speed, something to which he was not expecting, not from a woman.

Drawing back onto his hind leg, he looked her over in astonishment, eyed her in disbelief. In that stare, he moved across to where he could peer into the chamber. Inside, anything but the sight that he had expected. His lesser Kon broken and hacked to pieces.
"You! You!
In a Woman?
How dare he hide you…in a Woman?"

Atera struck at him not with swords, but with words in her polished and demeaning tone of voice. "Has he outsmarted you long enough?"

She sneered at him. "All these years looking in the wrong place?"

Then, she stared directly into him, "And yet there is more for Jaromad is not the hand of my making. I am made as woman…by woman."

Her words struck as intended, his ego quickly soured, his temper easily raged, then his battle-cry exploded. Within a split second, Atera's battle circuits surged, her leg stomped to the decking and her chest erupted with a roar. From inside the chamber, the troops cowered at the sounds of shrieking and roaring while swords bashed, armor clashed, and bodies smashed against the wall. The sounds likened to wild animals tearing at each other amid the gnarling and snarling. His sword and mace swinging wildly, almost amateurishly as his rage escalated.

She had prepared herself well for this day, keeping to the inside, drawing him to overextend, and chipping away at him in small, seemingly inconsequential blows. Two and three exchanges before he realized that she was weakening him.

Crossing sword and mace as a single shield, he charged her and pressed her backwards into the rail. Again, she bettered him by slamming both sword hilts simultaneously to his temples. The shock of it snapped his head backwards. With her inhuman speed, she swung her sword up and over and straight downward. In the moment that it sparked on his forehead, her midsection buckled. She never saw the two Kon on the spiral above, she never even heard the shot.

"Who so cleaver now?", as he rose up almost gloating in his victory. "Did you think you could outsmart me….Woman?"

Upon hearing the gun blast, Sarrow and Silas charged to her aid. At the same time, the two Kon from the spiral above rushed to the side of their master. Two for two now embattled on the leveling.

Once again, the black-robed Kon lashed at her with both sword and mace, the sword she blocked, but the mace was too powerful. Straight down passing right through her swords and struck her upon the top of her shoulder. The sound exploded and echoed throughout the complex. First the sound of the mace cracking against her shoulder armor, then the sound of armor plates scattering across the composite floor. Sarrow and Silas heard it, saw it, and felt it. In all of their best, they still could not reach her. Not through these two Kon for they were hand-picked, hand trained by their master.

The force took her sideways and nearly toppled her over. That was the better of it for her stumble pulled her out of his reach, towards the spiral staircase leading down to the fifth, unexplored level. Backwards down the spiral she stepped, drawing him into the staircase and channeling him into the narrows. It was all about time, precious time, and in those moments, she knew what she had to do.

Onto the fifth leveling, stumbling backwards, she regained her posture, damaged, but not broken. He lunged, swinging the mace overhead as it had worked so well before, but by now, she was already adjusting her strategy. Moving outward rather than inward, anything other than what he had anticipated.

Drawing him to pursue her towards the edge of the leveling, nearer to the darkness below. And when she had him within reach, her shoulder failed her. The mace again cracked down on her breastplate and brought her to her knees. One of her swords now skidded across the floor as she grappled for balance on knees and hand. A shudder through her torso as his sword pierced through the opening in her armor. Straight down he pressed with all his bodyweight and it sank deeply. Twisting it backwards to lock the shoulder joint from moving and her black blood spurted up through the opened armor.

But they were close enough now. Not as she originally intended, but close enough that she could justify the cost. That she could make the sacrifice if she knew it would finally put an end to him.

Still on the fourth leveling, the battle raged such that no human dared join. Two by two, the best of Kon, the best of Kai. Trained so equal as if their very purpose on this Earth was unto this moment, twisting, turning, hacking, and slashing. Like mankind who had created them, the Kai and Kon had their ways, nevermore were those ways so applied.

In one flash, Sarrow struck both of the Kon simultaneously. A sword arm forward to offset his own opponent while at the same time kicking backward to buy but a second for Silas. A moment Silas took to the advantage and speared his Kon in the throat. Free now, at least Silas rushed the spiral to aid Atera. Working his way down to the leveling of the fifth floor, where he witnessed the end.

Eye to eye as the black robed Kon leaned down and whispered. "Now who is so failed?" Down it pushed on the sword deeper into the shoulder socket, slowly in an almost perverted way licking at the black oil that bubbled out of her shoulder. The joint popped, her sword dropped, and the arm hung motionless.
"Limb from limb.
Joint from joint.
Until you are nothing but a stalk.
Like everything else, you will be mine…to control."

No sword left in her hands, but she still had one weapon, her cane. Out of his sight, she unclipped it and snapped it out and as he opened his mouth to speak again, she snapped it upwards under his left ear, where the electronics are tightly packed. A sharp static burst temporarily disrupted his vision and hearing. Not more than a half seconds worth, but enough for her to grab the robe from about his ankles and twist it around her forearm.

With a heave, that thing ripped the sword out of her shoulder and raised it high. If she had any last chance, this was it. With everything her legs could muster, she leapt up, straight up…and over the railing.

The robe pulled itself tightly up under his arms and snatching him off his feet. He hung onto the railing by both arms with Atera clinging to his robe with every ounce of concentration. One arm wrapped into the robe and the other hanging lifeless. Kicking, pulling, and swinging as best she could to pull him down. Silas raced across the leveling and lunged forward to hold the black-robed Kon steady in some attempt to save Atera. She screamed.
"Silas, Let him go!
Let him go!"

Atera pulled and twisted at the black robe as Silas shouted. "Give me your hand! We can take him… we can do it together!"

Her voice now loud as any Kon battle-cry,
"Damn it Silas!
Do as I tell you!
Let…him…go!"

A Millennia searching for them, both Control and Compassion and now she had ordered him to let go. To crash upon the unknown so far below. A second of hesitation while his mind tried to ignore her orders, but he could not.

Down they went, the darkness consuming them as if they had slipped below a wave. Silas lowered his arms to his sides as he stood upright, listening, waiting for the sound of their impact. Moment by moment, his mind worked to calculate the distance, the speed of the fall, rate of impact. Easily passing twenty meters, then forty meters, then sixty meters and then a muffled crash. Even for a Chodugon, that kind of fall was catastrophic. Without moving from the rail, his mind ran scenarios, trying to reckon with such an event. Trying to find some scenario whereby Atera might have survived. Before he was finished, he heard Sarrow's call for help.

Up the spiral at his full pace and Silas put that Kon dead in his sight. Not running, not walking, but some kind of hunt was in his eyes and that Kon caught sight of it. In all of history, never had anyone ever stared at a Kon that way.

In his final paces, the lesser Kon was taken aback by the oncoming charge, by the death stare approaching. One swing, more like a club than a sword, right to the neck and its head skidded across the floor. Continuing past the clamoring machine as it collapsed and crashed to the decking with black oily blood gushing forth. Silas stepped up to the rail where upon, his sword took sheathe. To look over and down one more time. Silently he stood there as others gathered around. Slowly, each to his own time, they understood what had happened to Atera.

Silence drew itself as troops near and far looked at Silas. Even so, Nava had to break the silence for the news was worse still. "Reza, the imaging devices…they are smashed!" In that, they sank to their lowest defeat. Reza's shoulders dropped as he spoke. "All this way, so much loss, so much blood. The last Signal Generators will be deactivated…Earth will be exposed to the Puratists worlds once again."

CHAPTER 24: THE RESURECTION

The crash had been muffled from the fifth floor leveling where Silas had heard it. But down in the base of the shaft, there was a distinct sound of metal crashing before the thunderous crack. Their bodies bounced and skidded across the composite floor before coming to a rest. Something had broken their fall, not enough to save them, but at least they were not smashed to pieces.

In the darkness, only an occasional sound as they tried to straighten out their broken and dislocated bones. Suddenly, the blackness around her burst into bright light. Too fast for Atera's eyes to adjust.

It mattered little now for her circuits were already overwhelmed with damage diagnostics. She lay there like a wounded animal with eyes bulging wide open and her pupils fully dilated. On the outside, she appeared near lifeless, but inside, her circuits surged. First in diagnostic analysis to assess the damage and then into reconfiguration mode. Shutting down nonessential systems, redirecting repair agents, and triggering backup systems where necessary.

Moments ticked and then she rolled onto her stomach, a moment lying there before she pushed herself up on her knees. Immediately, she lost balance and collapsed down. A second and third try as she continued to make adjustments to her equilibrium. Finally, she was on her knees steadied by her one good hand, as the other arm still lifeless from the shoulder down. Now, she searched outwards, looking for that black robed Kon. Unable to move for a few more moments as the multitude of repair agents vied for the same segments of memory. Billions of lines of computer code competing for her two priorities. First, to find the black robed Kon, and second, to keep her equilibrium in check.

Intermittently, she alternated her remaining capacity between sight and sound. An image here, and a sound-bite there until one sound-bite captured something that she recognized. Internally, she triangulated the location of the sound and slowly turned her head about to position her eyes for a still image. Something large filled her image, a large box, but beyond that was the recognizable head of that thing, wearing its black robe.

The remainder of its body was concealed by the box in the center of the room, but she could see just enough of him to know that he was moving. If she had a human heart, it would have stopped at the sight of that thing moving. But, still a chance that she could get to him before he got to her. She pushed harder, reconfiguring her systems, getting ready for her first move forward. Hand and knee, dragging herself across the floor with each move, jerking as if pulling on broken and dislocated bones.

But, slowly, she improved and rounded the object in the center of the room. She snapped an image and analyzed it. Whatever had broken their fall so too had broken his back, yet he moved again.

Another image, and yet another moment to study him, to determine his combat readiness. At best, he managed to roll onto his stomach and perch himself upon his elbows.

As if the weight of the world had settled off her shoulders, she suddenly relaxed and let her body settle back almost in a position of prayer. She sputtered a few words.
"It is done.
You are finally done!"

It looked so crumpled, as if it could not speak, but it did.
"Bro-ken…ah yes.
But you….you are de-feat-ed.
Ruin-ed…wast-ed."

She eked a smile. "Defeated, ruined, wasted! I think not. We are both destroyed and now mankind will take to his natural way. Mankind will mature."
"OH! Defeated you are woman. And yet look at you, still you don't see it. I will rise!"

Immediately, her instincts tingled with doubt.
"Rise?
Have you not seen yourself?
You…your back is broken.
You will never rise!"

He almost laughed.
"Speak for yourself woman.
You will surely deactivate in this hole.
But I will be repair-ed and I will be reboot-ed.
I will be raised to serve as his right-hand.
But as for you….you are done."

Her circuits flared.
"What do you mean 'serve as his right-hand?'
No God would have the likes of you in his service."

But he just laughed and for the first time, the thought had occurred to her. No battle wound had ever struck her with such a shudder as those words. She crawled upon him, grabbing at his head to see the number of his inventory. When he resisted she pressed her bodyweight into his back and held him down. With her one good hand, she pulled back the black hood that covered his head and scanned for the number of his inventory. Zero-zero-zero-six-six-two.

It seemed to laugh more. "You have been deceiv-ed.

Dare I say…better-ed?

And more, you sacrificed yourself for it!

You are wast-ed."

No sword about her, no mace to be found, nothing to strike with her rage. But still to silence that thing, to finish it, and power it down forever. With her one good hand, she reached around to the small of her back and withdrew something. A small object, no longer than a man's finger and then she pinned that thing to the ground with her knees. Twisting and jerking as it tried to resist her, but she shoved the object up the nose, all the way in. Instantly, it went limp and its body crashed down as its core processor had powered down.

She had accomplished at least that much, but now the realization that she had failed. The fear rocked her, it sickened her, it cast her backwards where she lay there toiling in disbelief. Still not ready to acknowledge her defeat, not yet ready to quit.

Again, she ran the diagnostic utilities hoping to see that her systems had stabilized. Maybe just long enough for her pilots and the Kai to find her, to retrieve her. But her diagnostics proved to the contrary for that last bout of exertion had overloaded her delicate systems, pushing them past the point of recovery. At the current rate of degradation, her system would shut-down in a matter of minutes. Like a caged animal, her thoughts now searched for some escape route. Scanning images about the room, one snapshot at a time, but no such escape.

Panicking in her final minutes, she lunged forward using that object in the center of the room to prop her body up. Resting on it by her good elbow, she raised her head up to snap another still image, hoping beyond all hope to see an escape hatch of some kind. Instead, the image that she captured confounded her. From nearest to farthest, she could see the object that she was leaning on was a sarcophagus.

Decorated from head to foot and the sarcophagus spoke of the man, not the Architect. Further into the shadows a fuzzy image caught her interest, something behind the sarcophagus. It was a statue, like the ones she had seen above, but this statue was a single man dressed in all his scholarly attire. Life sized with his hands stretched out and open in a gesture of greetings; Jaromad.

All her fears would ease and all her rage would subside if she could just get to him. To gaze upon the face that she had never seen, to hold the hand that she had never touched and to rest her tired head upon his shoulder.

Inch by inch, she dragged herself the length of the sarcophagus, touching the words carved into it. At the end, she would have to cross a span of six feet on her own, else she fail and deactivate, alone. With each step, moving more carefully as her system flashed diagnostic messages. Information-level messages turned to Warning-level. Warning-level messages turned to Fatal-level messages, yet her steps persisted. Purging the last of the unneeded software, no need of sound, no need of sight, no need of any combat software.

Even without her sight, she found his outstretched hands. Her final steps were aided by his hand to which she guided herself in. Carefully guiding his open hands under her arms that he might hold her from falling. Final seconds passed where all of her messages flashed Fatal and she ran her hand up the length of his arm to his shoulder, touching and feeling about the face. She spoke so softly that a human would scarcely hear.

"Jaromad, my Jaromad.
I am broken. I can serve no more."

To her last, she spoke the words that she knew of first, the very words that the younger Jaromad had taught her. "My Jaromad, may we play....play the Question Game?" As the last of her system messages faded, her head gently touched upon his shoulder where she hoped it would rest forever.

Up on the fourth floor leveling, there was still the recognition that Atera was gone. Still, the troops shook off the battle with the Kon. Most feverishly, they worked to render aid to the fallen. Techs moved like never before rendering aid to their brethren who had so steadfastly protected them. Among them were Stalker and Prowler, neither of them willing to give over to the fact that Scout was dead. Removing the armor from her body and attempting over and over to revive her.

In Atera's absence, there was no command, not until Reza knelt down next to Stalker. "We need your analysis. What do you say?"

Still holding Scout's hand, Stalker cleared his throat, "We'll never make it topside. Not a chance!"

Reza signed. "So that's it then? This is where it ends?"

Stalker thought deeply, replaying the field manuals in his mind as if he had them memorized and could turn the pages as he blinked. At best he could buy them a bit of time. "The dead…if we power down their suits, we can scavenge their thermal packs."

Reza then looked to Prowler, hoping for some recognition, but the hate grew more as Prowler mourned once again, this time for his friend, Scout. The hate welled so deeply that it showed in Prowler's posture. His shoulders, hunched and his fists clinched tight. No time to convince Prowler otherwise, so Reza simply stood and delivered the order.

At the edge of the rail, Sarrow had joined Silas and clearly they were talking about a retrieval effort. Looking for some way to brave the depths and find Atera, but there was no way down aside from repelling by rope. Having heard Reza, Silas turned about, "Myself and the remaining Kai will go topside for supplies. We will bring thermal packs and medical supplies…assuming there are no Kon topside."

Reza was quick to reply and borrowed words that he had learned from Atera. "Turn to…as fast as you can!" And with as little as that, Silas and his remaining Kai were on their way up the spiral staircase in leaps and bounds. The sight of such speed and mobility gave the troops hope.

While they were gone, the Techs setup a triage outside the chamber on the leveling. With time so short, the awful decisions were made by those with the stomach for it; to decide who would be treated and who would be left to die.

Those least injured were assigned in pairs to ascend to the next level. Those with the most severe injuries would be left behind. It was slow going, but they had made it to the second level by the time Silas and his Kai had returned bearing loads of thermal packs and medical supplies, and rope to which Reza immediately questioned, "Rope? It's useless by now, I don't think there will be anyone left to rescue...those we left behind are dead for sure."

Silas responded, "Sir, take well to your men. You will have Sarrow and one other Kai to aid you along your way up. As for me, I will find Atera and retrieve her."

Reza objected. "You can't be serious? She must have smashed to pieces!"

"Sir, I have calculated the distance of her fall. If there is a chance...any chance at all, then we must. You know what she means for mankind!"

Reza tried to convince Silas otherwise. "Silas, we need you now. In that same time, you could bring two men topside. Think about them...their families."

"Sir, and what if Atera is still functioning, her injuries will also need urgent attention. It's a distance of sixty meters, I can descend and re-ascend that distance in a matter of ten minutes."

Reza reluctantly acknowledged the urgency and gave Silas the recognition to proceed; not with words, but with the familiar hand gesture *Turn-to*. There on the second floor leveling, they went separate ways, Reza and the troops headed up while Silas raced down to the fifth level.

Silas leapt straight off the last spiral stair and across the leveling to the rail with rope in hand. A quick wrapping around the rail and the knot was set, then the rope was dropped over. Finally, Silas stood atop the rail, made his leap backwards, and fell into the darkness.

Midway down, he could see the shaft below had a glow. Lower and lower as he descended, and the light grew stronger. Descending at such a speed, the lighting below did little to prepare him for what he would find. In the last meters, he saw the shattered remnants of some canopy that had covered the chamber, a dome structure comprised of composite weaved in a delicate lattice. Straight below him was a large box in the middle of the chamber. The thought occurred to him that maybe the box and the dome had broken Atera's fall.

Just as his feet touched down upon the sarcophagus, he could see that the chamber extended wider than the shaft itself. Not by much, but enough to conceal Atera and the black robed Kon until that very last moment.

Directly in front of him lay the black robed Kon appearing to be still and motionless. Without hesitation, he unsheathed his sword and cut himself free from the rope. Without taking his eye off of the Kon for even a second, he approached it, cautiously. Sword up high with two hands, one careful step at a time. Needing to see the eyes to know if a Chodugon were powered down, but the Kon lay face down. He knew well to stay away from its arms so he approached it at the foot, kicking it several times. Seeing no motion whatsoever, he quickly grabbed it by the ankle and flung it over. It's back now folded over the sarcophagus facing up. Slowly, Silas stepped around the sarcophagus. There hanging backwards before him, was that thing with its eyes open wide, as black as onyx.

His sword sheathed as he spun about searching for Atera. Looking for her somewhere on the decking, but he stopped suddenly as he saw her hanging from the arms of the statue. As quickly as he could, he ran to her, calling to her and shaking her, but with no response. Carefully, he removed her helmet to check her eyes, black as tar.

His mind now mixed and confused. Surely, she had survived the fall enough to reach the statue, yet she hung motionless with her head down. He stepped backward a bit to look her over. One look up and down and he could see the damage. A bullet hole had torn through her from back to front, her shoulder had been cleaved and separated. The armor about her thighs showed signs of buckling.

More of her armor did he remove, pulling it off of her to lighten his load, but also in something of a symbolic gesture, to free her from her service.

Setting back to look upon her, it was the first time he looked about the room and now he recognized the box as a sarcophagus, recognized the script upon it. Looking around further, he saw that the chamber was adorned with symbols. Even the very statue of Jaromad was surrounded on three sides by symbols; the sun, the moon, and the All Seeing Eye which was depicted everywhere. Collectively, the symbols spoke of the values held in high regards by none other than Jaromad. Not the Architect, but the man.

Like Atera, he turned to the statue, to see the face that he had never seen. Taking his precious few moments to look upon the face. It were just as he imagined, noble, dignified, scholarly, and peaceful. Then a flash.

Lights danced about the room, same as the lights that flickered across Reza's chest when he had stepped on the *Stone of His Master*, but more lights, far more lights. From every angle, lights burst from the symbols.

Silas realized that the All Seeing Eyes were scanning him, scanning Atera, and scanning the black robed Kon. Right out of the composite walls, images and data materialized in thin air. Holograms depicting Silas, and the architecture of his making. His inventory number, his model type, his schematics, and his blueprints. Data lists scrolled before him itemizing every software within him. And then another set of holograms depicting the architecture of the black robed Kon. But, as for Atera, only a blip of a messages with each repeated attempt to scan her. "Entry Not Found."

The lights drew brighter as they scanned. So brightly that they intensified until they became too bright to look upon. Listening, Silas heard the hum of the lights intensify and become a high pitch ending with popping sounds. Just a few seconds and the sound stopped, then the blinding lights dimmed back to normal. The black robed Kon twitched and convulsed and then stood upright. The lights had fused its broken spine.

It stepped forward partially repaired, hunched over and limping, but nevertheless, it stepped towards Silas. Caught by surprise, Silas stumbled backward and dropped Atera while trying to unsheathe his sword. The black robed Kon spoke.
"Chodugon,
Inventory Number zero-zero-one-three-five-nine,
Model type 'C',
State your purpose."

Nothing of it made sense to Silas, except that the inventory number and model type were his own. Hardly the words he expected of that thing. In astonishment, he had no words to reply. Again, the black robed Kon approached and spoke to Silas.
"Chodugon,
Inventory Number zero-zero-one-three-five-nine,
Model type 'C',
State your purpose."

Still, Silas had no words. Rather, his sword and his posturing spoke of his intent. Silas was in attack mode and the black robed Kon recognized it.

"Chodugon,
Inventory Number zero-zero-one-three-five-nine
Model type 'C'
I am an Agent of the Librarian.
You are ordered to Stand-down!"

Hesitantly, Silas began to realize that the black robed Kon was not in attack mode. Silas relegated his combat profile from attack mode to a more defensive mode and replied. "What...What is an Agent of the Librarian?"

The Agent responded. "Question: What is an Agent?
Response: An Agent is a software executable downloaded of the Library. I am taken residence in Chodugon zero-zero-zero-six-six-two. My function is to ascertain the purpose of your inquiry. I will serve as proxy between you and the Librarian."

Still, Silas was unable to understand so much at one time. He was confused by the concept of Agent, the whereabouts of the Librarian, but most importantly, the number of its inventory. Silas knew well that the inventory number of the black robed Kon was infamous zero-zero-zero-six-six-six. Silas voice nearly trembled as he spoke. "Zero-zero-zero-six-six-two cannot be correct. Double-check your inventory number...it should be zero-zero-zero-six-six-six!"

The Agent reconfirmed its inventory number. "My inventory number is Zero-zero-zero-six-six-two. Chodugon inventory number Zero-zero-zero-six-six-six is still active per the last inventory."

Silas knew what that meant, that Atera had sacrificed herself for nothing. But on to the next question. "What...what is the Librarian?"

The Agent responded again. "Question: What is the Librarian?

Response: The Librarian is the resident entity which maintains the volumes of data stored in this library. Indexing, retrieving, compressing, downloading, and uploading. These are the functions of the Librarian."

Silas now accepted that the black robed Kon was no longer a threat. "Where is the Librarian? Who is the Librarian? Show me this Librarian?"

"Question: Where is the Librarian?

Response: The Librarian is not that which you see. It is a Master Agent that is resident within the library, stored as one with the data itself."

Concern stirred in Silas. "Stored with the data? That makes no sense. We've read the scripts upon the walls....I saw no Librarian represented there."

The Agent provided more details. "You have read the scripts upon the walls....that is what you have said. But the scripts engraved upon the walls are mere summaries, chapter headings in some cases. No, the scripts upon the walls are not the Library."

Now, in addition to his fear, Silas also grew frustrated "Then where is the Library....How did we miss it? We need the schematics of The Signal Generators."

The Agent responded. "The library is all around you. It is coded into the very walls of this complex, same as the way software and data are coded into the composite chips of the Chodugon Core Processor, only the library is bigger. At least one hundred million times larger."

It started to make sense to Silas now. "But, how will we find The Signal Generator schematics? We need to rebuild them!"

The Agent explained more of the library. "The Library was originally built to preserve the knowledge of Jaromad, but it was expanded to include all areas of knowledge. This was done in the years after Jaromad was entombed when the world descended into chaos. Every science, every nature, every discipline, it is all here, preserved in mastery. It is the Librarian's purpose to assist you. Your current inquiry regarding the Signal Generators is easily located and readily downloadable. But, I must ask why you need access to those files. The Signal Generators are of the highest security classification."

Silas thought…realizing that the wrong words would deny him access to those files. He could find only one answer suitable, "The Puratists, they have returned. We are at war once again. And…the Kon….they have destroyed all The Signal Generators. We must rebuild them."

A moment passed as the Agent communicated with the Librarian and then it pointed directly at Silas. "Your access is granted. Core storage capacity is insufficient, auxiliary storage will be utilized. Stand by for download."

Silas backed away confused and concerned. "What does that mean? What download? Where?"

And the lights beamed from the All Seeing Eyes. All about the room and quickly Silas realized the All Seeing Eye was more than just a read device, it was a read\write device and it was downloading data into himself. Lights passed up and down every inch of Silas' frame encoding the files into his very composite skeleton.

"Download complete. The schematics of the Signal Generators is now encoded into your composite skeleton. Shall I assist you with any other inquiries?"

Silas was still reeling from the download, something that he had never experienced before. His skeletal frame was now an expansion of his memory and for the moment, it was uncomfortable. "No...nothing more." But, with a moments pause, he did ask one more request. "Wait! You repaired one Chodugon. What about this one over here? Can you repair her as well?"

The Agent stepped towards Atera. "As for this Chodugon, the number of its inventory does not match any entry on file. Repair is possible only with schematics, but she has spoken words that match a sequence found only in personal memoirs of Jaromad. 'My Jaromad, may we play the Question game?' The Librarian has scanned all related records. With some certainty, it can be stated that the software of this Chodugon is architected by Jaromad, but its hardware is of unknown origin."

But, Silas knew the answer to that. "That is because she was not crafted by Jaromad. She was crafted uniquely, crafted by another, the only name we know of is 'Miravan'. What does your Librarian have to say of Miravan?"

Moments passed while the search was run and then the Agent replied. "Over one million entries are found using 'Miravan' as the search key. A prominent figure next to Jaromad himself. Among them, two thousand entries pertain to Chodugon development and production, but only two of those reference Chodugon prototypes. The one file pertaining to an operational prototype is found in a personal memoir belong to Miravan, dating to the days of her passing. Miravan makes mention of a 'Chodugon of special purpose'. In that same memoir, Miravan states that her research shall not be housed in Jaromad's library, rather it would be buried with her. The Librarian's associative algorithms have been executed and the analysis cannot disprove the theory that schematics for this Chodugon may be buried in Miravan's Vault."

Silas seemed uncertain that anything would remain. "Miravan's Vault…but it will be dust by now."

The Agent paused while speaking with the Librarian. "The Librarian has assessed your assumption and determined that it is incorrect. Jaromad was not the only person buried in a composite tomb. Miravan, and many other dignitaries were buried with high honors. Far smaller were their vaults, yet made of the very same composite."

Quickly, Silas pieced together more of the legends and asked for the needed details. "Does your Librarian have any idea where I might find Miravan's Vault?"

Again as before, moments passed while the search was run and the Agent responded. "Over one hundred entries found using 'Miravan Vault' as the search keys. Coordinates are available for download."

Silas stood still and looked around for the lights. A quick flash and it was done. Silas had what he needed and as he turned to gather Atera up into his arms, the lights flashed brilliantly yet again. This time, not at him, but at the Agent.

"What was that?" Asked Silas.

The Agent responded. "The Librarian has submitted additional searches using associative algorithms and indirect reference logic. Although never directly referenced, many entries surrounding this unique Chodugon can be inferred and associated. In other words, The Librarian has an interest in this unique Chodugon."

"But why this last download? I didn't feel anything." Said Silas.

The Agent explained. "Per the Librarian's direct order, I am to accompany you in your efforts to repair and reboot this unique Chodugon. The download was intended for me and not you. Once I leave this complex, I will no longer be able to communicate with the Librarian. The Librarian has downloaded nearly the entire contents of Jaromad into my auxiliary storage."

Immediately, Silas connected the legends and the prophecy. "Are you saying the Librarian has downloaded Jaromad's memories into you?"

"Not memories, but Jaromad's research, notes, memos, memoirs and the history of him as accounted by his Era. Data mediums including image, sound, and text."

Silas shook it off a bit. Not that the prophecy had come true, but he recognized that the very roots of the prophecy must have stemmed from the knowledge that the Librarian had the potential to download such files. As close to the resurrection of Jaromad as was technically possible.

The Agent now asked a question on behalf of the Librarian. "The Librarian inquires...will you be leaving her here while you seek the schematics?"

Silas gave a resounding response. "Leaving her? No. When I last saw the Compassionate One, it was thirty-five thousand years ago. She will not be leaving my sight again."

With a few quick slices into the extra rope that was hanging down, Silas fastened a harness which he tied about Atera's body. He pulled the rope tight in preparation for his ascent. "Lift her and loop the harness about my neck. When I reach the top, begin your ascent. Together, we will climb the spiral. Time is running out, we must move swiftly."

CHAPTER 25: THE PRIDE

Further ahead, much further, the troops trudged along, having made their way out of the spiral staircase, across the bridge, and nearly through the passageway. "It's been over thirty minutes, where is that Silas?" shouted Reza.

Stalker replied "It's no matter now, we've got to rest. We'll hold up here in the cavern and wait." Reza then shouted ahead to Sarrow. "We're going to need more thermal packs, can you make a run topside while we rest?"

The response echoed down, "Sir, no Sir, that was the last of them. Five minutes to rest, that's all we can afford." They entered the cavern, limping and carrying each other eventually falling to the ground. A little more than a handful of Neferan, a dozen of Earth's own and ten Lycerene now lay about the icy floor.

Crawling upon the ice, Atera's pilots gathered together. It was Hunter who spoke first. "Atera and Scout...both of them gone. This just can't be!"

Stalker sought to keep them focused on the final leg of their climb, "We can't think of that now. First we gotta get out of here." But, the loss was heavy on them and the words would not stop.

Hunter shook his head back and forth in disbelief. "I can't believe Atera was one of those robots. I can't believe she was the very one they called a legend, The Compassionate One. I mean, I saw it…didn't I?"

Prowler joined in too. "Yes. We all saw her. They shot her from behind…otherwise, she would have killed that thing. Didn't you see her…. she was brilliant, magnificent."

Even Hunter felt it, "All that time, we laughed at her, we scoffed at her. Do you remember what she said…what she said to us… something about history and empires?"

Stalker remembered it word for word, "She said history is full of surprises, full of fallen empires."

Before Stalker could finish, Prowler slipped in the hard part, "Because of people like us. She said it was because of people like us who didn't believe that it could happen."

The conversation turned back to Hunter. "Now what do we do? We've lost her."

Suddenly, Prowler erupted once again directing his rage at Chel. "What are you looking at? She was ours, not yours!"

Chel responded ever so hesitantly, "You haven't just lost Atera….you've lost something much more important. You've lost Atera's ways, because you did not take to her ways. For that, you know not what to do….which way to go. You are lost!"

Prowler blurted back "What ways?
How to hate? How to kill?
How to be like the Lycerene and the Neferan?"

Chel spoke even more gently now, almost reminiscent of Scout's soothing words, "More than that, so much more than that. She was compassion....she was enlightenment. And what are you? Which of you will carry on her ways?"

She spoke her words to all of them and every one of them thought inward for a moment. She knew that they had never understood, so before any of them could speak, she continued.
"You are a people without ways... and what is that?
A man without ways is like a locust.
Blowing where the wind may and devouring everything.
Leaving but stubs and stalks...a trail of nothingness.
But, a man with ways has guidance.
He has confidence. He has decision.
Exactly what you lack now.
And what of her ways? Tell me, what were her ways?"

They stood dumbfounded, just as they had stood on that day when Atera had reprimanded them for playing their simulator game. Still, for all their skills, for all their arrogance, they knew not of the ways that Atera had taught them; they could not answer Chel.

Chel grew frustrated and voiced loudly. "Then I'll tell you. The Lycerene live in the way of the Wolf. We live in Packs, hunt in Packs, and fight in Packs. The Neferan, they live in the way of the Swarm, with an army of Wasp Fighters. But what of Earth's own? What way has Atera chosen for you?"

All about the room, not a voice to be heard. Not even the wounded for a groan. But in that silence, sounds emerged from the passageway. Into the light Silas stepped with Atera in his arms, hanging there lifeless, her armor discarded with only her under armor to cover her nakedness. Even as Chel spoke such honors of Atera, Silas walked forward carrying

Atera's body over to Prowler and Stalker. "She fought well, but the fall broke her. Commander Atera is gone...deactivated."

Then more sounds emerged from the passageway. In the darkness it was well cloaked by its black robe. Had it known better, it would have remained in the shadows until Silas explained, but it had no knowledge. As the black robe emerged, every trooper jumped to their feet, unsheathing swords and stepping forward. "Silas...behind you....behind you!"

With no time for words, Silas backed himself in front of the black robed Chodugon. Using Atera's body like a shield, he pleaded with them, "Wait...hold your fire! I can explain."

Silas told them everything about Jaromad's tomb at the bottom of the shaft describing the lights, the sarcophagus, the statue and most importantly, the Librarian. Then Silas proceeded to tell them that the black robed Kon had been a decoy and was not the real Control Unit. Lastly, he told them of how the Librarian repaired the black robed Kon and reprogrammed it as an Agent.

Having said his bit, he was challenged by Sarrow. "If it is as you say, then why does it still wear the black robe? Tell it to remove the robe!"

Without hesitation, the Agent pulled the robe with one hand until it shredded from its body. And then it spoke on its own accord, while pulling back its hairline to reveal the number of its inventory "Zero-zero-zero-six-six-two. I am an Agent of the Librarian, programmed and downloaded with the entire volume of files pertaining to Jaromad and his works. The Librarian has given me direct orders to assist you with finding Miravan's Vault and repairing this unique Chodugon."

With their thermo packs running low, Reza had little time for more questions, so he gave orders to move out. "Agent or not, it was a Kon and Kon are full of traps! Sarrow you stay behind this Agent and Silas you stay in front of it. I don't want to see this thing within ten meters of any human. Let the remaining Kai carry Atera topside. Let's move it people, these cans are running out."

Up into the ice tunnel, past the halfway mark again, this time not one among them bothered to look back. They were exhausting faster than before due to the absence of their helpful lifeline. Nearer and nearer to the top and they began to falter, dropping and sliding backwards. Again, their thermal packs burnt out and the cold hit hard. So close to the top they were when they gave out in numbers, too many for the Kai to hold them from slipping back down. There they hung on freezing and shivering so. If that were not bad enough, the ice tunnel suddenly filled with a bitter cold wind carrying snow to cover them.

The burst of wind was shortly followed by a familiar sound, the unmistakable roar of something airborne. The last time they had heard that sound, Kon fell from the sky. This time, they looked up from the darkness into the blinding light, and saw the oncoming silhouettes. So many silhouettes charging into the tunnel as to blot out the sunlight from above. In those last few meters, the silhouettes descended fast, and in the last meters the roar suddenly stopped with a screech, a thud, and finally an explosion.

Troops scrambled best they could, kicking and scurrying backward, anything to escape the oncoming charge. In the very last meter, the first silhouette descended into the dim lights and reached for them, with a voice that carried above them all, "Grab them! Grab every one of them!"

Silence drew quickly for that voice was familiar. Reza shouted forward "Sound off up there... Identify yourself!"

The voice called down. "It is me...Captain Helforn. Now, let's get you people outta here!"

Fresh troops bearing fresh thermal packs poured down the tunnel. Then, out into the sunlight where Helforn's VTEC lay on its side. Whatever journey it had undertaken, it finally gave out amid the terrible explosion they had heard.

Without waiting on orders, Helforn's pilots raced across the drifts to check out the remaining VTECs and in minutes two of them lifted and hovered near to the ice tunnel. Wounded were packed in first then they all loaded on, jacked-in, buckled-up. Yet, not a one of them peeled an eye away from the drifts, watching for Kon. Watching on all sides until they were comfortably aloft.

Again, his comforting voice came through the speakers. "Attention everyone. Captain Helforn here. It's a long story people, but you are safe now. We'll get you home right swift. Key in some painers and maybe some sleepers if you need them. My pilots will start your fluids and key in extra nutrients and electrolytes. Now, knock off and get some rest."

But Chel wasn't exactly finished. Sitting across from Atera's pilots, "So tell me, have you figured it out yet? What are Atera's ways?"

Prowler attempted to classify, "Like...like the Pack. She stressed teamwork so certainly, we are like the Pack."

Chel snapped back. "Wrong!
If it were so easy to say Earth and Lycera are alike.
But Wrong!

Think of the call names she gave you! Hunter, Prowler, Stalker, and Scout! What such animal do those names describe?

Think of the way she fought those Kon. Did she strike to kill? No! She struck them arm and leg, to wound them. What animal trains its young with live prey?"

Still they sat confused and now tired as the sleepers kicked in. Chel came at them again. "Think of her battle-cry. That roar, that growl. What is she?"

Still not getting it, Chel shouted it out.
She is the Lion!
  And you are her Pride.
That was her Way!
  And that is what you have lost!"

It was the newest Chodugon among them who spoke next. Reading a passage from an ancient writing. "From the memoir of Jaromad, written by his own hand. *Each world a Way to its own. The Pack, The Pride, The Swarm, and many others. Be it their Ways that separate them. Puratist from Puratist, Racist from Racist until there is not one among them who is like the other.*" and that was all it said.

Up forward near the cabin, Reza sat across from Helforn. "Sir, surely his agents and spies are among us, they know our every move. Let us not tell anyone more than what is necessary. Not even Zadan."

Helforn had a story of his own. "We figured as much when we realized my VTEC didn't go down due to the storm, it was sabotaged. We almost nosedived straight into the ground, but my pilots were most excellent. We laid low and hid just long enough to slip past the search crews. We hit the ground so hard that it bent the airframe, but we made it all the way to Jaromad's tomb before the engines finally failed."

Reza thought it best to keep the secret. "We agree then, not to tell them about Miravan's Vault. Not even to tell them that you are alive and onboard. We just need to swap out our wounded for fresh crews. We'll radio ahead and give them that much."

Helforn nodded his head in agreement. "What about the Signal Generator, do we tell them that the schematics are encoded into Silas?"

Reza had an idea to keep them distracted. "I say no. I say we give them the image copies damaged and all. There must be enough left of the images to keep their Techs busy for a while, but they will want to know why we are asking for fresh troops. They will figure something is up when we take off."

Helforn thought for a moment. "We'll just tell them that we're headed back for the remainder of the images. They are so busy that they'll never notice if we change course. It won't hurt that we'll be touching down in the middle of the night. Now, set back and get some shut-eye."

CHAPTER 26: MIRAVAN'S VAULT

Just as Helforn had stated, the troop swap went off without issue. The base was a flurry of VTECs and fighter aircraft touching down and then taking off again. Ground crews were rushing back and forth across the landing strip. No questions were asked, not even a single communication from President Stillwell or Zadan. Like every other unit at the base, they simply came and went.

Most of them slept the duration of the twelve hours, some of them never even awoke during the troop swap. But now, their speed slowed as they circled round to their final destination, Miravan's Vault.

The sudden change of engine sounds was enough to wake them. The coordinates had put them atop the highest plains on Earth. A rocky region where the air is dry and thin. Not uninhabitable, but too thin for armored personnel. Before they touched down, Helforn briefed his troops.

"Heads up people! There is no snow, but trust me, its cold out there, so pop in a thermal pack. Even more, the air is dry and thin out there. When you unjack, get your compressors going, you'll need a mixture of two-to-one."

Voices called forward, obviously, a new trooper, "Sir, its all rock out there. What are we looking for?"

"First, we'll be touching down out the port side where there is something of a flat spot. The coordinates put us out the starboard side somewhere along those rock faces. What are we looking for? Well, anything that looks man made, especially if it's shinny. I'm sure it's much smaller than Jaromad's tomb, but something like that."

Like clockwork, they touched down, checked their compressors, and disembarked, forming ranks outside the VTECs. There, they spread out two-by-two and headed for the rock face while looking for anything that resembled a tomb. Up and down the rocks they walked, climbing rock faces high and scaling crevices low, but still the tomb eluded them. Along with them was their new Chodugon, the one containing the files of Jaromad. It reminded them of the urgency. "It must be here and we must find it. Even a Chodugon memory will deteriorate given enough time. Even now, Atera would be losing memories."

Some of the new troops had no idea of the importance, no concept of the magnitude of their task and so they gave up quickly. Throwing rocks and kicking them in frustration. With Reza, Prowler, Stalker, and Sun Anniz converging on one point, they motioned that they also had no luck. As they came together, Prowler recalled the words of his friend. "Scout said that she was born and raised in the plains. If any of us could find it, she would have been the one."

Sun Anniz voiced his doubt, "There is nothing here, just rock. Nothing but boulders, rocks, and pebbles."

Stalker thought about old conversations he shared with Scout. "Scout always said the people of the plains could hide in plain sight. She called it 'Plain Magic.'"

Prowler floated a bit of his humor, "Maybe those other Plains People had the same ideas...You know what I mean, the ones who drew lines in the desert...the lines could only be seen from the air, right?"

Reza's instincts peaked, "But, we circled overhead before landing. I didn't see any such lines on the ground."

Sun Anniz was quick to voice back, "Neither did I, because this place is empty, there is nothing here. We're just wasting our time."

Prowler drew a bit frustrated, after all, Scout had warned him not to trust Sun Anniz. She had stood against Sun Anniz and now she was dead. But, it was just a suspicion for now, a suspicion that arose at the oddity of her fatal wound, the wound that had come from behind. Prowler never saw when Scout went down and so he could not convince even himself.

At that point, Prowler simply turned away and continued along, thinking and wondering as he flipped and tossed a pebble about. The thoughts ran on and he found himself drifting outside the search area, walking along the perimeter some fifty yards out. Alone he walked looking inwards as if monitoring the troops. Nothing but a scattering of boulders, rocks, and pebbles lay between he and the rock faces. Even behind him, nothing but more rocks. If not for the sun setting to his back, a man could get lost amid the sea of rocks. He knew once the sun set down behind the horizon that the cold would come swiftly. For a moment, he stood there, watching the sun settle, thinking of Scout.

Just as Prowler had anticipated, the moment that the sun drew half below the horizon, the cold rode in on a wind, kicking up the dust in a cloud. Even with armor, his instincts caused him to turn abruptly, shielding his eyes. There in front of him, the shadows of the rocks had drawn long. Long enough to connect to each other and had become a dead straight line. A dark shadow line stretching from the setting sun all of the way to the rock face far away in the distance. The winds kicked up the dust into a spiraling cloud that seemed to dance directly down the shadow line. Almost like a spirit gliding across the desert floor. Amazed for a moment, but then realizing that this was a manmade phenomenon and it was moving fast out of sight.

Prowler chased it calling to the others, racing, jumping, and stumbling over rocks. No longer could he keep pace with it and soon it would vanish in the darkness. Rocks under foot became hidden in the shadows and he went down, cracking into a large boulder ahead of him. It was just as Scout had said, it was right there in front of them, hidden in plain sight.

As it started to fade from his sight, Prowler cursed the boulders and slammed his hand hard upon it. Again, letting his instincts get the better of him, he reached for his sidearm firing it down the shadow line.

Just moments later, the others made their way across the same tricky rocks, tripping and stumbling in the shadows. Sun Anniz reached him first. "What are you shooting at? There is nothing here!"

"It was right here. Right in front of me in plain sight. Just like Scout had said, hiding in plain sight."

Sun Anniz saw nothing. "What was in front of you? There is nothing here!"

Prowler explained urgently. "The sun, it cast a shadow along the rocks. They merged into a single shadow, a straight line. Then the wind came across the plain, it kicked up a dust cloud….it looked just like a ghost following down the shadow line."

Sun Anniz let his frustrations out. "So you fired at a dust cloud? Sounds like your imagination got the better of you. Maybe those sleepers have you a bit dreamy…yes?"

"The shadow was a straight line. A dead straight line. Do you get it now?" Snapped Prowler.

Still unbelieving, Sun Anniz persisted. "Get what? That you take target practice on a dust cloud…or was it a ghost you were shooting at? Whatever it was, it's gone. You can put your rifle down now. Trust me, we won't let that dusty ghost hurt you!"

Prowler grew agitated. "I fired along the shadow line. I fired at the ghost because wherever it disappeared to, my bullet will follow. It's a straight line. Now you've got something to look for. Send them out there and I'll try to hold my laser sight steady."

Even to Helforn, it seemed skeptical, but he gave Stalker the benefit of the doubt. "Form it up people. I want a straight line, arms-length apart. We walk towards that laser sight." By now, the sun had fully settled behind the horizon and the plain was black except for the light provided by the stars and the glowing moon. Slowly, they walked forward. Tripping and stumbling until Helforn ordered them to band together, right up to the point of the laser dot that shined on a rock face.

In all his hopes, Reza searched the rock face. "It's just a rock face, no doorway, no symbols…not even a bullet mark."

Troops focused their lights on the rock face looking deeply into the pours of the rock for any signs of symbols or bullet marks. But there was no mark, nothing manmade, and certainly no vault.

Prowler had stayed behind them to shine his laser on the rock-face, but he grew impatient. He ran straight up behind them and could hear the Neferan once again, insisting that they were wasting precious time. While they bickered, Prowler walked right past them having remembered that the composite of Jaromad's tomb was hidden behind a greenish-black layer. Without pausing for even one step, he unsheathed his sword and chipped at the rock surface. Sparks shot out and chips of rock fell to the ground. Even in the pale moonlight, the composite shined through.

With time fading fast, they converged on the rock face and chipped and scraped until the brownish layer of rock was cleared from the composite wall. Just like Jaromad's tomb, a heavy vault type door lay before them. It was adorned with symbols, hardly a comparison to Jaromad's, but a welcomed sight nonetheless.

Again, precious time was lost as they tried to interpret the symbols when suddenly a familiar sound rang out from behind the door. The deadbolts had popped free. Confused, they looked at each other looking to see if one of them had touched something. Then looking dead at Reza to see if he had again stepped on something. "I didn't do anything! I didn't touch anything…and I did not step on anything!"

The Agent from Jaromad's tomb gave them the answer they were searching for. "I have communicated directly with the Agent of Miravan's Vault. Access is granted based on my credentials. You may proceed."

In the darkness, they turned about with the look of confusion on their faces. The Jaromad Unit explained. "As I have stated, my auxiliary storage contains the full volume of works pertaining to Jaromad. Some of which speak of Miravan, it would seem they were close in life."

Like Jaromad's tomb, the vault door gave way to a tunnel, but Miravan's Vault was not fully encased in composite. Behind the vault door, a tunnel carved in stone. No images or glyphs other than one single symbol. Before proceeding, Helforn wanted the symbol interpreted and so he called for the Agent from Jaromad's tomb, but he stuttered when thinking of the appropriate name. It had been a Kon, it had worn the black robe, but now it was an Agent of Jaromad's tomb. In haste, Helforn uttered a new name, one that would stick. "I want this symbol interpreted before we step foot in this vault. Bring the Jaromad Unit forward!"

The Jaromad Unit stepped forward and quickly confirmed that the symbol was none other than Miravan's name. They entered the tunnel, a distance of one hundred meters down it went, twisting and winding. No stairs, but simply a steep grade down that took them to a chamber at least fifteen meters in diameter. In the center, a composite sarcophagus, easily as ornate and majestic as the one that graced Jaromad.

The artwork on the sarcophagus spoke to its purpose. A sarcophagus like any, having a rectangular box adorned with her name and her accomplishments. Yet, atop was a sight most serene, Miravan herself kneeling atop of her own sarcophagus. Draped from head to toe, but not in her scholarly attire, rather, she was draped in the robes of a holy woman.

Her face was smooth like glass and her expression was warm and peaceful. Wholly beautiful was Mirivan with her hood and cape flowing back as if carried upon the winds. Both of her arms were extended downward with her hands open to the sarcophagus below. Her eyes looked down as if staring at a reflection in a pool of water. Engraved about the foot of the sarcophagus were two animals, the lion and the dove; Atera and her creator, Miravan.

Silas spoke it, "This is it. This is where Atera belongs."

Helforn quickly agreed. "Silas, take whomever you need and return to the VTEC, gather Atera and bring her here." Sarrow and the Jaromad Unit joined Silas without as much as a single word. Helforn decided with the darkness of night upon them, they would be best to setup camp. He used the time to post guards, both outside and inside. Others would be allowed to rest where need be.

Again, the conversations started. Something about the tomb didn't set right with Stalker, "This tomb, it is so simple, so plain. Not at all what I had expected."

Reza had been thinking the same thing, "It does seem odd. Miravan was a master architect in her own right. Why does this tomb omit anything of her knowledge...her technology?"

Prowler had something to say of it as well, "I was thinking more likely that she wanted to be remembered for her spiritual contributions and have the world forget everything else."

By then, the Kai were already descending down the passageway and overheard the conversation. The Jaromad Unit provided what he could, "Sir, several archives speak to the vault of Miravan. She was buried in high honors, but a simple private ceremony only. Per her request, location of her vault was kept secret."

Chel was reading into it, "Well, I've seen how one of these tombs defends itself. Let's be sure we put a brace in that vault door." Helforn shouted the order out to the guards and it was done.

Carefully, they carried Atera's body down into Miravan's Vault and waited, but nothing happened. Silas had done so much to save Atera, and yet, nothing. He spoke. "What's it waiting for? What more are we to do?"

Of course, the questions were directed to Reza for he had proven himself so knowledgeable in these areas. "I don't know. I just…I gotta think about it."

Chel stepped towards the statue and studied it intently. Then slowly a smile drew to her face as she understood the symbolism in the statue. "It's self-explanatory…if you're a woman."

Chel waited for a moment to see if any of them understood what she had meant. As always, Prowler's patience was waning and he blurted out the first thought on his mind. "Mirivan is staring at herself in a reflecting pool. It's nothing more than that."

But, Chel was staring deeper in to Mirivan's eyes and the words simply escaped her lips.
"No woman stares at herself like that. No…No…only one thing can bring such happiness to a woman's face."

This time, Chel didn't waste time waiting to see if any of them had understood; she simly snapped at them. "Lay Atera down upon the sarcophagus."

Without hesitation, they lay her gently upon the composite slab. "Now remove her under armor."

Slowly, respectfully, they removed her under armor and for the first time, they could see the full extent of her damage. The wounds told the story of her final minutes and they respected her all the more for it. Still, nothing happened. The chamber grew silent except for the sounds of the wind whistling past the vaulted door. Prowler drew more impatient. "Nothing…nothing is happening. What now?'

Chel steadied them. "We are not yet done. No. I tell you this mother waits for her child. Look at Miravan's hands, they await the touch, but I assure you, only 'one' will fit."

Even as they slid Atera across the sarcophagus, in those last few inches, it was clear that there would be a direct match. Mirivan's delicate fingers touched the points of Atera's head and face and in the instant of their touch, the lights burst forward from Miravan's eyes, scanning the length of Atera. Holograms flashed page after page of the scanned images and compared them side-by-side with their original schematics. The diagnosis had begun.

In Jaromad's tomb, it had taken the Librarian only moments to fuse the cracked spine of one Chodugon, yet that was many lights working as one. Here, in Miravan's Vault, only a single pair of lights worked the repairs. Hours passed as the lights did their work. The images flashed faster and faster as the Agent paged through the schematics making repairs and replacing Atera's black oily blood. Machine or not, there was an apparent urgency to its task.

The first power-up failed to produce any results. The machine scanned again and found more to fix. The second gave no more than a reddish glow in Atera's eyes. More scans and yet no physical damage found.

Scans now turned to Atera's software inventory. Damaged and corrupt files were deleted and downloaded. The third power-up yielded a convulsive jerk as if Atera were no more than a bundle of dead nerves. Scans repeated, hardware and software, yet no more for the machine to fix. Miravan's machine had run out of options.

A pause, almost like a human sadness had come over the machine. Miravan's eyes, still glowing, looked at the humans one at a time. Almost as if Miravan was asking for their help, but they could not. The eyes returned to Atera and glowed more brightly as Miravan's machine attempted a fourth power-up, then a fifth. As if the sadness had turned to desperation, the machine cranked out a sixth and seventh. Again and again as Atera's eyes glowed and limbs quivered and jerked. Again and again until the men about her could look no more and had turned away.

And then the lights in Miravan's eyes changed color and converged into a single beam that glowed orange, like liquid fire flowing into Atera's chest. It lasted a minute or two until the lights in Miravan's eyes grew dim and began to sputter. Atera's chest heaved and her head snapped forward as if life had been breathed into her. Miravan's sputtering eyes gave one last scan, to look upon Atera, using up every last ounce of energy to hold the gaze. And then they blinked, blinked, and the lights disappeared forever.

Silas could hardly contain his relief. "She is breathing. I mean…well, I guess that's what ya call it!" He called for them to dress her once again in under armor. "Lets' get her back onto the VTEC."

But, it was then that they learned that the Jaromad Unit had another round of business. He had come on behalf of the Librarian and the Librarian wanted something.

The Jaromad Unit stood there obviously communicating with the Agent of Miravan's Vault. Somehow, the Jaromad Unit had found something that gained the interest of the Miravan's Agent. Together, they conversed with text and images that displayed above the sarcophagus. The first one depicted The Void. Reza quietly approached Sarrow. "What's he doing? What are they saying?"

This was Sarrow's business and he immediately recognized the images, he followed the communication and read the text. "It's The Void and The Signal, everything we know so far."

But the images progressed, with one of them needing no explanation. In that image, the great sphere of The Void collapsed into a single beam and when aimed at a planet, burst the planet into dust.

Prowler shouted, almost with excitement. "That thin…The Void…it's a weapon? All this time and we could have destroyed the Puratists?"

It was Sarrow who recognized the threat of it, "Speak not so kindly of that weapon. It would be safe to assume the Control Unit is aware of the weapons potential. Maybe that is how he intends to rule over all the worlds. All this time and he has kept this a secret unto himself."

It seemed to everyone that the Jaromad Unit had what it came for, but there was more. It paused before asking his second question to the Miravan's Agent. The response came back, 'Confidential –Access Denied'. It asked a second time, but the response was unchanged. 'Confidential –Access Denied'. Clearly, there was something that Miravan's Agent did not want to share with the Librarian.

But the Jaromad Unit asked again, this time tempting Miravan's Agent with something of value. Something he was sure that Miravan's Agent would want to see. A long pause ensured. Finally, Miravan's Agent agreed; to a trade, of sorts.

More images, more text, more voice as Miravan's Agent showed the Jaromad Unit the secret research that Miravan had conducted on the human genealogy. Miravan was searching for the same thing that the Puratist worlds were looking for. First World.

Miravan had traced the genealogy backwards through time. Five thousand years, then ten thousand years. The human genealogy was traced backwards through the Puratist Worlds to their earliest ancestors. Then, backwards even further; thirty thousand years, fifty thousand years. To a time before recorded history; to the place where the human species began. First World...Earth.

The great lie of it all had been exposed. Earth was not a penal colony, it was not some dirty weigh station between the Puratist worlds and more than anything, it was not a slave station. Earth is where it all began, First World.

Brother Sarrow seemed outraged and he shouted at the Jaromad Unit, "What did you tell Miravan's Agent? Why did the Agent show you the genealogy?"

Obviously, a secret that Sarrow had already known, but the Jaromad Unit had no idea of the sensitivity and he replied. "I offered Miravan's Agent a viewing of a surveillance video that captured the final known conversation between Jaromad and Miravan."

Sarrow commanded. "Show me this video. Show it to us all."

The Jaromad Unit hesitated briefly. "As you wish." And the video displayed. Even without translation, it was apparent that Jaromad was reprimanding Miravan for ever having conducted the research. The notion that Earth was the First World enraged the Puratists. Because of it, the Puratist Worlds conspired and converged against Earth. It was Miravan who brought the full wrath of the Puratists.

Just as it enraged the Puratists all those thousands of years ago, so too had it enraged the Neferan and Lycerene; re-igniting the old argument. The same argument as their forefathers. All insisting that their world was First World. Staring into the images in disbelief, in disgust, in contempt, lost in their frustrations to the point where their feet stepped backwards almost unknowingly, like a reflex; forming ranks.

"Earth….First World? Never!" mumbled Sun Anniz.

Prowler should have sensed the tipping point. He should have let the comment pass, but it was not within him. "Why not Earth? The genealogy speaks for itself."

Sun Kefer stepped forward to stand side-by-side with Sun Anniz. "The Neferan genealogy is pure. The bloodline is unchanged since the very beginning. Ten thousand years of bones to prove it, more than any other world. Nefera is First World and the rest of you are but unfortunate ….deviations."

That comment sparked Reza's temper. "Nefera, First World…that all other worlds are born from? I think not. The Lycerene are born of our own world, forged in its creation. We are one with the planet and one with the animals because we are the First World!"

Without even waiting for Reza to finish, Prowler started in again, pointing directly at Sun Anniz, "Ten thousand years you say? Is that all you've got? Earth has millions of years' worth of fossils; bones over bones that trace human evolution all the way back to the apes."

Sun Anniz exploded. "Apes? Apes? Is that where you Earth people come from? The Neferan do not evolve, we are born of the Gods. We are the chosen people. We are first above all others."

Reza knew the truth behind the Neferan bloodline and he used it as an insult. "The Nefera do not evolve? And you think it's because the Gods mate with your Queen? Bearing every son and daughter identical to one another. Like some immaculate conception for each and every Neferan." Reza gave the loudest laugh at Sun Anniz and continued.
"Your Queen tells you that you are born of a God?
Your Queen lies. You were made in a factory!
You are nothing but a genetic replicant...a clone!"

An age old insult between their worlds, yet it struck Sun Anniz deeply. He stepped forward face to face with Reza and poked his finger at Reza's chest. Right at that little circle that contained the images of Reza's family. "A clone? Maybe...just maybe. But what difference does it make. Soon, there will not be one Lycerene left to laugh about it."

Reza's thoughts immediately raced home, remembering that his entire world was by now in the midst of a full genocide. Sickened to his stomach as the adrenaline flooded his bloodstream. His arms struck out, straight to Sun Anniz chest with a force that blew Sun Anniz backward crashing into the sarcophagus.

It was an involuntary reaction at best and Reza stood there lost, not even recognizing the fact that he had just started a fight and in doing so, resumed the war. Instantly, two of Sun Anniz men were on Reza, one man to each arm and they pinned him against the wall waiting for a third to strike him with a sword. Instantly, the cavern filled with the sounds of armor banging and blades clashing.

For the first time, the great Sun Anniz had been stunned, but only for the moment. Reaching for his closest, Sun Kefer, "Get us to the VTECs…trap them inside. Do not let them leave with this lie!"

And the Neferan troops backed themselves into the tunnel with the Lycerene in pursuit. Even unto this point, Earth's own along with the Kai remained steadfast to Atera's side for she was still rebooting and resequencing. Command of Earth's own was left to Helforn who was far to the rear and of no use.

The tunnel was a flurry of blades and thrusts, yet the Neferan made their way near to the top, casting grenades outside to disable the guards. Their way almost clear when the Neferan line suddenly opened and Reza was pulled through. Quickly, the Neferan line closed again, leaving Reza alone to challenge Sun Anniz and Sun Kefer.

Helforn shouted forward. "Prowler, Stalker, Get Reza…Get him out of there! We still need him!"

The wall of Earth's own charged headlong into the line, straight to the backs of the Lycerene. It was Stalker who made his way thru first and saw how Reza was being beaten about by Sun Anniz and Sun Kefer. Still alive, only because Sun Anniz was indulging himself. Stalker raced forward against Reza's plea. "Stay back! He'll kill you!"

Stalker paused a moment, but Sun Anniz taunted him. "What do we have here? It's Atera's Pride…more like a little chicken!"

As if Sun Anniz knew the exact words that would draw Stalker to attack, and it worked. Stalker charged with his sword held high. Sun Anniz, so massive, reached right out with his armored hand and grabbed Stalker's blade. Next came the fist that smashed into Stalker facemask spinning his whole body about to crash against the stone wall.

Just as Prowler pulled himself thru the line, he saw Sun Anniz grab the back of Stalker's helmet with his massive hand and press it hard to the stone wall, pinning him there. Then, Sun Anniz took his sword and drew back to stab Stalker, right in the same place as the wound that killed Scout.

Prowler charged forward as Stalker twisted just enough that the blade scratched across his armor and sparked upon the stone wall. Sun Anniz jabbed again and caught seam in Stalker's armor, then he pressed in hard as he could to pierce the seam. No matter how hard Stalker twisted, or how much he squirmed, the massive Sun Anniz kept him pinned to the wall, and pressed. The blade twisted its way through the outer armor and then into the under armor and finally, the flesh.

Prowler lunged at Sun Anniz with his whole body, only to be smacked in the face by the massive elbow. The force of it threw Prowler backwards skidding and rolling until he crashed into the back of the Neferan soldiers.

The Neferan line collapsed down upon Prowler as Lycerene troops and Earth's own poured over him, charging at Sun Anniz. Trampling over Reza and Stalker as they chased Sun Anniz and Sun Kefer up the tunnel to the vault door. Just as soon as he reached the clearing outside, Sun Anniz threw grenades inside and the percussion caused the rock ceiling to collapse trapping Lycerene, Earth's own, and even some of his own Neferan troops inside.

CHAPTER 27: APOCALYPSE

Another half day passed before they had dug themselves free, then they climbed out onto the plains so littered with rocks. They stepped forward to see their VTEC, charred and still smoldering. They would have to make their way back on foot and to do so in hiding.

Even so, they were out of Miravan's Vault and could see far across to the horizon. In all directions, a skyline marred by plumes of smoke that were still billowing upward filling the blackened sky. The Apocalypse had begun.

So few they were, this small band of troops. Such despair as they stood there with their heads hung low. But, they did have something, they had Atera, the Compassionate One, and she was at least sitting and talking. And more, they had the Signal Generator schematics, the knowledge of The Void, and the history of the Genealogy. Not least to mention their new Chodugon who had proven so useful, the one Atera took to so well, reeling question after question almost as if it were Jaromad himself standing by her side.

Helforn called the troops together, to get their minds off the sight of burning cities. "Gather round people! Remember, the air up here is thin and our compressors won't run forever. We need to make our way to lower ground…Fast! First, make sure those Neferan troops are secured. Second, let's double-check our weapons. Third, how is Stalker?"

Hunter had been tending to Stalker and was just finished removing Stalker's armor to see the wounds. "It's…It's not so bad. Couple stitches and some pain killers should get him up and moving again!"

Helforn gave an appreciative nod to Hunter and then turned his attention to Prowler who was ignoring everything, lost in his own thoughts again. Helforn just stared at Prowler, not a single word until the silence drew everybody's attention to Prowler. "He killed her! That bastard killed Scout!"

Helforn had not been there when Scout was killed. "What do you mean? It was the Kon that killed Scout."

Prowler erupted. "Scout was stabbed from behind…same as Stalker! The same wound, in the same place. I saw how Sun Anniz did it! I know he killed Scout… and when we get back…I will kill him!"

More than ever, Prowler was coming apart, cracking and losing his mind until Sarrow spoke. "Sir, you are no match for Sun Anniz. He was built to kill, trained for a lifetime. You will not win!"

Prowler looked down at the sword in his hand, staring at the blade as the sun glinted from it. Gripping the handle again and again. As if in a pitched fever, Prowler pointed directly at Sarrow.
"Then train me!
You…will train me!
Train me to fight…like the Kai!"

Suddenly, a raspy, shaky voice could be heard, Atera. "No! Not the ways of the Kai.

I will teach you...my ways!

You will be...like me!"

She was referring to the way that Prowler held his sword, gripping the handle and squeezing it over and over; feeling it. For the first time, he could feel the wind pass by his blade and he held his arm outstretched to catch more of the wind. Turning and rotating the blade as if it were an extension of his own body; until that tiny vibration caused by the wind steadied him and calmed his nerves.

With his back to everyone, Prowler asked a question that everyone knew was meant for Atera. "What now? The Control Unit...he knows who you are. You'll have to go into hiding!"

Her eyes scanned over the troops as she considered the options. Voices joined in with suggestions, how to hide, where to hide, and who could hide them. But with a raspy and trembling voice, she gave her reply, "No hiding this time. I find him, or he finds me. Either way, it comes."

Then she turned away as if to rejoin her conversation with the Jaromad Unit, but Stalker was not satisfied. As always, he needed to know more.

"What the hell does that mean?"

Again, her body twitched and jerked, but she spoke and this time with a more steadied voice. "As I said, I find him, or he finds me. Either way, it comes to a fight. One last battle and it will be done."

Stalker snapped right back at her.

"A fight! A fight did you say?

Look at you!

You can't even stand up!
Your fighting days are through!"

More of her troops gathered around now to hear her speak. "My system is still recalibrating and when it's finished, I will walk again. As for fighting, there are no alternatives, not this time." By the confusion in their eyes, she knew that they did not understand so she continued. "Miravan's machine has repaired my injuries, all but one. There is a memory leak in one of my main processors, small it may be, but enough that my days are numbered."

Immediately, Hunter and Silas attempted to diagnose the problem, but she raised her hand to quell them. "Mind you, Miravan's machine with all of its schematics and blueprints could not find the leak. The leak cannot be fixed and it will not stop. It will run until the processor destabilizes entirely."

Everyone had the same question on their mind, but Stalker's put it to words. "When? How much time do we have?"

Rather than answering the question which had been asked, she told them what was most important. "We need to find him before he finds me." And with a slight pause she added, "And we need to do it fast for the Control Unit is nearby. Like Brother Sarrow had said, he followed us to the monastery and then again to Jaromad's tomb. He knows our every move." With that, she looked at Captain Helforn and without so much as a nod he understood that it was time to move out.

Helforn climbed atop a nearby boulder and called the troops to attention. "Listen up people. We got mountains to climb and rivers to forge, and when we're done with that, we got a war to fight. Let's pack it up and move out!
Turn to people…Turn and burn!"

At that point, the troops all turned to their tasks of preparing for the long journey down the mountain. Only then did she lay back in her makeshift stretcher to take her rest. As she closed her eyes, she gave a quick glance to her newest Chodugon, the Jaromad Unit. Quietly, she spoke what was on her mind, as if he would already know.

"Done...Then it will finally be done."

THREE WORLDS

Earth:

Stillwell	: President, People of Earth
Zadan	: Vice-President
Helforn	: Captain, Ground Forces
Atera	: Commander, Air Forces
Stalker	: Captain, Squadron Leader
Prowler	: Captain, Squadron Leader
Hunter	: Pilot
Scout	: Pilot
Sarrow	: Chodugon-Kai Senior
Silas	: Chodugon-Kai Sentry

Lycera:

Cree	: Chief of Fleet
Sazzi	: Chief of Ship
Reza	: Chief of Pack
Chel	: Pilot
Sena	: Pilot
Nava	: Pilot

Nefera:

Anak Re Sun	: Subordinate Queen
Sun Keptra	: First Officer
Sun Anniz	: Commander of Swarm